th his tall and wiry frame, clad always
an immaculate black suit, Harry Flack
ts an elegant, if for long unheralded,
ure in legal London. It was at *The*
rd that he made his reputation. As a
ght lawyer Flack has prowled the
dmns protecting freedom of speech
m threats for a
rter of a century. Everyone likes him,
t they don't know him very well. In the
dst of FLACK'S LAST SHIFT of guiding
e newspaper's team through stormy
gal eas, his past catches up with him.
old enemy licks a switch that he
off, corporate back-stabbing,
one hacking, and
osts from his past prompt him to t
s in the fight
save he loves.
ith wsroom twists and turns,
l riter Alex Wade his
nfidential source. With ma in the
wsroom and the courtroom, have they
der estimated good old Harry Flack???

FLACK'S LAST SHIFT

Alex Wade

By the same author

NON-FICTION
Wrecking Machine
Surf Nation
Amazing Surfing Stories

Flack's Last Shift

By
Alex Wade

BLUE MARK BOOKS

First published in Great Britain by
Blue Mark Books Limited in 2016

www.bluemarkbooks.com

This is a work of fiction. All characters in this publication
are fictitious and any resemblance to real persons
either living or dead is purely coincidental

A catalogue record for this book is
available from the British Library

ISBN 978-1-910369-11-1

Blue Mark Books Limited supports the Forest Stewardship Council®. The
FSC® promotes the responsible management of the world's forests.
All our books carrying the FSC® logo are printed on FSC®-certified paper

MIX
Paper from
responsible sources
FSC® C013604

Typeset in Minion Pro by Blue Mark Books Limited

Printed and bound by CPI Group (UK) Ltd, CR0 4YY

For those who toil by night

Contents

Continued...

FLACK'S LAST SHIFT

Prologue

4.05pm, Night Lawyer's Office

Flack was alone. Now was his chance. He could make a start and begin to destroy the whole thing.

He rose from his seat, took two steps to his left and looked out into the newsroom. A number of journalists came and went, all moving at speed, all preoccupied, most carrying pieces of paper and none noticing anything in their immediate environment. Dixon was nowhere to be seen and Flack knew that his colleague, O'Donoghue, was upstairs talking to the comment editors.

Flack stole another glance into the newsroom, an expanse the size of a small football pitch crammed at every turn with desks, chairs, journalists and computers, at whose outer reaches Richard Dixon could be seen, deep in conversation with a sub-editor. Her name was Clare. She and Dixon liked each other, perhaps as much as they liked the English language; he would be gone for at least another five minutes.

With Dixon so far away, immersed in conversation, and with O'Donoghue upstairs discussing a Comment piece, there was no need for excessive prudence. Unless Flack had gone temporarily insane and forgotten the presence of someone else in the office shared by himself, Dixon and O'Donoghue, it was devoid of any human form save his own, one of surprisingly spry capabilities, a full head of silver hair and a tall, slim frame clad in a well-cut black suit. Despite this, Flack hovered over Dixon's chair and looked over his shoulder back into the small, square office, as if in fear that a ghost had metamorphosed into a revise editor he had never met, one despatched to watch his every move on this, his last shift as a night lawyer for *The Record*.

Come on. Now is the time. Get on with it. How could anyone stop him? Flack sat down in Dixon's chair and grasped the mouse next to the keyboard, all the while staring intently at the computer screen which was used by *The Record's* chief revise editor. Within seconds he had manoeuvred the cursor to call up the Leaders. He already knew that the first one savaged the government's foreign policy in the Middle

East, while the third, as effervescent as it was ephemeral, celebrated the joy of the great British outdoors.

Flack ignored both in favour of the middle Leader. He pulled it up on screen and read it swiftly. As he knew from earlier conversations with Dixon and O'Donoghue, it was a rallying call in favour of the judiciary retaining wigs in criminal trials. They'd asked what Flack thought about this – 'What with you being one of m'learned friends and all,' as O'Donoghue had put it – and now, as he read the Leader, Flack reflected that yes, he'd always thought that wigs were ridiculous, but especially when worn by lawyers. This, though, was not the view espoused in *The Record's* middle Leader:

> *Banned for no good reason from the family and civil courts a year ago, the Lord Chancellor today calls for horsehair to be scrapped from the criminal courts. He is wrong. Justice must not only be done; it must be seen to be done. It has been seen to be done in an anonymized, deliberately unsettling fashion for centuries. A judge framed by a wig is not absurd. He is instead austere and authoritative, as the law must be. Moreover, a defendant does not arrive in a criminal court for a cosy fireside chat. He is there to be tried. He is there to be judged. He is there to behold the majesty of the law. The wig is one of the judiciary's sacred accoutrements by which this is preserved. It must be protected.*

Less than a day ago, Flack would simply have read the Leader in the same way as any other lawyer whose job was to assess its capacity for legal risk. Yes, he may have sighed at the notion of wigs – he had always thought that they were worn only by the foolish and the vain – but he would have signed it off as 'Legal OK' and moved on to the next story. Tonight, though, it wasn't so much that the text vexed him, more that its alteration was irresistible: it would be the first step in a scheme by which he intended to mark his last ever shift for the august *Record* in a way that its senior personnel could never have anticipated, least of all from a man like Flack. So having checked again that no one was watching, Flack created a new version of the Leader:

> *Banned for no good reason from the family and civil courts a year ago, the Lord Chancellor today calls for horsehair to be scrapped from the criminal courts. He is right. A judge framed by a wig*

looks like an idiot. He is ridiculous, as are people who wear wigs generally. And the fact is that a defendant arrives in a criminal court for a cosy fireside chat. Yes, he is there to be tried. Yes, he is there to be judged. But most of all, he is there to have fun, to have a laugh, to chat amiably with the judge and the barristers before going home with a grin on his face. A wig gets in the way of all this. It is high time that we said enough is enough, and made our courts more fun for criminals – after all, it is for them that the criminal justice system exists.

Though it felt as if it had taken an age to make these changes, no more than a minute had passed. Flack looked up from the keyboard and craned his neck to scan the newsroom. Dixon was still deep in conversation with Clare – perhaps about gardening, her passion beyond the confines of *The Record* – and there was no sign of O'Donoghue. Flack moved the cursor over the 'send' button. Once clicked, Flack would commit the paper to publishing his version of the middle Leader rather than that written to its editor's order.

He smiled at the thought but, a split second before he was about to condemn the paper – or, at least, its first edition – to an editorial position of stupidity, perhaps even madness, in walked Maya Berlin, a young barrister whose training as one of the paper's new night lawyers Flack was supervising. Startled, Flack all but leapt from Dixon's chair; certainly, his brisk departure from Dixon's seat did not go unnoticed by Berlin. However, years of absorption in the law – a passion since her teens, when, at the age of 13, she announced to her mother that she would one day become a barrister – had taught Berlin the virtue of an expressionless face. And so rather than appear discomfited by the sight of Flack at Dixon's desk, an apparition rendered yet more unusual by the speed with which he parted from it allied with a lightning-quick deletion of the changes he had made to the middle Leader, Berlin merely walked into the neatly laid out, glass-partitioned office and, carefully placing her coffee on the desk, sat down at the chair that had been made available for her. At the same time, Flack returned to his own position, one with only an obscure view of the newsroom.

Damn it! Flack almost said the words aloud. He had enjoyed his rewrite of the middle Leader. Granted, it was relatively innocuous compared with the other changes to *The Record* that he planned to engineer, but as a start it wasn't bad. But then the girl had turned up.

Who was she again?

A minute or two of silence passed before Berlin spoke.

'Can I ask you about this story?' she said, gesturing with two sheets of A4 paper in Flack's direction.

'Of course,' said Flack. He looked disconcerted, as if he wasn't sure of something. His voice, though, was even. 'What is it?'

Berlin moved her chair closer to Flack's and placed the papers on his desk. Flack noticed her slight wrists, lightly tanned, and inhaled a subtle fragrance, a perfume made by a manufacturer whose identity he would never guess in a thousand night shifts but which he instantly adored. Berlin edged a fraction closer, so close that to lean over and kiss her would be easy, if not the most logical or even sensible course of action, for men of rectitude such as Flack do not kiss female colleagues when they have only just begun their training shifts, not even in their wildest dreams and especially not, as was Flack's fate, when he was old enough to be Berlin's father.

How old was she? Flack couldn't say, but he admired her smooth-skinned, olive face as she started to explain the background to the story. It concerned a celebrity who'd had an affair with a teacher. Both were married but while the celebrity had been eager to preserve the status quo, the teacher had left her husband in the hope that one day their love would be conducted in an open, above-board relationship. The celebrity had not shared this desire and eventually, her imprecations having fallen on deaf ears, or stony ground – the celebrity having concluded, in so far as matters of the heart are concerned, that the best devil is the one you know – the teacher had sold her story to a tabloid newspaper. *The Record* sought to do a follow up, but its content perturbed Maya Berlin, freshly qualified as a libel barrister from 9BR, one of the most eminent specialist defamation chambers in London.

'I think, if we publish this as it's written, we're sure to be on the end of a claim,' she said, when Flack asked her what was troubling her about the story. 'The paper could be sued for libel or privacy, or both. I don't feel comfortable with it at all.'

Flack furrowed his brow and peered at the copy. To Dixon and O'Donoghue – who, at that precise moment, reappeared from their respective tasks and entered the office – it appeared as if their long-standing colleague was deep in thought, mired in legal minutiae, resolving, for the umpteenth time, the kind of problem he'd spent a lifetime dealing with for journalists at *The Record*. The truth, though, was otherwise. Flack was unable to take in anything on the sheets of A4 in front of him. The words swirled as randomly as a blind man wandering in a funhouse. None made any sense, all that mattered was that Flack had just hit upon another weapon in his plan. She was attractive – she was beautiful, so beautiful that he could barely take his eyes off her – and she was sitting next to him, so close that he could kiss her, if only she would let him. His mind drifted. Would she? Yes, he was much older than her, but the world is full of liaisons between men and women of differing generations. What would a kiss with Berlin be like? Surely it would be wonderful: their lips would meet, hers hesitant and yet inviting; his more careful, experienced but gentle; they would clasp and kiss and stop after no more than a minute, somehow aware of what could grow between them, conscious of an extraordinary bond, as if they had known each other forever and were destined to be together. Could Flack risk trying, perhaps later? Could he somehow embrace and kiss this gorgeous, unexpected arrival, whose dark hair shone like polished serpentine? But no, such thoughts were fanciful and anyway, Berlin would be useful to Flack in ways she could never imagine. Her innocence was essential; it had to be preserved; it would see him to victory. Kissing Berlin was preposterous, if she would even let him. What had he been thinking?

Armed with resolve, suddenly Flack jumped up. He stood in the doorway, turned and looked at each of Dixon, O'Donoghue and Berlin. And then, before rushing off as if on a mission which meant the difference between life and death, he said:

'Leave it to me. I'm a night lawyer, don't you know! You can take your Middle East foreign policy, put it in a pipe and smoke it! I'm the night lawyer round here! And I'm a very experienced one at that!'

Part 1

CHAPTER 1

11.00am, Editorial Conference

'Our new leader will be here in a minute,' said Liz Lewington, *The Record's* picture editor, sotto voce.

Flack turned to her.

'It's none other than The Collector himself, Eddie Conrad, late of *The Echo*,' said Lewington. She and Flack went back years. 'Have you dealt with him before?'

Before Flack could answer, the door was pushed open by a tall, greying, moderately overweight but impressive male, a man who was perhaps some ten years older than everyone else in the room, except for Flack. At once, silence descended. Ordinarily so in thrall to gossip, the assembled hacks sat still in their chairs, like a bunch of rebellious adolescents whose daily torment of a weak teacher has been quelled by the unexpected arrival of the headmaster. To those who scrutinised him, whose number included Lewington, Flack, the news editor and the sports editor, Conrad's mouth wore a smirk as he ambled to the chair left vacant for him, as if he were mildly amused that his presence could have such an effect. The curious half-smile stayed in place even as he sat down, and expanded into an outright, unabashed grin once he was in situ, able to clasp his hands underneath his chin, survey the personnel gathered around him and say: 'You all know who I am. If you don't, you don't belong here. If you don't belong here, I'll know by the end of this conference, and you won't be able to fake it anymore because I'll tell you to fuck off. And fuck off is what you'll do. Right. What have we got? Let's start with news.'

The news editor rose to the occasion. Relatively young by comparison with his colleagues – a mere 30 – he was as hard and unscrupulous as a phone-hacking private detective or, if there could be such a thing, journalist. Niceties concerned him no more than ethics; fair play he regarded as for losers or, as he put it, 'the other papers'. In truth, he was every inch a certain kind of tabloid man, and a renowned one at that, but his move to *The Record*, which surprised industry observers and spawned no less than three diary items in *The Gazette*, had been a success. He was widely credited with having given the paper's home news coverage a much-needed shot in the arm, thanks to a series of stories that were controversial and hard-hitting. He was fearless, too, afraid of ruffling neither feathers nor libel lawyers; all in all, he was the kind of man who management had earmarked as an editor in due course, so long as he stayed on the straight and narrow.

The news editor updated Eddie Conrad on three stories before announcing that he had saved the best for last. 'By which I mean, of course, the Murder of the Century trial,' he announced, looking meaningfully at his new boss. 'You'll know all about it, of course, but you might not know what we've got.'

Conrad seemed impressed. 'Tell me,' he said.

'We've got the last victim, the woman who escaped. On tape, her full story. The works.'

'Well, well, well,' said Conrad. 'We were trying to get her at *The Echo* for ages. I won't ask how you did it. But well done. Pictures, too?'

'Everything,' replied the news editor. 'The jury is expected to retire this afternoon, so as soon as the verdict's in we can run one hell of a story – the splash and six or seven inside pages, maybe more. We've got details of all the bastard's previous convictions, too – sexual assaults, GBH, theft. Really nasty stuff. Victims on record, too, about his love of extreme porn and how he was obsessed with knives. We've also got a former girlfriend who's told us about a weird, horrible incident, to do with killing his pet dog.'

'What was weird and horrible about it?' asked Conrad.

'The dog barked during an episode of *Eastenders*. Thing is, it wasn't the barking that got him mad. It was the tone of the bark. Apparently he went mental because the tone was wrong. It was too high, and made him think of a singer he hated, so he picked up the dog and strangled it.'

'It was a small dog, then?' said Conrad.

'No, it was an Alsatian.'

'Good grief.'

'When it was dead, he turned the TV off and barked at it. Then he got it stuffed and put it next to the TV. From then on, whenever *Eastenders* came on, he'd bark at the dog, then say, "Go on, wag your tail now! Bark at me now, you bastard! You can't, can you?"'

'Unbelievable. What a fruitcake. And you've got the girlfriend who saw all this?'

'Yes. And a photo of the stuffed dog.'

Conrad leant back in his chair. Gazing as if into the distance, but at the news editor, he said: 'Our Mr Terry is a horror story. A real, live, hideous and horrible horror story.' He paused, then added: 'The public loves a good horror story.'

No one said anything. It was unclear where Conrad was going with this statement. But then he said:

'So why should we wait for the jury's verdict?'

'Sorry?' said the news editor. The proposal implicit in Conrad's words – to ride roughshod over the contempt of court laws – suggested that he was joking, but he sounded serious. The news editor was unable to hide his confusion. 'Sorry,' he repeated. 'I don't understand what you're getting at.'

Conrad shuffled in his seat and leaned over the table. 'What I mean is this,' he said, speaking quietly. 'It seems to me that there's no point waiting for the jury's verdict. The contempt laws say we should, but I say we shouldn't. I say we should show a bit of contempt for the contempt laws. The accused, our lovable Peter Terry, resident of Ealing, father of three, husband, taxi driver, dog strangler, "bastard", as you rightly call him, murdered a woman a year for twenty-five years. He stuffed his pet dog and put it next to the TV. If there's one thing the British public hates, it's cruelty to animals. So that, and the small matter of being a serial killer, makes this the perfect horror story for our times. And guess what – everyone knows he's guilty. The evidence against him is overwhelming. All anyone has to do is go online and it's all there. All the trolls have been sleuthing away, tweeting this, blogging that. You'd have to live on another planet not to know that he's as guilty as sin. Who are we kidding if we think that the jury will possibly be influenced by what we publish, in this day and age? It's a farce. Pathetic. And think of the sales. If we publish tomorrow, with everything we've got, we'll have the best sales figures for a decade. We'll out-sell everyone.'

The news editor was speechless. So was everyone else in the room. To a man, they wanted nothing more than to be guided by an editor who was prepared to take risks, to put his head on the block in the name of freedom of speech and yet with a weather eye on the bottom line, but to make a mockery of the contempt of court laws was another thing altogether. This, though, was precisely what Eddie Conrad was proposing to do.

'Who's our lawyer?' said Conrad, to no one in particular.

'I am,' said Flack. He was staring at Conrad with what Liz Lewington was startled to see was outright rancour. Later, indeed, she fancied that Flack looked as if he hated the man whose first day as *The Record's* editor coincided with his last shift as one of its night lawyers. Hated him with the most extraordinary venom.

Conrad met Flack's gaze with equanimity. 'I suppose,' he drawled, 'that you're going to tell me I can't possibly publish the escapee's account and details of Peter Terry's previous convictions until the jury's verdict is in.'

Flack said that yes, that was right. He added that he didn't need to justify his advice.

'Of course you don't!' exclaimed Conrad. He began to laugh, as if Flack had just uttered a tremendous joke, one it was impossible to resist. Soon enough, the journalists were also laughing. It was best, on such occasions, to join in.

'Sorry,' said Conrad. 'My little joke. Of course we won't do anything stupid like publish before the jury's verdict is in. The Attorney-General would have our guts for garters and I've only just had a run in with him. Mock up a splash and a few pages just in case the verdict comes in before the end of the day, with the dog on the centre pages with a couple of *Eastenders'* actresses. Get a quote from Barbara Windsor. Let's hope the trial is all done and dusted in time, but if it's not, of course we must do the right thing. We must do what the law tells us. Isn't that right, Mr Lawyer?'

*

Flack had been awake, but only just, when the phone went in his central London flat, about an hour and a half before he encountered Conrad.

'Hello, is that Harry?' asked the woman on the other end of the line.

'Yes, hello Pat, how are you?' replied Flack, a man taught early in his childhood that one should always enquire of one's interlocutor's health at the outset of a conversation, for in this way embarrassment – such as launching into a speech about how you've just got a pay rise, or won the school prize, or met the woman of your dreams, only to find that the recipient of this information was ringing to tell you that his or her mother had just died – would be avoided.

'Not so good,' said Phillips. 'Evan will be at court all day on the

Murder of the Century trial. He Between you and me I don't see why he has to be there. The court sends us the latest orders and the journos all know how careful they've got to be with this one. I bet it's curiosity, pure and simple – it's got the better of him and he wants to be there when the jury gives its verdict, which is likely to be today. He feels we need to be seen to be there because of Leveson and all the scrutiny on the press at the moment. The journos all know how careful they've got to be with this one, and they've been doing a great job, but Evan's right – *The Record's* legal department needs to be there. Trouble is that as well as that, Jim is still in hospital.'

'I'm sorry to hear that,' said Flack. He barely registered that Evan Brooke, *The Record's* most senior lawyer, would be out all day at court, but he felt sorry for Watson, the third-in-command in the paper's legal department, a fine lawyer but uncannily prone, over the past year or so, to one accident after another. He had been in a car crash and broken his left ankle; recovered but then dislocated his right shoulder while playing tennis; and bounced back only to snap the medial ligaments in not one but both knees, this while skiing in the Dolomites. His obsession with sport and inability ever to let his body recover was as compulsive, it seemed to Flack, as Brooke's dedication to ensuring that *The Record* was as immaculate in its court reporting of the so-called Murder of the Century trial as possible. As Phillips, second to Brooke in the paper's legal department, confirmed, Watson was at that very moment barely twenty-four hours clear of a second operation on one of his knees (Phillips did not specify which), and was likely to be bed-ridden for another month. 'And the worst of it is that I can't get in to work today,' concluded *The Record's* much-respected senior legal advisor. 'I've got to take one of my sons to hospital as well.'

Flack was relieved to hear that there was nothing seriously wrong with Phillips's eldest son, and knew what was coming next.

'The thing is, Harry, we're in a mess. The paper hasn't got a lawyer at all for the day. There's a trainee coming in but we can't go and put her in charge. So I was wondering, given that you're due in for the night shift, if you could come in and legal for us for the day as well?'

'Of course,' said Flack, 'I'll be there as soon as I can.' He was about to hang up but Phillips wouldn't let him go.

'Harry, I appreciate this,' she said. 'You've really helped us out. And by the way, don't think that I've forgotten tonight is your last shift. I'm really sorry to do this to you on your last day.'

'It's not a problem,' said Flack, 'don't worry.'

'We're taking you out for dinner next week – the Champagne will be on me personally,' replied Phillips.

Again, Flack told her not to worry. Yes, it was his last shift, his final night's work as a night lawyer in twenty-five years, but he didn't mind coming in for the day. Perhaps it was even appropriate, in some way. Whatever, he'd look forward to dinner the following week, a dinner which both suspected would be his last among those who work in media London. A new life, a long way from the capital, beckoned. But thoughts of last suppers, final farewells and the fulfilment of long-held dreams were left unsaid, Phillips choosing instead to remind Flack to attend the morning's editorial conference at 11am, qualifying her words with an apology: 'I know you won't forget – sorry. I just can't help but say these things.'

'Don't worry,' said Flack. 'Now you'd better go and take your son to the hospital.'

'Thanks Harry,' said Phillips. 'Oh – one last thing. We've got a new editor. You've seen so many over the years that it'll make no difference to you, but I thought I'd better let you know.'

Phillips had rung Flack at 9am on a damp day in June; by 10.15am he had made it to *The Record's* HQ in Wapping. As was customary among night lawyers asked to deputise for their diurnal brethren, he ensconced himself in Phillips's office and, there being little to do for any lawyer in any newspaper at this time of the day, settled down with a cup of coffee to read the day's papers. He was a locum lawyer about to begin his day shift; a complaisant individual who had, that morning on the last day of his working life in London, willingly agreed to help out a colleague of many years' standing who was in a jam.

*

It had been so long since Flack had attended a morning editorial conference that he had forgotten where they were held. Because it wasn't within a night lawyer's remit to be at one, their location was a mystery; it was information that did not need to be known. Despite this, over the years one or two NLs, as they were known, had found themselves present, correct and, usually to their relief, invisible at an editorial conference. Such appearances transpired if they were completing a locum day shift, one which, like that which marked the end of Flack's career, proved to be denuded of all the staff lawyers. On these occasions the editorial conference could not proceed without the availability of lawyerly input, and so an NL would be instructed to navigate *The Record's* endless corridors until he found himself deep in the newspaper's beating heart, a windowless room with a large oval table, a TV screen, a couple of telephones and chairs which would be occupied by a gang of about fifteen senior journalists.

Over the course of his long career Flack had taken up the baton on several occasions, for so favoured was he by James Madison – the first head of legal for whom Flack had worked – and all who succeeded him that he was regularly left at the paper's legal helm, there to withstand the cut, thrust and, often enough, extraordinary demands of whoever happened to be the editor and his team. But by the day of his last shift it had been some time since Flack had been the voice of law and, he liked to think, reason in a morning conference. The cookie simply hadn't crumbled his way. If he'd been asked to come in for a day shift it had been when at least two of the three-person legal team were also present.

So when Flack set off for morning conference at 10.35am, he was not taking any chances. He had a rough idea of where the conference would be, and could always ask one of the editorial PAs on the way, but being late was not an option. Not only was it not Flack's style, but a straggler, or, worse, the last person to arrive, was in for trouble. The subtle humiliation of forfeiting the right to a chair was one thing but also, depending on who occupied the editor's hot seat, there was the ever-present threat of being castigated for one's tardiness, not because anyone especially cared but because this modest sin made for easy material with which to ridicule a colleague.

Legend has it that at one newspaper, this routine was taken an extra mile by a managing editor who, following a nudge in the ribs by the editor, stood bolt upright as a PR executive walked in five minutes' late. He bellowed her name and shouted: 'You're late! You're late! You're late!' Dumbfounded, she replied: 'I'm sorry. I was taking a call from *The Mail*. I thought it was important. Perhaps I misunderstood.'

This excuse counted for nothing. 'I don't care!' screamed the managing editor. Then, striding furiously round the oval table, for oval tables are *de rigueur* in the highest echelons of the corporate world, which also, like it or not, includes the newspaper fraternity, he stopped a few feet from the exquisite object of his wrath, next to a cupboard door. This he yanked open. 'Get in!' he told the PR woman. 'Go on, get in the bloody cupboard!' Casting him a look which mingled bewilderment and contempt, the lady said, 'Excuse me?', whereupon the managing editor, having caught the eye of his mirthful boss, explained that 'everyone who's late has to stand in the cupboard. It's company policy. Now get in. Now!' The woman refused, saying, 'Somehow, I don't think so,' and continued, slowly but surely, on her journey round the table to take her seat. Five days later she was sacked for an unspecified, though presumably no less serious, crime.

Flack did not expect such shenanigans at *The Record's* morning conference. This was likely to be an altogether more sensible affair, though tempers could still fray. No wonder, for even of a morning a newspaper is a frenetic establishment, one in which a leisurely moment is to be found solely in the amiable pages of the weekend supplements, never among the frantic daily routines of its employees. Having found his way to the conference room, there were already some five or six journalists ahead of Flack, people, like him, who knew that to be late was a luxury which came with a price. Among them was Liz Lewington, the picture editor, a woman Flack had known for the past twelve years. Theirs was a relationship of such cosy cordiality that it had been suggested they were once lovers; neither had ever confirmed or denied the rumour.

'Harry!' said Liz, a wide smile on her face. Not for the first time, Flack mused at how she managed to look so outdoorsy, when, like just about everyone else at *The Record,* all she ever saw was artificial light.

'Why hello, Liz!' replied Flack, with an element of the flirtatiousness that, to the prurient, of which there were one or two at *The Record,* betrayed a former or perhaps even extant intimacy. 'How are you?'

'I'm very well, Harry, very well. Won't you sit next to me?'

Flack sat down next to Liz Lewington, a distance, he rapidly calculated, of some eight chairs from the editor's seat. Perched at one end of the table, he was where the day lawyer usually sat – out of the firing line, and yet on the edge, observing all.

'Well, what an auspicious day this is!' declared Liz, clasping Flack's arm beneath the elbow. 'The day we bid you farewell, is it not?'

Flack confirmed that today was his last shift as a night lawyer for *The Record* – and anywhere else, for that matter. He explained, too, that none of the day lawyers were around – they were ill, or in court, or dealing with the difficulties of their offspring – hence his appearance at morning conference. 'It's been a while, though,' he concluded. 'I hope they don't ask me anything about the law.'

'Oh Harry, don't be so modest. You know that they respect you in this room as much as they used to love James Madison. But anyway, next week is your farewell lunch, isn't it? Wednesday, I think?'

'That's right. You'll be there, of course, won't you Liz? I won't come unless you say yes.'

The pair would undoubtedly have carried on with their easy banter, had it not been for the arrival of Mike Redmosson, deputy editor. A short and pugnacious man, Redmosson lost no time in berating the deputy news editor for a mistake that he'd seen in the morning's paper. 'A fucking disgrace, you idiot,' he said. 'I mean, since when do we run a story about a sex offender with a picture of the woman who's just been through hell in court? Haven't you heard of the victim's right to anonymity? Our legal eagle will tell you that.' He looked in Flack's direction, registered the night lawyer's presence and turned again to the deputy news editor. 'Don't let it happen again.' The man getting this flak began to mutter something about having obtained the woman's consent, in writing, but Liz Lewington took the opportunity to whisper in Flack's ear: 'Same old Mike. Can't resist a fight. I bet they had her consent, and I bet he knows it. They wouldn't be so stupid.'

Flack nodded. The room by now was full, every chair save for one taken by a group of journalists who, aside from Lewington, were all male, Caucasian and between the ages of 30 and 50. The empty chair awaited *The Record's* editor – a newcomer, as Lewington reminded Flack.

*

In he had walked. Conrad. Eddie Conrad. Eddie 'The Collector' Conrad.

The man who had ruined Flack's life.

Eddie 'The Cunt' Conrad. That's what Flack would call him, a long time ago. Except that he hadn't thought about him for so many years that he'd all but erased his existence. Conrad was dead, even though he was alive. He'd been at other papers, collecting his writs, increasing sales, making his enemies, making friends of politicians; he'd been doing his job. But Flack hadn't thought about him. So he didn't need to call him anything.

And now, he didn't like saying *Eddie 'The Cunt' Conrad*. He didn't like swearing. Hated it. Worst was using the C-word. Flack was old-school. It was just unnecessary.

But Eddie 'The Cunt' Conrad was back in his life. A life that had begun in the law, in hope. A life that over twenty-five years ago had promised so much. Until Conrad had come along.

CHAPTER 2

Dr Tax

'A night lawyer? And what, pray tell, is a *night lawyer*?'

Early in his legal career, Flack was asked this question. His interrogator was the senior partner of the medium-sized, well-regarded London firm with which he started out in the law. The senior partner was a lofty, intimidating man who had made his name and fortune advising the great and the good and even the royals. For all the grandeur of his position – or, perhaps, one or two cynics suggested, because of it – he insisted on introducing himself to every new recruit, whose customary blend of deference and terror would provoke anything from charm to rage but rarely indifference. One afternoon he wandered into the office that Flack shared with his immediate boss, who herself was absent in court.

'I see that the fragrant Melanie is not here,' said the senior partner, who was not known for his fidelity to feminism.

'No, she is in court,' said Flack. 'I believe she is due back at five.'

'What case?'

'The Spiller case. A libel trial.'

'Libel, a ludicrous and arcane branch of the law. But good money in it, so the lovely Melanie says. Not as much as in tax, that's where you'll get rich, but she does manage to get some good fees in. Who are you?'

'My name is Harry Flack. I've just joined the firm.'

'Have you? They didn't tell me you were coming.'

'Er, yes. I've been here for three months.'

'Three months! I've not seen you anywhere. What on earth have you been doing, polishing your nails and hiding in a cupboard?'

Flack was unsure how to reply. He had, in fact, caught the senior partner's eye and shyly nodded a greeting in the lift on one or two occasions. The greeting had even been returned, once, with the faintest of nods.

'Well, where have you been? Do tell! You must have been in here, lingering over files into the twilight with Melanie, perhaps sliding up against her when she bends over to pick up one of those particularly heavy ones! Can't say I blame you, Melanie is as fine looking a woman as you're likely to see around here. Lovely arse or, if you prefer to be polite, *derriere*. What's your name again?'

'Flack. My name is Harry Flack.'

'Of course it is. I remember you now, you're the one who went to Bristol, isn't that right?'

'Er, no. I graduated from Oxford.'

'Of course you are, I remember now. Harry Flack from Oxford, good degree, didn't play rugby, not even for the second fifteen, likes jazz and cricket, enjoys gazing at Melanie's admirable assets. And what do you think of it so far?'

There was a pause as Flack looked nervously at the senior partner, a specialist in tax law who routinely made rich people even richer with only the slightest of inconvenience to the authorities. He was adored by his many clients but feared by the majority of his employees, as much for his mercurial temperament as for an abiding ruthlessness that did not hesitate to cull when culling was called for, even in circumstances where his conduct had been less than professional, such as – so Flack had heard – when he had dismissed his mistress of a few months, a young solicitor of great potential whose career foundered as soon as she'd decided his clutches were less than congenial. The senior partner survived this and other scandals, steering his crew through the most turbulent of waters as if he were merely pushing a toy boat in a garden pond, all the while managing to earn twice as much as his colleagues. As a consequence, his position of supremacy was nigh-on inviolable, and it allowed him the indulgence of a streak by turns cruel, amusing and Machiavellian. Underlings might gripe, and all but a minority of his employees abhorred his chauvinism (which Flack and Melanie regarded as outright misogyny), but the senior partner had earned the right to wear his eccentricity as proudly as his Savile Row suits – and did not blanch from either calling. As Flack hesitated, the senior partner swooped forward towards the edge of his desk, as if he were about to seize the file that Flack had been studiously reading. 'Well,' he said, stopping himself in the nick of time and casting a withering, imperious look at Flack, 'what do you make of it so far?'

Given their respective roles, this was not a question to which there was a series of answers baying for Flack's attention. And nor could he afford to linger any longer. 'I'm enjoying it very much,' he said.

'Good-oh,' said the senior partner, before executing an about turn in the direction of Melanie's desk. This was placed opposite Flack's, near the door to their office. The senior partner, who was known to all in the firm as Dr Tax – owing to the Hippocratic devotion with which he served his clients – sat down in Melanie's chair and placed his feet on her desk. A small model of the Eiffel Tower, acquired during a visit to Paris by one of Melanie's sons, toppled to the floor. Dr Tax gave no indication of being aware of this act of disruption. Instead, he tapped the keyboard of Melanie's PC and peered at its screen. What he saw did not appear to please him. He groaned, gritted his teeth and peered censoriously through his black glasses around the office, eventually alighting on Flack, whom he affected to notice as if waking from a dream.

'Still here! Has the lovely Melanie got you working hard? Or – damn the wench! – just hard?'

'Yes,' replied Flack. 'I mean, yes, she's got me working hard, yes.' It was obvious he feared the turn the conversation was about to take.

'On what, exactly?'

'Some litigation.'

'I know it's bloody litigation, she's one of the litigation partners! To what poor sod's claim has she harnessed your talents?'

Flack blushed. He had been warned of Dr Tax's habit of dropping in on newcomers when they least expected it, or, worse, when they were unprotected by the buffer of their immediate supervisor. Flack had told himself to stay on his guard and had even rehearsed one or two choice anecdotes with which to regale the senior partner come the day he faced his cross-examination. Now, anxious to impress, he was incapable of even a stammer. Dr Tax was overwhelming. Flack felt out of his depth and where before he had sometimes, ever-so-slightly resented her presence (being a young man with a preference for solitude), now he positively yearned for Melanie to return.

'What's wrong, cat got your tongue?' said the senior partner.

'I'm sorry, sir,' said Flack, at once hating himself for calling the senior partner 'sir'. He was not a sir and had done nothing to deserve being called one. This thought flashed through Flack's mind, and yet despite himself he had called Dr Tax 'sir'. How demeaning, and yet how inevitable. Flack tried to muster his wits but searched in vain for the bons mots that had flowed so effortlessly when he was alone in the lift, or sitting in the canteen, or on the tube to work, or even in the bath at home, a place in which one of the firm's lawyers, if he found himself thinking of a client's case, would charge the activity at double his usual hourly rate ('Anything less would be a travesty,' he would say, if ever asked whether this practice was ethical). Now, confronted with the moment that every bright young thing had to face, Flack was failing dismally. Not for him an injection of l'esprit de l'escalier but instead a statement so analgesic that it inevitably provoked further scrutiny. 'Melanie has given me a lot of interesting work,' he said.

Dr Tax groaned.

'Not bloody libel?'

Flack felt there was no option but to confess. Yes, Melanie had indeed tasked him with much background research in the Spiller case. So, too, had he been asked to analyse the defence in another libel claim, this involving an allegation that, in coughing loudly on air – as reported by a tabloid newspaper – a radio presenter in Devon was guilty of a lack of professionalism. The presenter, a minor celebrity (in Devon, at least), denied both the cough and its alleged volume and objected to what he claimed was a portrayal guaranteed to subject him to ridicule and contempt. So strongly did he feel that he had consulted the estimable firm presided over by Dr Tax, one of whose junior partners, Melanie Masters, was intent on carving out a libel practice. Melanie had doubts about the merits of the claim, but was not about to turn away new work. Flack had helped her draft the Writ, as it was known in the days before its rebirth, as the twenty-first century dawned, as the prosaic Claim Form, and legal proceedings had been issued. Now the defence had been served, claiming that to publish the allegation that someone had coughed on air – even if that someone was a comparatively well-known radio presenter – was not defamatory. *The idea that such an allegation would make anyone think the worse of your client is risible,* said the local paper's lawyer, in a robust letter to Melanie, who had asked Flack to research any available precedents. Flack had found one case involving *The Jewish Chronicle*, but otherwise was not faring well. This latter point he did not tell the senior partner.

'Sounds ghastly,' said Dr Tax. 'Haven't these people got better things to do with their time? I mean, if he'd been accused of rape and pillage, I could understand him suing, but saying that he coughed on air? Who on earth cares?' And then Dr Tax added: 'You know, in all my time, I've never advised a client to sue for libel. Sticks and stones, that's what I say to them, sticks and stones. Or if you really must, go and see Melanie.

She knows her libel and, rather more pertinently, has a great pair of tits you can dream about if she's boring you with legal analysis. That's what I say, and they usually take my advice. Always, in fact, and they never regret it.'

Perhaps Flack looked as bludgeoned as he was feeling. After all, the senior partner had been in the law for years, and although Flack was sure he was being confrontational for the sake of it (or, perhaps, owing to his allegiance to a game in which the partners participated so as to test new employees), the fact was that he was fresh from law school. He had little or no idea of how to deal with the astonishingly irascible and outrageously politically incorrect Dr Tax. And maybe Melanie was right: 'He dresses immaculately and rules the roost, but he can't stand women. That's the bottom line.' She'd said this to Flack two or three times, and who, confronted with such behaviour, would argue with her? With these thoughts in his mind, Flack chose to say nothing. Instead he simply nodded, only to find that this response galvanised the senior partner yet further.

'You don't mean to tell me you find this stuff interesting? All this bloody libel? You look like a sensible chap to me, the sort who might smile sweetly at Melanie but who would be better off helping me and my clients avoid the bastard taxman. Note – avoid, not evade, a distinction too often forgotten by journalists but that's another story. Am I wrong?'

Flack had been in the law for only a short time but already knew that he would never be a tax lawyer. He could think of nothing, or very little, that could possibly be worse. He had also, it is true, always been intrigued by the media. He liked the work Melanie had given him, and ever so tentatively said as much.

'But why?' said Dr Tax, softening his voice a little. 'Do tell me – seriously, I'm interested.'

Flack said he found libel interesting because it shone a light on how the media works, something that very few people understand.

'Go on,' said the senior partner.

Encouraged by the change in Dr Tax's tone – and the fact that he had removed his feet from Melanie's desk – Flack expounded on his curiosity for the world of libel law. He pointed out that we read the newspapers every day, especially on Sundays – for much of which many of us are surrounded by mountainous and seemingly impenetrable supplements – and yet know little of the hidden craft of journalism. Why are some stories given more prominence than others? How does an editor decide a newspaper's political agenda? Is it down to him? Why are there so few female editors? Today's media has such power – some might say that it is even more powerful than the government of the day. Is this right? But leaving aside such intriguing, and yet essentially futile speculation, to look at the minutiae of the Spiller case – in which it was alleged that a well-known actor was a convicted blackmailer – is to see the various frontiers over which words must pass before a newspaper is published. An event happens and copy is written to an editor's decree. The copy will be changed, tweaked, honed, before reaching the sub-editor, who, in some cases, rewrites it so that what a newspaper's readers find is comprehensible English rather than a haphazard collection of words, vaguely appended to an event. Then the words go to the revise editor, who checks the facts and house style, at the same time as the night lawyer reads the words for lurking legal dangers. Only once this process is complete is the story *a story*, in the sense of a publishable, readable story or, as has uncharitably been suggested (but not, all those years ago, by Flack), tomorrow's fish and chips' paper. 'It's been fascinating getting a better understanding of all this,' said Flack, concluding with a flourish that he regretted even as he was saying it: 'I should think many people don't even know that a night lawyer exists.'

Dr Tax was either surprised by Flack's sudden loquacity, or genuinely mystified. 'A night lawyer?' he exclaimed, incredulously. 'I have never heard of such a thing. What, pray tell, is a *night lawyer*?'

Flack explained that, thanks to the work Melanie had got him doing, he now knew that every national newspaper has a rota of lawyers, who generally arrive at four o'clock in the afternoon and stay until around 9.30pm. Those lawyers – who are on call, once they have left the paper, until the early hours – are a mixture of barristers from the two or three pre-eminent sets of libel chambers, or solicitors who have a background in media law. While the barristers are working on libel cases during the day and moonlighting in the evenings for the experience and contacts the work gives them, many of the solicitors have chosen to forego the security of working for a firm – complete with pension plan, private healthcare, gym membership, a company car and even, sometimes, luncheon vouchers – to strike out on their own, shuttling from newspaper to newspaper evening after evening, largely uninsured and unregulated, subject definitively only to one unwritten rule that says that if they get something wrong, they will never again darken the doors of the unfortunate newspaper they have so sullied. Their task, so long as mistakes are not made, is to read each and every page of the newspaper, and to advise on the legal risks in a given story. There might be a risk of being sued for libel, or there could be a danger of prejudicing a criminal trial, for example by publishing details of an accused's previous convictions. *Contempt of court,* as it is known, explained Flack, for which an editor can even be imprisoned (though none has been for a very long time). There could be a court order prohibiting the identification of certain individuals, breach of which would also be a contempt of court, leading to a fine at the very least. A rape victim entitled by law to lifelong anonymity may have been inadvertently identified; there might be an infringement of the Press Complaints Commission's Code of Practice, something which editors appear to take much more seriously than in former days (though there are those who would argue that the PCC is not merely toothless, but, given its composition by the very people it ostensibly regulates, inherently flawed); there could be a misuse of someone else's laboriously crafted creative work sufficient to found a claim for infringement of copyright. The law of confidence was a problem, too – one which some commentators believed would develop exponentially in the coming years. All these issues jostled at the tip of the iceberg and beneath there were a myriad of other, more subtle but no less deadly problems with which a night lawyer could be confronted, all to be processed at breakneck speed as journalists raced to get the paper off stone and into juggernauts and onto the streets and into newsagents who themselves, Flack noted in uncharacteristically showy fashion, were also theoretically liable in law for the publication of defamatory content. 'It was,' hypothesised Flack, 'probably quite a demanding job.'

The senior partner did not look convinced. 'Hmmm,' he growled, his eyes drifting to a photograph of a woman in her mid-twenties on Flack's desk. 'Friend of yours?' he asked, gesturing towards the dark-haired woman in the picture frame.

'My fiancée,' replied Flack.

'When's the happy day?' enquired the senior partner.

'In nine months.'

'Very good. And what do you think of the night lawyer in Melanie's Spiller case?'

'I'm sorry?'

Dr Tax sighed loudly, before booming: 'What do you think of the naughty night lawyer in marvellous Melanie's sexy Spiller case?'

Yet again, Flack was perturbed. He regretted the enthusiasm with which he had revealed his precocious knowledge of libel law. He blinked, blushed and blurted out that he didn't quite understand what the senior partner was driving at. Dr Tax was only too happy to enlighten him.

'I'll tell you what I'm driving at. It goes like this. Based upon your explanation of the ins and outs of newspaper publishing, the night lawyer must have seen what was published, that in respect of which, unless I am mistaken, Mr Spiller is now suing for libel. He is certain to win and *The Record* will pay substantial damages and all our costs. If the night lawyer were half the man you are suggesting he should have been, he would have spotted the danger, alerted his immediate superiors and helped avoid calamity. Would he not?'

Flack was taken aback. Did Dr Tax know much more than he had let on about the workings of libel law and, more precisely, the role of night lawyers? Clearly, at any rate, he knew more about Melanie's caseload than he had indicated. Flack felt that he was facing a perversely complex and difficult adversary, and had no idea of how to respond.

'I agree, perhaps the night lawyer may have made a mistake.'

The words were ecstatically received by the senior partner.

'A mistake! By the night lawyer! Well, there's a bloody surprise! What did he do, this wonderful night lawyer? Fall asleep on the job? Accidentally take a sleeping pill before he turned up? Ha ha!'

Despite this burst of invective, Flack found himself rising to the unknown night lawyer's defence. 'Perhaps there were so many stories to advise upon that night that he didn't get a chance to consider this one properly,' he said, with more conviction than either he or Dr Tax had thought possible. Dr Tax's laugh ended as abruptly as it had begun, and he swung his long legs back onto Melanie's desk. 'Well, you know, young Flack, it's a good thing he was too busy, or asleep, or down the pub, or simply, like most night lawyers, an idiot, because if he'd been any good at his job our Mr Spiller wouldn't have much of a claim, now would he?'

'No, sir, I suppose not,' said Flack, feeling thoroughly cowed, not least by another lapse into calling Dr Tax 'sir'. Dr Tax, though, was on a roll.

'Let's look at the facts, Flack,' he announced, getting up and striding towards the twenty-five-year-old articled clerk. Dr Tax was a large, well-built man with a shock of black hair, and the rapidity with which he spoke and approached Flack's desk was terrifying. 'Here we have our Mr Spiller, a well-known actor who has appeared in countless films, highbrow and lowbrow and even some that lurk unclassifiably in the middle, on television and in the cinema. He is a force to be reckoned with, an actor who, if not of the highest order, is from the top drawer, if you will forgive the mixing of my metaphors. He has been honoured by his peers and feted by a nation. He does not disdain to open supermarkets and even, occasionally, writes sagaciously on issues of film finance in our best financial newspapers. And along comes *The Record* and says he is a convicted blackmailer. Nothing could be further from the truth or, if it is true, perhaps due regard should have been paid to the Rehabilitation of Offenders Act and the law on publishing details of spent convictions. God knows that such does not fall to the journalist, who cannot be expected to recall such technicalities having passed a mere diploma in journalism.

'No, this is the territory of the night lawyer. He, or sometimes she, should know every provision of an obscure statute like this like the back of his, or her, hand. In the Spiller case, the night lawyer did not know the law. It is as simple as that. Thank the good Lord, because Melanie will come back from court triumphantly and, thanks less to her undoubted physical beauty but rather more to that of the system, we will all be enriched. But if I were *The Record's* editor, I would be annoyed, and I would cast a long and unforgiving glare at my night lawyers. I might even cast my eye further afield, increase my budget for legal services and appoint some reputable lawyers. For the truth is that night lawyers are mavericks. They are unable to sustain the rigour of a serious life in the law. Their mental fragility and chronic emotional instability leads them to drift to the twilight zone of the profession, where gut instinct is too often confused with legal acumen. And most of the time, they do not even have the instinct.'

The senior partner seemed as if he were about to thump Flack's desk for emphasis at a number of junctures in this speech. Flack sat still, dumbfounded, for perhaps a minute, until the silence was broken by the arrival of Viraf Mehta, one of Melanie's close friends in the firm.

'She's not here,' said the senior partner, with the utmost calm, adding: 'She is in court on the Spiller case, making us a fortune in fees from a cock-up by one of *The Record's* night lawyers.'

Mehta laughed, as if at an in-joke. 'Not again?' he said, before leaving a note on Melanie's desk and leaving the office. Dr Tax once again sat down at her chair, and picked up the note. It was in a sealed envelope. 'What do you think it says?' he asked Flack.

'I really don't know,' said Flack, as neutrally as he could.

'Better not open it, had we?'

'Er, no, I don't think so.'

'Quite right. But aren't you curious?'

'No, I'm not.'

'I am. Like to know what's going on round here. Took me years to build the place up. You never know what people are getting up to. Still, you're right, better leave it where it is.' Dr Tax paused, before rising from Melanie's chair and walking to the front of her desk. He picked up the model of the Eiffel Tower and returned it to its rightful position. He looked over at Flack again. 'Well,' he said, 'I wish you all the best with your fiancée. What's her name?'

'Helen.'

'A nice name,' said the senior partner, who added, as if it were an inconsequential afterthought: 'Tell me, if we were good enough to keep you on once you've finished your articles, in what area of the law do you wish to specialise?'

Flack frowned, and then, shyly, smiled. Despite the gruelling few minutes he had spent with Dr Tax he was an honest young man who was no more capable of lying than he was of arriving at work wearing not a well-cut black suit but a pair of Bermuda shorts. 'Libel,' he stuttered, his lower lip quivering imperceptibly, like a child trying not to cry.

The senior partner shook his head and strode from Flack's sight. After he had gone, Flack noticed that the note from Mehta to Melanie was nowhere to be seen. He picked up the phone to dial Helen's number, and found himself wondering whether night lawyers had to deal with the likes of Dr Tax.

He would have liked to tell his fiancée of his remarkable conversation with his law firm's figurehead, but his number – the number of the flat that he shared with Helen – was engaged. He waited, and tried the number again. Again the line was busy. Flack thought it strange, momentarily at least – he was sure Helen had taken the day off work, and couldn't imagine who she might be talking to – but there was nothing for it but to get back to work. Not that Flack minded: Melanie had asked him to research the defence of fair comment, and just before Dr Tax had arrived he'd discovered that it could be defeated by proof of malice. Flack soon lost himself in case law revealing that this was not merely malice in the everyday sense, but also that which indicated a dominant improper motive, or even, sometimes, mere recklessness as to the truth.

CHAPTER 3

Before the Law

It wasn't as if there was anything wrong with her fiancé as such, but just that – well, Helen couldn't say exactly what it was. Flack was kind, he was steadfast; he was intelligent and he would have been popular, if only he would engage that little bit more with the world around him. Being occasionally mistaken for a cold fish was no great crime, and it was certainly the kind of de minimis behaviour that Helen could forgive. Even as she reflected on her fiancé's character she smiled, for while she – like him, a solicitor – avoided using legal language in everyday situations, Flack seemed unable to help himself. Phrases such as *de minimis, caveat emptor, in camera, sui generis* and *ad seriatim* flowed as naturally from Flack's careful lips as rain through a pristine piece of plastic guttering; sometimes he would even go further, observing *amantes sunt amentes* and *credo quia absurdum est*. And that was the problem, said Helen to herself: 'There's no sex in the man. All is clear and functional and ordered, as if ordained by an obscure system known only to Flack, but there's no spark, no ardour, such scant impetuosity and so very little joie de vivre.'

'He'd rather get up early and sweep the yard on a Sunday morning than mess around in bed,' was a lament that the more intimate of Helen's friends had begun to tire of hearing.

One of them, a considered young woman with a passion for Portuguese literature, instinctively took against her friend during her laments over Flack's apparent failings. All the while that Helen would be moaning about Flack's irritating habits – not least, his quest to sweep every leaf from the courtyard to the rear of the couple's ground floor flat, as if this were not a gesture of futility but a noble embrace of the natural world – Martha would inwardly tut and groan, until finally she could stand it no more.

'Helen,' she would say, in a vexed tone, 'what, really, are you so upset about? Harry Flack is a good-hearted man, who will be loyal and constant. He loves you. He will cherish you, in his own way.

Admittedly he's not very demonstrative, but you knew what he was like before you accepted his proposal, didn't you? What has changed since then? Not Harry, but you.'

Despite an impulsive, some might say hot-headed streak, Helen nevertheless possessed the solicitor's analytical mind and could not help but agree.

'I know, I know, I know, it's me who's the problem, not Harry. He's the same old Harry. Sweet, kind and taciturn; boring, faithful and dull; attentive in his own inattentive way. But Martha, he really *does* sweep the yard on Sunday mornings. On Saturday nights he's always watching the clock, he's always on the brink of saying "Come on, dear, we'd better be going home". That's assuming we've even made it out. He's so predictable! And his Latin phrases – I'm so sick of them. Do you know what he said the other day? "Ad usum". Yes, that's right – ad bloody usum. Do you know what it means?'

Martha had a good idea, but usually felt it best to demure when Helen was in full flow.

'It means "according to custom", Martha,' said Helen. 'He said it before he got up and went into the yard last weekend. "Ad usum, darling, I'm going to sweep the yard." I mean, honestly, it's too much! I just wish he'd do something different, something wild or eccentric, something red-blooded, something *not* according to custom, maybe even something subversive. You don't know what a smile it would bring to my face if for once in his life Harry decided to step out of line.'

As ever when the conversation reached this point, Helen would feel the beginnings of guilt with as much force as the feelings that had animated her earlier condemnation of her fiancé. How could she say such things? Wasn't Harry, after all, her future husband? Granted, their engagement had an air of ethereality – in the sense that it had seemed to drift toward them and weigh anchor, rather than the couple having consciously set a course for it – but nevertheless, they were engaged. They had even set a day for the wedding. It was to be two years after they began work in the law, a decision made with rather more forethought than Flack had shown in his efforts to secure Helen's hand (or she, his). Did they love each other? Yes, we did, said Helen to herself, surveying the past. They had fallen in love, or into a sea-drift of sensible compromise, in their penultimate year at Oxford, where both read law. While many student liaisons are doomed to evanescence, theirs rapidly consolidated itself as a serious, estimable affair of the heart, one that even the most resolute philanderer would grudgingly admire. *There go Harry and Helen, the happy couple – and how happy they are*, went the largely uncritical refrain, as their peers could not but acknowledge that this was a case of genuine empathy and affection, perhaps even love. Flack, as ever ordered and orderly, seemed somehow to have subdued the flighty Helen, but the subjugation was consensual, such psychological restraint as underpinned the relationship at once covert and welcome. The couple's bond persisted to Law School in Guildford, where they not only sat next to each other in lectures, as was their wont at Oxford, but went the extra mile in renting a Spartan but adequate flat in the centre of town. It was above a newsagent's and of a Sunday morning, fresh from having carefully watched his alcohol intake the night before, Flack would pop downstairs and out of the adjoining door, from there to take an immediate right turn and enter the shop. Inside he would peer at the newspapers, marvelling at the profusion of words unleashed on the nation on God's day of rest, and scrutinise each for telltale signs of politics in the headlines. Often he would notice little else in the shop, and later, if asked to describe who had served him, he would not be able to say if it were a man or a woman, still less what age they were, whether they were attractive and if they had spoken to him. But Flack unfailingly noticed the headlines of each and every newspaper. He absorbed them carefully, devotedly, and would think nothing of buying every paper in the shop, thence to return, arms laden but content, to the flat he shared with Helen. For Flack, a Sunday spent reading several newspapers from cover to cover was the most perfect way to spend a day imaginable.

Early on in their relationship Helen was happy to join her fiancé on the couple's somewhat bedraggled sofa, a beige thing purchased from an antiques shop in Guildford. She too would plough through the papers, stopping every now and then to discuss a story with Flack. If she cast her mind back to the very beginning, she could, so she told Martha, recall that on at least two occasions she had managed to make her future husband cast aside *The Sunday Record* in favour of sex. 'But it wasn't *hot*, if you know what I mean,' she said. 'Harry always made me feel as if I'd interrupted a ritual, as if sex, outside the time he'd allocated for it, was an inconvenience. And as for when we moved to London, forget it.'

London was the obvious place for the bright young couple to begin legal careers which their parents assumed would be lucrative and perhaps, given the day and age, even glittering. Helen secured a training contract with a 'magic circle' firm, one whose hours would be a torment but whose salary and prospects would surely make it all worthwhile. She was savvy, quick-witted and, when the mood took her, amiable; she was academic, too. At no point during her law degree, or in her post-graduate studies, had she stumbled over legal principles, a fate not shared by Flack, for whom contemplation of the law of trusts and tax remained only marginally more appealing than spending a day sitting in a moorland bog. His disinclination was not, however, matched by ineptitude. It took him time to muster the will to tackle trusts and tax, but tackle them he did – tolerably well, if not with brilliance.

For Helen, it all came easily. She even wrote well, too – a skill often said, by barristers, to be lacking in solicitors – and bridled only at the thought of advocacy. 'A few interlocutory hearings will be fine, but I don't see myself being the next Rumpole,' she would say, words which resonated with those interviewing her for they, too, if they were honest, which sometimes happened, would admit that theirs was not a vocation for the courtroom limelight but rather the joy that comes of being a general behind the lines, marshalling his forces, deploying them to the best possible effect, crushing opponents and returning with the spoils. If Helen could only suppress an occasional tendency to impulsiveness ('And she will, trust me,' said her father, a former naval captain who had retired, with his wife of forty years, to Portugal), she would have no problem in this environment. In time, she too would rise to be a general.

Her husband-to-be was apparently cut of even more predictable cloth. Unlike Helen, whose rash decisions had never influenced her academic or societal progress but which had seen her make one or two poor choices in men ('Why does she pick these dreadfully driven chaps? They're always so much trouble,' was periodically, if also rhetorically, uttered by her mother until Helen settled down with Flack), Flack was temperance personified. His interests – cricket, jazz, literature – were pursued with measured fidelity rather than ostentation. He was as capable of discoursing on the etymology of the word 'cricket' as much as reciting lists of England's finest players;

he could rhapsodise with the most diehard jazz buff on the intricacies of Gil Evans's 'La Nevada' and the several incarnations of Miles Davis, though, if he were feeling heretical, he would admit that he struggled with 'On The Corner'. And he shared, too, Martha's love for the literature of the Iberian peninsula. The poems of Fernando Pessoa were often at his bedside, so too his *Book of Disquiet*. But Flack rarely spoke of such things. Martha had once heard him say that he agreed with the Coimbra law student turned writer Eça de Queirós, who declared that everything about English society 'is disagreeable to me – from its limited way of thinking to its indecent manner of cooking vegetables'. Eça de Queirós even – said Flack – said that he detested England, and yet could not help but conclude that 'as a thinking nation, she is probably the foremost'. But if ever Martha tried to engage him further on these topics, a gentle half-smile – of courtesy, diplomacy, the desire to avoid confrontation – would flit on Flack's lips before he changed the subject.

His very taciturnity commended him, however, to the legal profession. This was a man whose sense of discretion needed no bolstering by a course on the law of confidence, still less exposure to the professional conduct courses which lawyers must complete, lest they forget how to be ethical. It was innate, as much a part of him as his eyes and ears. Those tasked with appointing the next intake of solicitors from the ranks of Oxford's undergraduates saw at once that Flack was of the right stuff. 'He's clearly able, if a little weak on trusts, dresses well and exudes tact,' they would say. They might go further and suggest that he would not excel amid the cut and thrust of litigation, but surely Flack had all the makings of the suave commercial lawyer, the man who, in time, will have the ear of captains of industry, financiers and politicians. 'He has the potential to be a first-class lawyer of the utmost dependability,' was the conclusion to many a memo written by a lawyer lucky enough to interview the young Flack. Better yet, he was engaged to be married. He liked cricket. Flack was the safest bet of all.

Those who backed him – or, perhaps rather, those whose backing he acquiesced in – turned out to be a medium-sized player in legal London. His peers assumed that Flack would follow Helen's suit and accept any of a number of offers from magic circle firms, but he confounded them, opting for the Holborn offices of Bowles & Parkes. The firm was respected, certainly, but even its staunchest advocate, or retained PR advisor, would blanch at arguing for heavyweight status. No, Bowles & Parkes was one of London's many decent, honourable, long-standing and independent firms, one which had merged occasionally, as if it felt obliged to keep pace with the times, but which had never seriously threatened to do much more than make a tidy living for its thirty or so equity partners. Its employees were paid well, but not over the odds; bonuses were reasonable and welcome but never, even in the best of times, outlandish; the firm's health, safety and discrimination policies were au courant but not slavishly adhered to; the Christmas party could engender embarrassment but only of the transient (if no less mortifying) kind peculiar to the professional classes.

But for Flack, Bowles & Parkes was perfect. It had a libel practice. And this, felt Flack – even as an undergraduate, perhaps even when he was at school, certainly in the midst of his studies at Guildford – was the most fascinating branch of law of all.

CHAPTER 4

Club Hydra

Aside from the unpredictability of Dr Tax, life at Bowles & Parkes was everything Flack had hoped it would be.

He was busy, but not unfeasibly so; he was well-liked, in a quiet, respectful fashion; and better yet, he was capable. Flack's mind was so well suited to the law that he was able to breeze through even those aspects he found boring. They were, in no particular order, the law of conveyancing, which he endured as part of his articles of clerkship; the law of wills and probate, which was likewise compulsory; and the law of trusts, which often dovetailed with bricks and mortar, death and inheritance. These subjects Flack found tedious, dry and a little depressing, but there was no avoiding them and in accepting their inevitability Flack not only found that he understood them but also ensured a more tranquil passage through the years of his articled clerkship than at least one of his colleagues, Ryan Verter, who found it impossible to pretend that he was even vaguely interested in clients who wanted to buy houses and make wills. Verter's antipathy to quotidian law was, according to Melanie Masters, sure to get him into trouble: 'If there's one thing the senior partner loathes, it's people who think they can run before they can walk.' That Verter lost no time in bemoaning his fate to colleagues in protracted after-work drinking sessions was also, it struck Flack, unhelpful to his cause.

But if Flack marched to a steadier drum, he was also as incisive a lawyer as Bowles & Parkes had seen in its long and moderately venerable history. His obligatory stint in conveyancing, wills and probate over, Flack's next seat was in the firm's employment department. There he dazzled his boss, a sallow man called Caines, with an immediate grasp not merely of the law but of its human subtext. Even Caines, a man in his late fifties who was so jaded that he would regularly announce, to anyone who would listen, that he would like to leave the law but that he had to remain in practice 'to my dying day because otherwise how am I going to keep my wife and brats in the style to which, having taken my money, they've become accustomed?', even the despairing and oft-disobliging Caines was impressed by Flack's ability to empathise, as he noted in a memorandum to the senior partner, summing up Flack's six months under his tutelage:

> *I endorse the prevailing view of Harry Flack. He is quiet and thorough, but not so quiet and so thorough that he is a nonentity. Instead, he demonstrates great legal acumen. I remind you of the Wright case, in which his research on the law of constructive unfair dismissal was excellent. He is also abundantly in possession of what is sadly all too rare among today's young people: empathy. Flack gets to the nub of things quickly and can put himself in the client's shoes. Such compassion, in an employment law context and given this firm's bias towards acting for claimants, is an asset. In short, it's been a pleasure having Flack in my department and I would welcome him back, should the firm ultimately decide to keep him on. Which is more than can be said for that fool Verter – but that's another story. Perhaps you might have time to discuss our current intake of articled clerks at the usual place on Thursday after work? I gather that Verter has, once again, married conviviality with indiscretion.*

Flack's easy progress among the foot soldiers of Bowles & Parkes was not matched by Helen's experience at her magic circle firm. Perhaps this was no surprise, for rather than real engagement with the law Helen often found herself wedded to the photocopying machine, her task, as a putative City solicitor, being the copying and collation of bundles of documents for a corporate fraud trial. There could be no doubting the importance of this work, for without it barristers would have nothing upon which to focus their efforts in court, save the accused and sundry witnesses, and thus the edifice of the law would prove to be a chimera or, worse, intangible, but if this is a truism it is just as undeniable that standing by a photocopier (even those of the highest of standards and slickest of mechanisms) and inserting document after document, so that a facsimile can be created which, once it has come into existence, is then placed in the appropriate place, perhaps a lever arch file, or one of those old buff folders that somehow, even in today's increasingly paperless world, survive, yes, even with the most wizardly of contemporary equipment it goes beyond a rebuttable presumption to state, without equivocation, that this role soon becomes tiresome to anyone with a university degree, whether it is in Law or, as has become common among lawyers, another subject, such as History, English Literature, Physics or even, in the case of a notorious solicitor from Wales, something known as Surf Science. We might add that photocopying grows wearisome for anyone, legally qualified or otherwise, condemned to its practice but for her part Helen – commendably qualified in the law, and only the law – took initially to her role with gusto, mindful of her father's hope that come the day she entered the legal profession on a full-time basis she would settle down, her flightiness vacating her personality as a rain-puddle on a pavement evaporates under a burning City of London sun in the height of summer. If, as a trainee solicitor in a magic circle firm, Helen had a vision in which she made rapid, not to say instantaneous, steps to glamour, power and wealth, her acquiescence in such mind-numbing labour arose from the fact that she was bright enough to accept that a few weeks' at the photocopier was par for the course – if not quite, as she drily noted under her breath, 'part of the magic'. But as the case wended its way through interminable interlocutory hearings, each necessitating the creation of yet another vanload of documents, weeks became months. Helen's acceptance of her role turned into resentment. She thought of her fiancé, at his medium-sized, increasingly niche (for Melanie Masters had just won another high-profile libel trial) firm, and wondered if she might have been happier at a similar kind of outfit. After all, even if he had found conveyancing boring, at least Flack was properly engaged with the law. At least he was learning his trade. By way of sorry contrast, Helen found it very hard to see what possible use interminable hours spent photocopying was to the development of her legal skills.

The conclusion of one twelve-hour Friday at the photocopier saw Helen only too keen to drown her sorrows at the nearest pub. She was not a dedicated drinker but when she got going tended to keep going, and, over the past few months of glorified secretarial labour, had ventured to The Hanging Dog for three or four extended sessions. Thankfully, each had been on a Friday, for Helen had not been in a fit state for work the following day. Indeed, she had, to Flack's unexpressed chagrin, failed to return home, opting instead to stay with Martha, her friend from university who found herself living in London at the outset of a career in publishing.

'It's OK, Harry, she's with me,' had been Martha's words, uttered, with Helen giggling in the background, the last time she had stayed out drinking. 'We're in a cab on the way back to my place. I'll send her home when she's in a fit state tomorrow.' As ever, Martha was sober, careful and considerate, her friendship with Helen one of opposites attracting and her compassion for Flack perhaps, to those who like to infer hidden meanings in the most prosaic of circumstances, signifying an unrequited ardour for him. 'No, you can't talk to him,' Flack heard her say to Helen, just before the line went dead. 'You're too drunk.'

Flack's trust in Helen was sufficient to withstand any green-eyed stirrings and it never occurred to him to cross-examine her upon her return, somewhat worse for wear, early the following afternoon. This, though, was another of Helen's criticisms as her third glass of dry white wine was poured by a waiter who, she couldn't help but note, was rather handsome.

'Look, it's not as if Harry even cares if I stay out all night, so what's the problem?' she asked, not of Martha, who was unable to join her for what Helen happily predicted would be 'a bender' but of three work colleagues, two female and one male. All were articled clerks and all, to varying degrees, were finding that magic circle firms weren't always magical at the outset of one's career.

'So it's settled, then?' said Simon, an Alpine, angular young man who listed rowing as his primary passion. 'We're going to the club?'

The women – all three of them, Helen, Natalie and Angela – nodded their assent. Natalie, however, thought it best to double-check that Helen was as sure as she seemed.

'Won't Harry be annoyed? Didn't you promise him you'd be going home for dinner tonight?'

'I did, but he won't mind,' replied Helen. 'Honestly. He'll just read his Portuguese poetry or listen to his jazz or do whatever else he does when I'm not there. Let's go! I'm in the mood for letting my hair down.'

This was music to Simon's ears. 'Perfect! I don't know about this Harry, whoever he is, but you sound like my sort of girl!'

'Harry is Helen's fiancé,' said Natalie. 'He's nice.'

'Yes, *nice*,' said Helen, 'but he doesn't know what it's like to stand next to a photocopier all week long and, frankly, darling, he wouldn't know a good night out if it hit him in the face. Come on, drink up!'

Within half an hour the party had entered the swish and exclusive Club Hydra, so named less in honour of the chthonic Lernaean water beast but more because its proprietor owned a substantial villa on the Saronic Greek island which, if the rumours were true, was once much favoured by Canadian singer-songwriters and European artists alike. Inside the ambience was well-heeled and thrusting. The opulence passed for discreet, the crowd were too young to be decadent and the cocktails were apostrophized. The exclamatory fervour transmitted itself to the clientele, who seemed long ago to have crossed the boundaries of conversational restraint. They bayed and brayed and barked and bawled, almost as if in unconscious emulation of Lake Lerna's many-headed serpent, that which gave Heracles such a miserable time of it until, if Greek mythology tells us anything of use, the resourceful and much-tested hero pioneered the techniques of both surgical decapitation and cauterization, apparently with a little help from his nephew, Iolaus.

'Christ, it's loud in here!'

The author of this statement was Eddie Conrad, journalist. He was welcomed by Simon with a guffaw and a pat on the shoulder, as if he had just said something of great wit and brilliance. But Conrad was not one for sycophancy. 'Simon, get on with the introductions!' he shouted. 'Who are these lovely ladies?'

Above the din Simon introduced each of Natalie, Angela and Helen. With practised ease Eddie Conrad, a man who had been a reporter with *The Morning Star* for four years, air-kissed the women, clasping each by the waist with his right hand as he did so. Only a dullard would have failed to observe that Helen's eyes bore a dreamy sheen as she pulled back from Conrad's pseudo-kiss and admired his fresh, olive complexion and smooth cheeks. Above them sat a pair of dark-brown eyes which, even the same dullard might have said, returned her gaze with equal interest.

*

Flack was alone. Now, for the first time, there had been no phone call. Neither Helen nor Martha, nor anyone else, had called. With the suppleness that comes of youth, he sprang from his bed and made his way into the living room. Was there a message on the answer phone of the south London flat he'd shared with Helen since the couple had begun their respective jobs in the law?

Nothing. He looked outside, into the morning-drab street. 'What am I doing? Am I expecting to see her here?' he asked himself. He concluded he wasn't, and sat down on the large beige sofa that had accompanied the lovers from Guildford. Absent-mindedly, he turned on the TV. Absent-mindedly, he watched it. And then, thoughtfully, he wondered where on earth Helen had got to.

'I'd better ring Martha,' he said to himself. 'She's bound to be there.'

Martha's voice merged concern and tenderness in a tone that a more astute listener might have found revealing. 'No, she's not here, Harry. She rang last night and asked me out for a drink, but I couldn't make it. Haven't you heard from her at all?'

'Not a word. I'm sure she's fine. If she happens to call, could you just ask her to call me?'

'Of course I will, Harry,' said Martha. 'But are you sure you're all right?'

'Oh yes,' said Flack. 'Don't worry about me.'

By way of a distraction Flack set off to buy the morning papers. This was less a diversionary tactic and more the enactment of a cherished ritual. Once, Flack had even counted the number of steps it took him to reach the newsagent's – 552, to be precise, though precision in such matters is elusive, for an unexpected encounter with, say, a mother pushing a pram, or a happy couple out jogging, or even, heaven forbid, a threatening gang of youths, or, yet worse, a determined mugger, all of these things can set a man off his stride and talking of which – the male perspective, that is – it is also correct to say that sometimes the mere sight of a beautiful woman on the other side of the street can result in a wandering eye which, in turn, can be disastrous when it comes to the simple act of putting one foot in front of the other. Then, if a man of lesser probity than Harry Flack allows himself to turn and stare as she walks, sans seductive intent but nevertheless brimful of femininity, all manner of perambulatory chaos can ensue. Some men, in this situation, have walked into dustbins, while others have banged their heads against lampposts. Still others have careered off the pavement and into the road, only narrowly avoiding serious injury, whether as a result of a car travelling in excess of the designated speed limit or because, at that exact moment, a cyclist is pedalling as fast as he can in pursuit of a powerful and yet obscure quest, one destined to lurk forever beneath his helmeted visage.

Happily, however, Flack did not have an errant eye. In fact, it was fair to agree with Helen when she observed that, as he strode each Saturday and Sunday morning to buy the papers, he looked as if he had found a calling from which he would never, in a thousand trips, be distracted. On this day, too, it took no more than a few of the 552 steps ahead of him to forget all about Helen's whereabouts and start wondering what might be in the papers. This curiosity embraced almost everything the press had to offer, from the calculated rants of the weekly columnists to the property, finance and business pages, even including the outdoors features and especially, of course, anything about cricket. Flack regarded himself as well-informed – indeed, he could not be otherwise – and another of his passions lay in trying to second-guess the lead news stories, something which he hesitated to ascribe to an unfulfilled editorial urge owing to the awareness of other aspects of his character which, so far as he knew, would always be in the ascendancy.

At what he subsequently imagined (for he had not been counting) was approximately the 460th step, his ruminations were shattered. There, walking unsteadily towards him, was Helen.

It is not known whether Flack's instinctual and immediate emotion was one of concern or astonishment, but conjecture suggests that his mind was swamped with a pair of tautologous clichés. First, he said to himself: 'She looks as if she's been dragged through a hedge backwards' then, moments later, he thought: 'She is most definitely not a sight for sore eyes.' Helen herself would not have disputed either contention. Her eyes were bloodshot, her face was devoid of colour and her blonde hair, always so neat, was wayward and ungovernable.

'Harry, I'm so sorry,' she said. 'I bet I look like death warmed up. Can we go back to the flat and talk?'

Flack gave her a hug. 'It's OK,' he said. 'I knew you'd be fine. Why don't you go on home and I'll just get the papers? I've walked this far so I might as well.'

If Helen's eyes hadn't been so dropsical, it might have been possible for Flack to note that they widened – only slightly, admittedly – in amazement at this suggestion. But then again, he had turned on his heel and was on his way to the shop so quickly that Helen barely had time to murmur 'typical' before continuing on her way.

CHAPTER 5

Deer Tracks

Within minutes of returning to their flat Helen had stripped off and climbed into a hot bath. Foremost among the emotions assailing her was a desperate desire for water. She felt as if she wanted to drink it forever, and greedily gulped a bottle of chilled still water, one of Flack's ever-present supplies; she wanted to hear it, too, and relished the sound of the liquid cascading from the taps of the bath; and, most of all, she wanted to feel her body covered, from head to toe, in water so hot as to be almost scalding.

Lying still in the bath, a static image of Flack's face – solicitous and yet preoccupied, with what she wasn't sure, though it was probably the cricket or another of his routines – kept appearing whenever Helen took her mind back to the events of the night before. How she wished Flack wasn't so insistent, how she yearned for him to be more as he was in life, a minor character, intelligent and quiet and unthreatening, undemonstrative, the kind of man who listens before he speaks and certainly isn't the type to intrude upon an erotic reverie – for what memories she had ... But gradually, as she revisited them with the persistence of a paparazzo in pursuit of his quarry, Flack departed from her mind's eye. One man dominated her thoughts, the tall, quick-talking, black-haired and adroit Eddie Conrad, a man unlike any she'd met before. Where on earth had he been all her life? And how could she think of wasting it with Flack? Dear Harry, so faithful, so nice, so dull, so boring. What was she doing with him? What did they ever actually *do*?

'He's back in my mind again,' sighed Helen. 'And soon he'll be back from buying the papers. And then we'll sit around, doing nothing but reading them, all day. We won't even talk about where I got to last night. Oh Eddie, where are you?'

The night before had gone like a dream. Club Hydra had been fun, abandoned, devil-take-the-consequences fun, so much so that even the disapproving Natalie had let her hair down. Had Natalie, now she thought of it, ended up with the young investment banker they'd met halfway through the evening? Helen wasn't sure. She remembered Natalie's disappearance in a cab with him, but perhaps things had gone no further. As for herself, as Helen lay in the bath, soaping her arms and thighs, she remembered the look on Eddie's face the first time she saw him. So commanding, almost stern, and yet he had the most delightful, insouciant smile, one that suggested mystery and mischief in equal measure. They'd flirted from that moment on, their banter easy, amused and, for one or two of their group, exhausting. It was as if they were two long lost friends, eager to catch up on a lifetime of anecdotes. They even spent five minutes discussing how they must have met, sometime, somewhere – was it at university? Or sixth form college? Or on a holiday? Had they been brought up in the same area? None of this proved to be true but their connection was instant and impregnable. No one else could get a word in edgeways, and so exclusive was the duo's conversation that Angela even asked Simon how they knew each other.

'They've only just met,' he confirmed, adding, with a peculiar hint of spite, that 'it looks like love at first sight, don't you think? I wonder how Helen will square that with her tedious husband-to-be.'

But the last thing on Helen's mind was Harry Flack. And yet again, as she replayed the evening's events in the bath, Flack the interloper appeared in her thoughts. 'Oh, go away!' she muttered, as Flack's studious, kindly, constant face interrupted the rhythm of her memory, one which was intensified by the realisation that she had two faint bruises on both hips, where the bones merged with her abdomen. 'Eddie's hands, gripping me tight, pulling me towards him,' remembered Helen. 'He'd turned me over. I was on the sofa.' But there was Flack. 'Go away!' said Helen, audibly. But her pleasure was sure to be compromised. Within minutes Flack would be back, she'd hear him turn the lock in the door, come in and sit down on their old beige sofa. When she emerged from the bathroom, she'd find him ensconced in its decrepit folds with a mountain of newspapers. But there was still time to cast her mind back, to think of the feel of Eddie's body next to her on the back seat of the cab. Eddie asked the driver to drive home along the Embankment – 'I love the river at night, don't you? Let's take a detour' – before dropping him at his home in Chelsea and then continuing to take Helen to the Fulham flat she shared with Flack. On the way they'd slid ever closer, until their hands were interlocked as if it were the most natural thing in the world. What had they talked about? Why, everything and nothing, but then, yes, that's right – the poem. Helen could remember only the first two lines:

Beautiful, sobbing, high-geared fucking

'It's called *Deer Tracks* and it's by an American writer,' said Eddie. 'Have you heard of it?'

Helen had said no, it had never crossed her radar; coquettishly, she added that it sounded promising. 'Go on,' she said, squeezing Eddie's hand. 'How's the rest of it go?' And then, of course, she remembered: Eddie had only read the first two lines in the cab. He couldn't recall the rest, but it was in a book, in his flat – would she like to come in, just for half an hour? He'd find it and read it to her. 'It's the kind of poem every woman should know,' he said. 'Then I'll call you another cab and you'll be home before you know it.'

Conrad's second-floor flat, in a Chelsea mews, was reached via a narrow staircase lined with wine-red wallpaper. Its front door led to a corridor, at the end of which was a bedroom. Peering ahead, as she followed Eddie along the corridor, Helen fancied the bed was unmade, but they turned right before the bedroom, into the sitting room. There, as she sat on a brown leather sofa waiting for her host to bring her a shot of vodka ('Just one for the road – it can't do any harm,' he'd said), Helen noticed a parquet floor which, where it wasn't suffering under the weight of books, papers and CDs, was thick with dust. Just as she was musing on how Harry would never have allowed such caprice to prevail, Conrad handed her a drink.

'Do you like Miles Davis?' he asked.

Inwardly, Helen groaned. She had heard *Kind of Blue* so many times courtesy of her fiancé that she had come to loathe it and everything about its creator.

'Yes,' she replied. 'Have you got *Kind of Blue*?'

'I have, but let's not bother with it,' said Conrad. 'It's been played so much it might as well be lift music.'

Helen couldn't prevent a look of relief from crossing her tired, and yet exuberant, features.

'I knew it!' said Conrad. 'You're suffering from Death-by-Miles-Davis. It's a common syndrome, especially in attractive young women. They find themselves so over-exposed to Miles by would-be Casanovas and nice but dull partners that they begin to yearn for anything-but-Miles. Am I right?'

Helen confessed that he was. 'In that case,' said Conrad, 'I have the perfect antidote. Wait a sec.'

Soon the flat was filled with the minimalist sounds of Brian Eno's *Music for Airports*. Helen wasn't sure what to make of it, and her ambivalence wasn't lost on Conrad.

'It's great, isn't it?' he declared. 'It's like abstract art. It means absolutely anything you want it to mean.'

Helen wondered what Eddie meant, but before she could decide he'd jumped up and was rooting among his books. 'I didn't bring you here to listen to Brian Eno, now did I? I brought you here to read you a poem. And that's what I shall do.' In less than a minute his search had proved successful.

'I've found it!' he said. '*Deer Tracks*, by Richard Brautigan. Are you sure you've never heard of him? Before he died, of a self-inflicted gunshot wound at the age of forty-nine, he wrote some weird and wonderful books, things like *The Hawkline Monster* and *Sombrero Fallout*. Also *The Revenge of the Lawn*. A jealous boyfriend once took a pair of scissors to my copy. He left the cover intact, by way of a little joke. I imagine he chuckled at the thought of me picking up the book, which I'd been raving about to his girlfriend, only to open it and find that it had been cut in half. People are strange, don't you think?'

Helen remembered asking if Conrad made a habit of provoking jealousy among boyfriends. He grinned and told her to close her eyes. She did as she was told. 'Listen to this,' he said, before reading:

Deer Tracks

Beautiful, sobbing, high-geared fucking
and then to lie silently like deer tracks
in the freshly-fallen snow beside the one
you love. That's all.

She kept her eyes closed for a long time, wondering if there was more, beginning to realise there wasn't, and all the while hearing the words float over the strange, tranquillising texture of *Music for Airports*. She only opened them, briefly, when she felt Eddie's lips kissing hers.

*

Flack was alone. Now was Helen's chance. The chance to confess, to set the record straight, perhaps even to engineer that most miraculous of circumstances, the clean slate. With the kind of feline grace which, when we are young, survives a night on the tiles, she slunk into the sitting room. Instead of taking her place, next to her fiancé on the beige sofa, she looked out into the street. A number of people came and went, sauntering along, foot-loose and fancy-free. None of them saw her and, if we are to remain faithful to the hardest taskmaster of them all, factual accuracy, we should not be surprised, for the living room window of the Flack flat was blessed with that most English of inventions, the net curtain. From behind the sanctuary of its veil, Helen was invisible, or, again if we are to be scrupulously honest, barely visible. Either way, she was able to look on unseen at the Fulham street in which she had made her home for a little over a year. What she saw did not please her, but, at that juncture, nothing other than the sight of Eddie Conrad bounding up to her front door, whether or not he was brandishing a bunch of flowers, would have pleased her.

'I'm in love,' she said to herself. 'It's crazy, I know. I've known him for less than twenty-four hours. But I *know* he's the one. Christ, what am I going to do?' But even as she felt a terrible sense of desolation a smile nudged her lips, one prompted by the twinge she felt in her hips and stomach and the way Eddie had kissed her: softly, delicately at first, as if merely kissing would always be enough, until then he'd gently bitten her upper lip, two or three times, before their tongues met in what Helen, replaying what had happened, saw as a kind of perfect violence. 'Christ, it was incredible,' thought Helen. 'Such passion but something else, too, something I've not had before. I wish I was with him now.'

But again, even fixing her eyes on the vacant street outside their flat could not prevent Flack's unbidden arrival. There was his face, hovering behind the kisses she was recalling; and there he sat, behind her, reading his papers.

Helen turned to face Flack. Now was her chance. As she turned she felt a now familiar, pleasing ache on both sides of her hips, and as she had predicted, Flack sat, Buddha-like, surrounded by the Saturday papers. He'd managed an 'All right my love?' when he'd heard her leave the bathroom but that was it. How long had she stood gazing out of the window without either of them saying a word? Did he even know she was there?

'Harry,' she said decisively. 'We need to talk.'

Flack did not look up, but he did reply. 'Of course, dear. Do you mind if I just finish reading this story first?'

Helen groaned, took an angry step towards Flack and then exclaimed: 'Yes! I do!'

Startled, Flack looked up at her. She stood before him, radiant after her bath, wearing a dressing gown with her eyes ablaze, hands on her hips and shoulders taut and angular. He had never seen her like this before. She could be acerbic, dry and catty, and once or twice he'd seen a flash of the hot-headed streak rued by her father, but he, Flack, had never witnessed anything resembling temper, still less genuine rage. But a wild-eyed and angry woman now stood before him. What had happened? What could he have done wrong? He'd not said a word about her night out, had not even cast a mournful glance at her when they'd met on the pavement. His trust in her was absolute – he would never interrogate her about where she'd been in a thousand years. Surely she knew this, and respected him for it? Did Helen imagine that he was making her wait before subjecting her to an onslaught of cross-examination? So was this then a pre-emptive strike?

Flack gazed at Helen, his mind grappling with guilt. He had been inattentive. He had not asked if she'd enjoyed her night out and he'd failed to appreciate that she must be suffering from a hangover. And as he gazed at her, a look of torment on his face growing with every unspoken second, he realised, afresh, that he loved her even in this most unexpected of incarnations.

'I'm sorry,' said Flack. 'I've been ignorant.' With these words, he rose from the sofa and walked towards her. Within a couple of steps they were standing face-to-face. Flack clasped Helen, and, pulling her freshly scented body towards his, whispered in her ear: 'I love you. Nothing else matters. Does it?'

With her head on his right shoulder, and their cheeks touching, Helen looked past Flack, out of the living room and down the corridor to their kitchen. From this vantage point she could see that Flack had done the tidying up, that he'd vacuumed the carpet and washed and neatly stacked the dishes. Perhaps he had also swept the yard. Helen didn't know. She closed her eyes and, returning her fiancé's embrace, she sobbed, so quietly and softly that Flack would never know.

CHAPTER 6

Broken Glass

Even Flack, a man so immersed in a series of routines and rituals that he often failed to notice anything beyond them, could tell that things were different. One minute Helen was as playful as ever, the next she was sullen and withdrawn. She had taken to staring out of the sitting room window for minutes at a time, her eyes and forehead protruding above the net curtain, her body tense and expectant. But nothing ever happened. No one came, the nothing new was the always the same. Whatever Helen was hoping for failed to materialise. After perhaps five minutes of apparently purposeless immobility, she would turn, take the few steps to the beige sofa and sink into it with a sigh. But then, just as she was prone to staring blankly into space, she was also capable of sudden coquetry. Flack would find himself subject to a barrage of advances, from subtle teasing to overt sexual posturing. Most, he resisted, for to succumb on an ad hoc basis to erotic urges was neither in his nature nor something he commended. There was a time and a place for such things, and it was not when Flack was reading the papers. Occasionally, though, there was nothing to do but sate Helen's thirst. Try as he might Flack was powerless to resist, and afterwards, as the pair sat, bathed in unforeseen exhaustion, on the sofa, he reflected that actually the suspension of one's normal habits wasn't such a bad thing. Perhaps he should give in more often? After all, wasn't sex a natural and wholesome urge? Maybe, if he could only be that little bit more spontaneous, not to say abandoned, Helen would be happier?

For unhappy she was. Even Flack could see that things were awry. From Monday to Friday she slaved at the photocopier for her elite and magical law firm; on weekends she either paced the flat, like a boxer in his dressing room before a fight, or stood stock still at the window, as if she had been discommoded by an unseen punch and was taking a standing count, eyes glazed, affixed to the street outside but seeing nothing. Then she would snap out of her trance and either harass Flack or sulk. What was wrong with her?

Flack assumed that dissatisfaction at work was the cause of Helen's discontent. Almost anyone would bridle at the prospect of spending hours at a time photocopying documents and putting them in files, no matter how well paid they were or to what greater good. He said as much one Saturday morning, after he'd read two of the five papers he'd bought earlier.

'Perhaps you could talk to your supervising partner and tell him you're unhappy with being a glorified paralegal?' he offered in the direction of Helen's back: she was, as so often these days, staring out of the window.

She did not respond. But Flack was determined to try and make some headway.

'Darling, I'm just wondering,' he said, 'if you're so fed up with your lot, why not have a word with your supervising partner? I'm sure he'd understand.'

'She's a she,' snapped Helen, turning to face him.

'Oh,' said Flack. 'Well, anyway, why don't you have a chat about how things are going? She's not unapproachable, is she?'

Helen sighed. 'No, I suppose not,' she said. 'I'll go and see her on Monday. I'm sure she'll click her fingers and solve all my problems. By the end of the day I'll be handling the juiciest case going, one that is the envy of everyone in London, and I'll be oh-*so*-happy.' She strode past Flack to the kitchen. He could hear her clattering around, opening drawers and slamming them shut with such force that it was as if a dervish, rather than a temperate articled clerk engaged to be married, was on the loose. Before long, there was the sound of breaking glass. Flack jumped up and ran down the corridor to the kitchen.

'It's nothing,' said Helen. 'I just dropped a glass.'

At her bare feet were shards of a wine glass, from which she had been drinking the night before. Flack found the dustpan and brush.

'You didn't cut yourself – that's the main thing,' he said, looking up at Helen as he swept up the glass.

'Yes, that's the main thing, Harry, isn't it?' she spat.

Flack stopped what he was doing. He looked at her. She cast a withering glance at the man she was set to marry within a year and said: 'I'm going out.' He watched as she put on her shoes and coat and marched out of the front door.

*

The following Monday, Helen did not discuss the lacklustre circumstances of her daily workload with her boss. She did, however, confide in Natalie, whom she would meet for lunch whenever they could escape the ennui of their legal lives. Deep inside the recesses of a dark and spacious City café, after Natalie had bemoaned the absurdity of achieving a first in law only to spend hours in court taking notes of proceedings that were, in any event, being transcribed by professional stenographers and which no one would ever read because there were so many senior lawyers present anyway, all of whom were perfectly capable of taking their own notes and indeed, often did, using them in conjunction with the daily court transcripts to review the evidence, facts which, said Natalie, meant that they'd never, in a thousand chargeable hours, ask for her opinion, whether based upon her meticulously compiled notes or insightful observations of how the case was going, as to which she was sure that the fifth witness was lying, because he kept on scratching his ear whenever he spoke, after all this had poured forth from the wearisome Natalie at last Helen could say: 'I'm sick of him', prompting Natalie to ask, not surprisingly for there were one or two men in their firm who could be the object of anyone's ire, 'Who?'

Helen then launched into a tirade about Flack. He was dull, boring and uninventive in bed. He was interested only in one thing, and no, it wasn't sex. She used to wish it was but it wasn't. Would never be, not in a million stupid Sundays and pointless under-the-sheets-with-the-lights-out Saturday nights. All he cared about was reading his stupid papers. Why? What was the point? I mean, it wasn't as if he was a journalist or a libel lawyer, though then again he kept going on about libel, as if it were the be-all and end-all of legal work. He was working with some woman called Melanie and they'd won a case, all because Harry had found an interesting precedent to do with fair comment, or was it qualified privilege, Helen couldn't remember and who cared anyway, libel was a preposterous branch of the law as far as she was concerned and as for Flack's constant, stupid, irritating habit of sweeping the yard, what was all that about? What was he trying to achieve? Why did their yard have to be the most leaf-free in Fulham? He drove her mad, and as for his jazz, if she heard another Miles Davis track again she'd kill him. Still, at least jazz was marginally more interesting than his other hobby, if that's what you could call it – cricket. Why couldn't he be interested in a proper sport, like rugby, not one where the players dressed up in white slacks and jumpers, I mean they looked as if they were about to attend a pyjama party, and anyway the game, if that's what it was, was so complicated only a mathematician could possibly understand what on earth was happening. And then, on top of all that, was his love of Latin legal phrases. Only yesterday he'd said, out of the blue, 'ex turpi causa' when reading the papers. Just like that. It was insufferable.

Natalie was taken aback. She had met Flack on a couple of occasions and liked him. She warmed to his pleasant, unruffled nature, and was herself quite partial to Latin legal phrases. Indeed, for a second her agile legal brain skipped to Lord Asquith's famous dictum to the effect that if two burglars, Bob and Alice, agree to open a safe by means of explosives, and Alice so negligently handles the explosive charge as to injure Bob, Bob might find some difficulty in bringing a personal injury claim against Alice. Natalie smirked inwardly as she imagined Flack encountering a modern day instance of the *ex turpi causa* principle as he read the Sunday papers, but even as the spectre of the disastrous Bob and Alice discovering that no good can come of dishonourable conduct was looming in her mind she was also conjuring a different line of thought. Natalie hadn't seen Helen for a couple of weeks, since their Friday night at Club Hydra. Although she'd heard one or two barbs about Flack, she had assumed they were no more than the everyday fare cast by women in the direction of men, the kind of harmless insults that keep the world going round and which are just as often uttered by men about women. Now, though, Helen was in full flow. Flack could do nothing right. He was awful. He was the most tedious man alive. If Helen wasn't engaged to him she wouldn't cross the street to speak to him. Did Natalie realise that he actually *counted the steps* from their flat to the newsagent's? Who in the world is as boring as that? I mean, he'd even said, as if he'd won a wonderful prize, like a holiday or new sports car, how many steps there were, though he'd also been careful to point out that the precise number could vary, depending on unforeseen circumstances encountered en route. God save her, it was like living with a robot! And then Natalie remembered: Helen had spent an awful lot of time with that tall and savvy journalist that night. What was his name? Eddie – that was it. Eddie Conrad. Had something happened between them?

At first, Helen said no, of course not – what on earth was Natalie thinking? But it took only one 'Are you sure?' from Natalie for the truth to come gushing forth.

'Promise you won't say anything?' said Helen.

'Of course,' said Natalie.

'Then all right, yes,' said Helen, 'I slept with him. Oh Natalie, it was wonderful. I've never had sex like it! He was amazing.'

Despite herself, Natalie couldn't resist a smile. 'Really?' she said. 'Helen! That is *so* wrong!'

Helen's face wore a mock frown as she agreed that yes, it was wrong, she knew it was, of course she did, but it was so wrong that it was right and didn't she deserve to be happy? Don't all of us? How could a man who spent his free time watching cricket, listening to that idiot Miles Davis and reading not just one daily paper but just about every single one that was printed make her happy? She needed excitement in her life; she was young and had everything going for her, and, thanks to Eddie, she'd realised in an instant that marrying Flack would be a catastrophe. She didn't want to be middle-aged in her twenties! She wanted passion, sex, and yes, maybe even love.

'Helen, you can't have fallen in love already,' said Natalie, interrupting Helen's monologue at the first opportunity. 'I mean, it's only been a couple of weeks. No one believes in love at first sight, least of all lawyers like us. We're careful, we think things through. Don't we? But how often are you seeing him?'

At this, Helen's lips curled downwards, and then outwards, and then, for a moment, froze. The look on her face, allied with her silence, could mean only one thing.

'Helen, are you saying you've only seen him the once? The night we went to the club?'

Helen sighed. 'Yes,' she said. 'I know. It's pathetic. I just wish he'd call me! Why won't he? Natalie, I didn't imagine what happened between us. It was incredible. He read me a poem and then ... Oh, his touch. He was so intimate, so attentive, strong, gentle, everything, you name it, he's *so* good in bed and let me tell you, I've known a few men in my time, good lovers too, even Harry wasn't so bad once upon a time. But he said he'd call me, he said we'd meet for a drink. But – nothing.' She held her head in her hands; before her, both the cappuccino and the brie and bacon baguette she'd ordered were untouched. Natalie, a skiing enthusiast, suddenly conceived an image of a skier lying prone at the foot of a black run, a sight she'd encountered on her most recent trip to Méribel, but felt it best not to mention this. Instead, she consoled her friend with the observation that the majority of men fail to call when they say they will, to which Helen sank so swiftly into a deeper realm of woe that Natalie heard herself suggesting that in this case, however, there was probably a very good reason for Eddie's reticence – perhaps he was too busy, or away on holiday.

Natalie was not hopeful that these sops would be of any use, but, remarkably, Helen's eyes were ablaze. From being slumped over their table, suddenly she sat bolt upright and beamed with joy. Natalie was astonished at the change but, as she looked at her friend, she realised Helen's gaze was occupied by something in the distance, near the door of the café. Natalie turned to see what it was.

There, his eyes scanning the busy eatery, was Eddie Conrad. He was with an older man in a grey suit, and the pair was evidently looking for somewhere to sit. Conrad's head stopped moving the moment his eyes alighted on the two women, whereupon he turned to his companion and said something incomprehensible. The older man shrugged his shoulders before shaking Conrad's hand and leaving. Conrad then strode confidently to their table.

'Do you mind if I join you?' he said, to which Natalie, at least, managed a neutral assent. Helen's demeanour gave rather more away but, as she moved her chair to make room for the prodigious guest, her metamorphosis was complete when Conrad clasped her hand and whispered: 'I'm so sorry I didn't call. I lost your number. I've been thinking about you every day. I just can't get you out of my mind. How are you?'

As Helen was protesting that she was fine and asking, in turn, how Eddie had been, Natalie remembered an important call that she had to make and got up to leave. At the door of the café she risked a quick look at Helen and the man who had so afflicted her repose. Yes, she reflected, they look as if they are in love. And he, this young reporter, was as assured as he was handsome. Perhaps he was the right man for Helen. Maybe she would be happier with him than with Flack. Natalie couldn't say, but, as Conrad caught her eye for a split second before turning solicitously back to Helen, she couldn't help but feel sorry. For whom, precisely, she wasn't sure.

CHAPTER 7

An Uneasy Engagement

Helen's parents were late. This was unusual. Her father, Maurice, had not spent a lifetime in the navy without having his inborn sense of punctuality honed to a T. And far from corrupting it, his three years as a civilian – one who lived abroad – had seen its apotheosis, so that now every aspect of his life was minutely regimented, from the exact time and route of his morning walk with Charles, the family hound, to the mid-morning tuning into the BBC World Service (at 11am, to be precise), through to lunch with yesterday's *Daily Telegraph* (1pm), another walk with Charles (3pm), afternoon tea at 4.30pm ('There is nothing to be ashamed about when it comes to British routines,' he would say, 'They are to be preserved') and a gin and tonic, facing west, at 6pm. His wife, Mary, was moderately more adventurous, sometimes departing from her own time-worn treadmill in favour of whatever was happening in the Portuguese village to which the couple had retired, but for the most part also enjoying the stability of a life which had a time and place for everything including, every evening at 7.15, dinner. At this point, Maurice and Mary sat down and enjoyed the quiet communion of the tactfully married. Few words were spoken but those that left their lips were soft and respectful and imbued with understanding and affection. Having watched television after supper, Maurice and Mary would retire to their separate beds at 10pm, content with the passing of another day.

'Where the hell are they?' said Helen. She was staring through the net curtain of the Fulham flat she shared with Flack, who meanwhile had slumped into the sofa, surrounded by newspapers.

'They were supposed to be here half an hour ago,' she continued. 'Dad's never been late for anything in his life and now the one time he ought to be here on time, he goes and gets lost.'

Flack did not respond. He was engrossed in a story in *The Record* about a couple that had vanished from a restaurant without paying the bill. It had made the paper because of the restaurant in question – The

Ivy – and the size of the bill: a sturdy £984.76. The well-dressed pair had asked a waiter to help them with their coats, so that they could have a breath of fresh air before returning for coffee, only to disappear into the night.

Helen had no idea what story Flack was reading, but though she may have conceded that this one had a certain persuasive interest, whatever it was would not have excused Flack's silence. Flack could have been reading the confession of a newspaper baron, at last unable to live with his crimes and, prior to electing to fall over the side of a yacht, determined to issue a dramatic *mea culpa* via the very papers he had so mercilessly stripped of staff, integrity and circulation – only so long as the word 'exclusive' was appended to every page – Flack could have been reading even this, a story of irrefutable prepossession and compulsion, and yet Helen's reaction would have been the same.

Turning to face him, she said: 'Why the hell can't you say something? All you do is sit there, reading your papers. I'm sick of it.'

Of late, Flack had grown accustomed to Helen's moods. She was frequently catty with him, ever-ready to jump down his throat for no apparent reason. Flack put her anger down to how miserable she was at work, but felt powerless to help given that he was thoroughly enjoying his legal life at Bowles & Parkes. Melanie Masters' practice was booming, and Flack was proving to be indispensable, even as a lowly articled clerk. He had a knack for libel law, one which Melanie said was as instinctive as any she'd come across, perhaps something of a strange comment given that those who possess an instinctive flair for libel law are surely few and far between. But this aside, how could Flack empathise with Helen, when all was so rosy in his world? When he, as tight-lipped as Helen was extrovert, the supposed drudge to her live-wire incisiveness, was prospering in the law, not her?

Moreover, the pair was grappling with their wedding arrangements. Flack had heard from friends who had already taken the plunge of family angst about seating plans and he had read, not too long ago, of a disaster engendered by the bride's insistence that her ex was invited (he had turned up, got drunk and abused the groom, behaviour which was predictable enough given his past – he was a dangerous and unstable man – but what no one could have imagined was the groom's reaction: outraged at the onslaught to which he had been subjected from the back of the church, he had smashed a candlestick into the ex's head, killing him outright), but he could never have imagined that the reality of getting married was so stressful – not in his life, anyway. Everything, from choosing the date of the great day to the type of service and whether to get married in a church or register office (Flack favoured the latter, while Helen would settle for nothing less than a white wedding), was fraught. She cavilled at her parents' choice of florist, she rejected her mother's suggested wedding shoes as ridiculous; she said the design for the wedding invitations was a disgrace and, to Flack's unspeaking horror, she declared that on no account, at any stage during the reception, would the sounds of jazz be heard, anywhere, at all. 'I don't want music for old farts,' she said. 'The only music at my reception will be good-time music. I want people to be happy and remember the day, not be miserable and go home early.' In vain did Flack protest that jazz was as good-time as it got (if not, admittedly, his treasured and yet largely melancholic *Kind of Blue* album but any number of world famous standards besides), but Helen's rigour did not stop there. She intended to ban Flack from receiving any cricket results on the day – it was, they agreed, to be a summer wedding on a Saturday – even if they were merely relayed to him by David or Jonathan, two friends who shared his excitement for all things Wisden. But then again, Helen also said she didn't give a damn what he did on his stag do, so long as she could have some time away with just a couple of her best friends. Flack could even, she announced, have a weekend in Yorkshire to watch the cricket, if that's what he wanted.

'Darling, what do you want me to say?' said Flack, putting his paper to one side. 'Your parents must have been held up by the traffic, it's as simple as that.'

Far from ameliorating Helen's sense of injustice, Flack's words seemed only to add to it.

'Oh, so it's that simple, is it?' she sneered. 'It's that simple. I see. So instead of worrying about whether something's happened to them, instead of thinking that maybe Dad's just too old for this kind of journey and has crashed and is in a terrible state, that maybe he's on his way to hospital right now, instead of thinking anything like that I should just think "oh, it's OK, they're held up in traffic". Well, Harry, what bloody traffic? It's a Sunday morning! There's nothing on the roads!'

Flack let a small sigh fall. It was not one that Helen would have noticed.

'Darling,' he said, 'they're driving from Heathrow. Their plane could have been delayed, there might be problems with the hire car company, maybe there's been an accident on the M4. Anything could have happened. But your father is in his fifties. He's still a young man. He and your mum are sure to be fine. Please don't work yourself up.'

This brief speech seemed to have an effect. Helen nodded, slowly, a touch ponderously, and, abandoning her confrontational pose, sat down on the sofa next to him. She reached out her left hand and clasped his arm. He was wearing a navy shirt, bought only a week earlier from Marks & Spencer. A navy shirt and dark blue corduroy trousers, black socks, slippers; this is my man, thought Helen, squeezing his forearm through the shirt, which Flack had ironed the previous night. This is my man on a Sunday morning, fresh from sweeping the yard while I lay in bed and thought of the kind of sex that Harry, in a thousand nights, could never give me; this is my man, with his ironed shirt, making an effort for my parents, my father, recently of the navy, my mother, still of the staff room, even in Portugal; this, Harry Flack, his newspapers strewn around him, his absorption in their content inviolate and impregnable, is my man.

'You're right, Harry,' said Helen. 'I mustn't work myself up. It's not good for us ladies, is it?'

*

'For God's sake, when are we going to get there? How much further is their damn place? It's so *rude* not to be on time. I can't stand it. I knew it. We should have set off much earlier instead of dithering in the airport café. Then we'd have avoided all that trouble. I knew it'd turn out like this.'

Mary was all bluster and regret as she neared what her husband enjoyed calling 'the Flack flat'.

'That's what it is, isn't it?' said Maurice, as they parked their car in a road nearby. 'He's called Flack and they live in a flat. Ergo, it's "the Flack flat". And it'll be even more so "the Flack flat" when the happy day has been and gone. It could even be "the two-Flack flat", or "the double-Flack flat". Or simply "the Flacks' flat". And then imagine if they have junior Flacks! Didn't Helen talk to you about children recently? It might soon be "the many Flacks' flat".'

Mary's reply was curt. 'For God's sake, Maurice, shut up. We're over an hour late as it is. You know what Helen's like when she makes an arrangement. She'll be tearing her hair out.'

'My dear,' said Maurice, 'that may be true. But there is nothing we can do about our tardiness. It was not of our making, and our daughter will understand as soon as we explain what happened.'

'Not of our making? You can say that again. How you can be so flippant is beyond me!'

'Just trying to lighten things, dear,' said Maurice. 'That's all.'

By now the couple had climbed out of their car, a spotless low-mileage vehicle hired from Heathrow, the manufacturer of which Mary would never guess in a thousand journeys, so uniform were its controls and undistinguished its appearance. In this, thought Maurice, modern cars are not disappointing; they may lack anything resembling character but at least they work. Mary slid her arm through her husband's and together, as they had always been, even when Maurice was away for months at a time at sea, they made their way to their rendezvous with their only child and her fiancé, a man Maurice rather liked, while Mary had her doubts. Flack struck her as a little too serious, earnest even; she would not have liked a carouser but knew that her daughter needed someone with a bit of spunk, someone with enough not merely of his own mind but of his own desires, needs and friendships. Too often, though, Flack was self-contained and withdrawn, perhaps even disengaged, as if his emotions had been placed in quarantine; certainly, he was not the type one would describe as the life and soul of the party. Yes, he was pleasant – his manners were faultless – but Mary had a sneaking suspicion that Helen would tire of a man who never put a foot wrong, for the simple reason that he never put a foot anywhere.

Her ruminations lasted no more than a few seconds. Unfamiliar with the streets of Fulham, the couple had walked away from the Flack flat, not towards it, as Maurice realised when they neared Bishop's Park. 'My darling, we appear to have taken a wrong turn,' he announced, with the utmost calm. 'I think perhaps we should turn back.'

In the midst of their about-turn Mary criticised the inadequacy of her husband's route-finding skills. 'We're already late enough as it is! Why can't *you*, a so-called navy man, get us there? I thought you knew how to navigate your way round the world, let alone through a few London streets in broad daylight.'

Arms once again linked, they left Bishop's Park behind and retraced their steps. Soon Maurice experienced a Eureka! moment.

'There!' he exclaimed, pointing with an arm as strong and angular as a ship's canon. 'That's the corner of their road. Once there, we turn right, walk a few yards and hey presto, we're at the Flack flat.'

'Will you please stop calling it that,' said Mary. 'It's not so much the words, but the way you say them. You make it sound as if it's stupid, or doomed.'

'Neither stupid, my dear, nor doomed. It's just the Flack flat. And look, after all our travails, here we are. Number 19. This is the entrance of the Flack flat.'

Imperiously, Helen's father strode to the door of his daughter's flat. He noted that it needed a lick of paint, but resolved not to mention this to Flack. 'He might think I'm meddling,' he said to himself. 'Besides, he's a capable chap. He's sure to sort it out himself.' Having jettisoned this thought, he rapped his knuckles on the door with the kind of force that comes easily to men from Her Majesty's services but which lesser mortals find difficult to emulate and slightly intimidating.

Flack opened the door and bade them a cheerful welcome. 'Come in,' he said, 'come in. You must be tired after your journey. Come in and sit down.'

Holding the door ajar, Flack stooped to kiss Mary on each cheek as she passed him, and then accepted the proffered right hand of Maurice. The two men clasped hands firmly, but perhaps not firmly enough for Maurice's liking, for he found himself unable to refrain from mentioning the indifferent state of the front door to the young lawyer. 'Needs a lick of paint, that door,' said Maurice, gesturing back at it. 'Nothing major, wouldn't take five minutes. But I apologise, old chap. I'm sure you've got it in hand. Old habits die hard, you see. Need to keep things spick and span. Be professional at all times. You know what I mean.'

'Quite so,' said Flack, without irony. He had been meaning to paint the door for a while. 'But look, let me take your coats, and let's go and find Helen. I'm sure you're dying to see her.'

*

'Yes, it was quite frightful. I have travelled the world but have yet to see a pile-up as bad. I imagine it'll be on the front pages tomorrow.'

Maurice's account of the accident that had caused the delay in his and Mary's arrival captivated Flack and appeared to satisfy Helen's lawyerly need for causation. Shortly after the couple had left Heathrow, they had found themselves travelling behind a lorry that had, unaccountably, jack-knifed. Expert driving by Maurice had seen them avoid a collision and, indeed, overtake the disintegrating vehicle. A few other cars had similarly missed it, but then the carnage had begun. As Maurice came to a halt on an open stretch of motorway almost half a mile beyond the lorry – by now impaled in the crash barrier – he could see that it was being battered by car after car. One even landed on top of its upended carriage, to perch unconvincingly until the momentum of another crashing car sent it thudding to the road's surface. Soon the slim area beside the lorry, through which Maurice and a few other drivers had threaded their cars, was occluded by wreckage. The road was an impassable mess of mangled metal.

'Those poor people!' said Mary.

But Maurice, though not unsympathetic to the accident's victims, was pragmatic. Various drivers from cars that had evaded the pile-up were rushing to the scene; the emergency services would be but minutes away. There was nothing he or Mary could do, save provide succour – and wasn't he at least half a mile, probably more, away from the impact zone? Besides, their only daughter was waiting for them – they hadn't seen her for some time, and were due to meet her and her fiancé to go through plans for their wedding. They should press on. He put the car in first gear and started to pull away.

'What are you doing?' said Mary. 'We can't leave the scene! We should go and see if we can help.'

Maurice stopped the car. He turned around and once again craned his neck to survey the debris. Mary did likewise. 'I'm not sure,' he said. 'I'm not sure there's anything we can do.'

They stared for some time at the lorry, whose cabin had been crushed upon hitting the galvanised iron of the crash barrier. Its cabin was shattered; its driver, surely dead. Broken cars lined both sides of the motorway, and yet, with traffic having ground to a standstill on both sides, an eerie silence hung over everything. It was broken when Maurice opened his car door, got out and stood up to view the accident.

Through the stench of exhaust fumes, spilt petrol and diesel the screams of the dying and injured could be heard, even from where their car had stopped.

Everything in Maurice's being told him to go to the maimed and help them. He knew that Mary must be thinking this, too. But he didn't move.

Picking up the story over their roast beef, Maurice revealed that just at the moment when he'd decided to help, the emergency services had arrived. He'd been seconds from rushing towards the lorry, but a policeman had yelled at him to stay away. 'What could I do but obey?' he asked, as Mary nodded. 'I made sure to give my details to another officer, as a witness, but he was also intent on getting to the scene. I imagine we'll get a call soon, so that we can tell the authorities what we saw. But there was no point in hanging about. We decided to press on and, I must say, I'm glad that we did – this meal, Helen, is delicious.'

There was a pause as the four diners tucked into Helen's juicy roast joint and took in Maurice's explanation for being an hour late. It was, of course, entirely reasonable that such a calamitous event should result in a delay, one exacerbated, said Mary, when they reached Fulham and took a wrong turn, but Flack was ill at ease. His prospective parents-in-law seemed so unfazed by what had happened, as if multiple car crashes were all part of the daily grind, and yet more worryingly, this appeared to be Helen's response, too. Her lack of compassion was startling, her acknowledgement of the magnitude of the events described by her parents confined to a series of disinterested mumbles. Moreover, Flack could not understand how Maurice, a man for whom service and duty were second nature, had dithered. Why had he not run headlong to the scene? Surely his years in the navy would have made him better equipped than most to help? Wouldn't they have conditioned him to render such assistance, however slight, that he could?

Flack found himself reflecting on what struck him as being dangerously close to a lapse in professionalism, something that Maurice's former colleagues in the navy would struggle to accept. And yet, as he watched Maurice and Mary help themselves to a second course of succulent beef with crispy roast potatoes, cauliflower and sautéed carrots, it was as if nothing had happened, that there had never been a motorway pile-up with an horrific death toll that would be the lead item on the TV news and on the front page of every newspaper for the next few days, not to mention on every home news page and on the comment and editorial pages, too, as junior ministers announced official inquiries and polemicists blamed our obsession with the car and environmentalists banged their drum and thunderous editorials flowed from all and sundry. Was it a lack of professionalism, or was it an absence of empathy? If the latter, did behaving as an exemplary *professional* mean acting without care for others? Flack's contemplation got him nowhere. And for their part, Maurice's wife and daughter seemed to accept that he could not have done anything other than, as he put it, 'press on'.

'This beef really is exquisite,' announced Maurice, as he polished off his last slice. 'Do you know, I might even have thirds. Would that be all right, darling daughter, do you think?'

'Of course, Dad,' said Helen.

Again Maurice devoured the meat. Sated once more, he declared that it was time for the quartet to discuss the most important thing on their minds – the wedding of the happy couple. 'Quite right,' said Mary. 'Shall we retire to the sitting room and talk there?'

Her mother's notion of 'retiring' all of three yards, from the kitchen-diner where they'd had lunch to the sitting room, with its expectant veiled windows and too-often empty street, irritated Helen, but before long all were seated with a common purpose: to finalise plans for the wedding.

'Let's start with numbers,' said Maurice. 'Your mother and I have been thinking. Of course, we want you to have a wonderful day. That goes without saying. But then again, we're not wealthy. Well, not particularly wealthy. So we need to get the numbers right. How many people are you hoping to invite?'

To Flack's surprise, Helen replied that they were hoping to have a total of 178 guests. He could not remember settling on this or any other figure. It seemed on the high side, but Maurice and Mary met it in their stride. 'Jolly good,' said Maurice, who proposed that next they discuss the venue for the reception. Just then, though, there was a knock on the door. Helen all but jumped up from the sofa, where she had been sitting side by side with her fiancé, and volunteered to see who it was. Flack was curious, too, and thought of going to the window and peering through the net curtain, but, realising that to do so would be discourteous, remained where he was.

*

Helen opened the front door to an unexpected visitor.

'I told you to check with me before you came here!' she gasped, as she beheld the handsome features of Eddie Conrad.

'I know,' he whispered. 'But I just had to see you. I took a risk that you'd come to the door. If you hadn't, I'd have made up some nonsense. I'm sorry! Are you busy?'

'Of course I'm busy – it's a Sunday!' exclaimed Helen, adding that besides, her parents had flown over to discuss her wedding. She told Conrad to make himself scarce. 'It's too risky, you being here – it's madness! Go now before any of them come out.'

'Just one kiss, and your agreement to meet me tomorrow, and I'll be gone,' said Conrad. Then he whispered: 'Remember, *Beautiful, sobbing, high-geared fucking and then to lie silently like deer tracks in the freshly-fallen snow beside the one you love.* That's us, Helen, that's all it is – us.'

With that he leant forward and kissed Helen on the lips, yearningly and delicately, aware of the moment's fragility and yet as if to promise that their next kiss would linger from dusk to dawn. Her eyes bright with love, Helen said 'I love you' as Conrad turned and scurried from the threshold of the Flack flat.

Back inside, Flack, Maurice and Mary were relieved to note a marked improvement in Helen's mood. She was positivity itself, greeting each idea for the wedding with a charming blend of childlike enthusiasm and lawyerly capability. Nothing was too much trouble and all was sure to be wonderful. Why, Flack could even have a jazz song or two at the reception (though not, please, Miles Davis) and tune in the radio to find out what had happened in the cricket.

'Women,' said Maurice to Flack, as the pair examined the front door and its need for a lick of paint, a task they had set themselves in a spirit of familial bonding while mother and daughter did the washing up. 'They're all the same, whether your mother, your daughter, your wife or your sister. You can never tell what they're going to do or think from one minute to the next. I'd wager that knock on the door was a friend who gave her a quick pep talk. But don't worry. Helen can be flighty but she's a good sort. Her heart is in the right place. It'll be all right on the night.'

Flack agreed.

'I love her very much, you know,' he said.

CHAPTER 8

In Flagrante

The ease and rapidity with which Helen and Eddie Conrad became lovers was a surprise to them both. Once, exhausted after making love one afternoon at the Flack flat, in the very bed that she shared with her fiancé, Helen turned to Conrad and said: 'It's amazing, isn't it? Only a couple of months ago we didn't know each other. Now here we are, and I can't imagine my life without you. How long do you think we'll be able to keep doing this?'

Conrad, lying naked next to Helen, turned to her and, stroking her hair in the fingers of his right hand, said: 'As long as you want. As long as we both want. Hopefully forever.' To Helen, her lover's words were poetry. She felt anxious when away from him; complete in his presence; ecstatic when she knew he was on his way and overjoyed when he arrived. These emotions had not accompanied her courtship with Flack, even in its early days, when passion is at its height. The comparison may have been invidious but, it struck Helen, it was all the better for it: Flack was exposed as a poor second when stood side by side with the young journalist.

Not that Conrad was a mere hack. What so impressed Helen was his flair, his élan, his confidence, but also – not that she was a literary type – his extraordinary knowledge of books, writers and poets. Sometimes it seemed that Conrad had a poem for every occasion, from Brautigan's *Deer Tracks*, so perfect a piece of first-night seduction, to Pablo Neruda's 'Tonight I Can Write', which he read to her, quietly and conspiratorially, after they'd made love for the fourth time. He knew the most obscure of books, and remembered lines from them as if he'd written them himself. 'Journalism equals intellectual male prostitution of speech and writing,' he was fond of saying. 'That's a line from a very fine but difficult novel, *Under The Volcano* by Malcolm Lowry. Do you know it?' As with almost everything he quoted, Helen's answer was to confess ignorance, something which, it later occurred to her, seemed to please Conrad. 'What do you think Lowry meant?' he once continued, and though Helen had an inkling she opted for an uncommitted response, one which allowed her lover to expound that while Lowry, an alcoholic and disturbed man, was happy to condemn the profession of journalism, he did so out of bitterness, because of his own failure to achieve the acclaim that his talent could, perhaps, have justified, something that would not be Eddie Conrad's fate, for no, he had it all worked out, he would rise through the ranks of sundry newspapers at the same time as retaining his integrity and writing a novel, the idea for which he had been obsessed with since the age of thirteen and which would see him one day feted as the voice – perhaps even the embodiment – of his generation. 'That sounds arrogant, I know,' said Conrad, 'but it is important to have faith. Am I stupid to do so? Am I naïve? I don't think so. I will get there. I have to believe that I will.'

Sometimes, Conrad's sense of the greatness of his destiny was not so unshakeable. These moments – of weakness, he called them, 'weakness, pure and simple, nothing but rank, pathetic, abominable weakness' – were seldom, but saw him trade exuberance for uncertainty in a fashion that Helen, had she thought about it deeply, might have seen as an indicator of instability. She never forgot one evening ride in a cab, after a stolen dinner in the West End, towards the end of which Conrad had sunk into a fog of moodiness and inarticulacy. Leaning against him in the taxi, Helen had kissed his cheek and said: 'Eddie, what's wrong? Is it me? You haven't said a word for half an hour. You seem so unhappy. Please tell me what's wrong.' Conrad said nothing until they reached his flat, this being an evening which Helen had manipulated so that she could stay with him, for Flack had gone away for the weekend to watch some cricket and see his parents. Quickly, they undressed and found themselves in bed, but far from the high-geared intimacy to which Helen had grown accustomed she met with flaccidity, mental and physical. Conrad was sombre and withdrawn. Finally, unable to stand his seeming indifference any more, Helen exclaimed: 'Eddie, what the hell is wrong?! Please tell me!'

Conrad's answer surprised her.

'It's *Krapp's Last Tape*,' he said, in tones of resignation bordering on defeat. 'It's on at the moment. I've been thinking about going to see it. I heard the couple next to us in the restaurant talking about it. Do you know what it's about?' Helen said that no, she didn't. 'It's a play by Samuel Beckett about a failed writer. He's called Krapp. As in, K R A P P. It's a short play, not too much to stomach if you find the inherent artifice of theatre a bit wearing, maybe fifty minutes long, no more. A play about a writer who sells seventeen copies of his book, eleven of which went to libraries. And his failed love affairs. And a banana and a long viduity and the impossibility of communication. "Perhaps my best years are gone. When there was a chance of happiness. But I wouldn't want them back." That's what Krapp says. That's what he concludes at the end of his life. He's a failure, and can't reach any other conclusion. Helen, I don't want to be like Krapp.'

For many years, Helen recalled this interlude, one which ended when she took Conrad's face in her hands and said: 'Eddie, you'll never be like that. You're meant for more, so much more. Besides, I won't let you.' Then they made love, as high-geared as ever, and Conrad never mentioned Krapp, or self-doubt, again.

Their affair escalated. Not once, even at its outset, did either of them question it. To the extent that Helen thought about Flack, it was only to determine his whereabouts – would he be working late, or be at an evening function, or – bliss! – going away? If so, could she get home in time for Conrad to visit? If not, could she rearrange her working day so that there was time to get to Conrad's flat? She didn't care where they met, so long as they could see each other, kiss, caress, make love, cuddle afterwards, lie together so entwined it was as if their limbs had been conjoined. It seemed so natural, so inevitable, that she and Conrad were together that Helen assumed it was only a matter of time before they confessed all and became an item. Her engagement with Flack was a mistake – this was as plain to see as the leaves in the yard which he so zealously swept each Sunday morning. He, too, would come to understand this – surely he would. He would settle down with a different kind of woman, a boring one who liked to read the papers, who understood cricket and even, if it were possible in a woman (though Helen doubted it), liked jazz and that confounded Miles Davis. He would forget all about her; Helen, meanwhile, would live in rapture with the beautiful Eddie Conrad, so commanding, so handsome, so obviously meant for her. So complex, too, but wasn't that part of his charm?

Helen's friends were not convinced. At work, Natalie marvelled at her colleague's shamelessness; the same was true of her friend from her school days, Martha. 'I don't understand how you can sleep with him in the bed you share with Harry,' said Natalie, over one of their lunches. 'I mean, what do you think, later, when Harry climbs into bed with you? Doesn't he notice things, the scent of another man, ruffled sheets, that sort of thing?'

'Harry notices nothing,' would be Helen's reply. 'I could shag Eddie in front of him and he wouldn't know. All he cares about is reading his papers. Besides, Natalie, I'm not stupid – of course I take the sheets off and put them in the wash.' As she said this, Helen thought, but did not dare say: *Harry complements me on making sure the sheets are always clean. He says I needn't go to such trouble. He is so solicitous. I can't bear it. It's ridiculous. And to think: I repay him by sleeping with another man. I hate him all the more for the fact that I don't feel guilty.*

Helen's sense of Martha's scruples meant that she refrained from telling her of her lovemaking sessions with Conrad at the Flack flat. Instead, she portrayed their affair as one which occurred solely on her lover's territory. Even so, Martha was unimpressed. She had a soft spot for Flack and a predisposition to monogamy. If a relationship wasn't working, she felt it should be ended before a third party got involved. 'I can't stand people who finish things by finding someone else,' she once said. 'It's so cowardly.' She liked Helen, almost in spite of herself – so different were their characters – and so humoured her enough to listen to her friend's updates, but could not condone the affair. 'If you know that Harry is the wrong man for you, break off the engagement,' she said. 'Tell him. Do the right thing.' Helen would say that yes, she was going to – it was just a case of getting the timing right. She had to talk to Eddie, her beloved Eddie, and make sure he was in agreement. Of course, he would be; he knew as much as she just how special their love was, that it was unique, that it was *meant to be.*

Despite this, Conrad found various reasons to put the brakes on, to ensure that Helen did not confess all. These ranged from due regard for their respective careers (not doing anything to disrupt their progress at this vital early stage), to remembering the truth of the old adage that one marries in haste only to repent at leisure (thus, although it was obvious that they were meant for each other, they should wait a while and allow their love to grow even stronger, lest they jeopardise it by acting prematurely), to acknowledging that if it ain't broke, don't fix it (after all, weren't they onto a good thing, so why did they need to upset the applecart?). There was also the novel he was writing – which it would be wrong to interrupt by such a radical upheaval – not to mention his work, too, which was just as important, for if Conrad could swiftly ascend the Fleet Street ladder, he would create a platform for the best possible future for himself and Helen, as well as their children, for yes, Conrad liked children and looked forward to the day he would have them. Ideally, he wanted a daughter, a little girl who would be his princess, an only child he could adore exclusively, but if Helen wanted more children that was fine, too. It was just a case of getting the timing right, that was all. Occasionally, Helen would bemoan her lover's hesitancy, but never for long. For the most part she was swept helplessly away on a riptide of emotion, mollified, if needs be, by the merest kiss, assuaged by the tenderness of Conrad's touch, only too willing to suspend any hint of disbelief and plunge headlong into a fantasy which, if there was any justice in the world, would surely come true.

But the fantasy was dented by Flack. His existence alone was enough to give Helen pause, if not for guilt but for anger, not least because increasingly her supposedly blind fiancé showed signs of being able to see things perhaps not clearly but in a way which put him in danger of groping his way to a semblance of the truth. That Flack was demonstrating a hitherto unrecognised perceptive streak, albeit a clumsy and adventitious one, may once have gained Helen's respect; now, though, it was yet another reason to loathe him. Her detestation was not only a frequent topic of dinner-table conversation when she met up with Eddie, it was also more and more an aspect of daily life with Flack.

'Why don't you just leave me alone?' shouted Helen, one Saturday morning when Flack had uncharacteristically abandoned his pile of newspapers and suggested that they do something different, like go for a walk in Hyde Park, or go to a matinee, or visit the Tate and afterwards amble along the Embankment.

Flack was taken aback by Helen's exclamation, but persevered. 'I was just trying to think of something that we could enjoy doing together. I know work has been tough for you, for a while now, but I don't want you to think that I don't care. I do. I'm worried about you. And I'm worried about us.'

So vituperative was Helen's reply that it astonished her as much as Flack. 'Well, it's a bit late, don't you think? But if you read your papers I'm sure you'll find an answer to all our problems. Or maybe it's in the yard, buried among the leaves?'

Flack was not a man given to histrionics. He disliked arguments almost as much as he objected to the idea of cricket players wearing multi-coloured kits. But in the face of the bile in Helen's voice he snapped. 'You're out late all the time! You don't make a single effort to be loving and now you throw my effort to get on with you back at me as if I've just asked you to join the Nazi party. What the hell is wrong with you?' For good measure, he slammed his right fist into one of the cushions on the sofa.

This time, Helen was silent. Never, in all the years she had known Flack, had she seen him lose his temper. Equanimity was his middle name. That he had exploded was all the more frightening for being so out of character. As soon as she realised this, she made capital.

'You've never raised your voice at me, not once,' she said. 'I've never seen you clench your fist, let alone punch something. I'm scared. I'm scared by you, by the way you looked just then. I'm scared by the way you spoke to me and I'm scared by the way you punched the sofa. What next – more abuse? Will you punch me? I think we need time apart. I know I do.'

It was late on a Saturday morning. Helen was already dressed as if to go out, perhaps for a lunch with Martha, something she'd made a routine of lately. As she strode past her fiancé and reached for her coat, slung indecorously on the stand in the hall, Flack elected to agree with her, if only to keep the peace and also, perhaps, because he was upset at having lost his cool: it simply wasn't like him. He couldn't remember a similar occurrence, ever.

'OK, darling, you're right,' he said. 'I'm sorry. It was wrong of me to act as I did. Please forgive me. Let's sort all this out tomorrow. Or later tonight. What time will you be back?'

But Helen again saw an opportunity that was too good to resist. 'I think it best if I stay with Martha tonight,' she said. 'Or one of the girls from work. I think a bit of space will do us good. I'm sure you agree, don't you, Harry?'

Flack nodded. 'OK,' he said. 'But Helen, I'm sorry I shouted. And I'm sorry I hit the sofa. Darling, I could never hit you. You must know that about me. You must believe me. I couldn't hit anyone, let alone you. It's not me.' He even made a joke, saying his wrist hurt, before concluding: 'Have a good day.'

Helen all but ran down the street once she'd got out of the door of the flat. Its remaining occupant did not, however, notice. He had already immersed himself in the day's papers, content to be distracted by them amid the welcoming cushions of the beige sofa. There were few finer pleasures, he thought, as he started with a preview of the day's cricket, especially when dealing with the flightiness of a woman like Helen and the extraordinary loss of one's own lifelong temperance.

*

Within minutes of leaving the flat Helen was in a phone box, frantically dialling Eddie Conrad's number. It rang and rang, but eventually Conrad answered. He sounded groggy, his voice hoarse as if from too many cigarettes and too much alcohol. Helen was mildly surprised, but not enough to make anything of it. 'It's me,' she said. 'I've got away for the day and, believe it or not, the evening too. I'll come round now, yes?'

Conrad was lukewarm. He muttered that he wasn't sure – he thought the paper had work for him later, a doorstep or something. Besides, his flat was in a state because of building work downstairs. All in all, he wasn't sure. Could Helen call back in a couple of hours? He'd know what was what then. Maybe the builders would have gone, too – they surely wouldn't work all day on a Saturday.

Of course, Helen understood. She knew that even if Eddie had dreams of making it as a writer, his career as a journalist was also vitally important. She understood, too, that his was not a profession of regular hours. He'd stood her up once or twice, maybe a few times in fact, but on each occasion because of a work commitment that had come out of the blue. As he was fond of saying, 'In my business the people who say no to an editor are the people who are out of work the next week.' Eddie Conrad never said no. Then again, why would building work to the ground floor flat mean she couldn't come round? Why did they have to wait for the builders to finish work first? But it was pointless to worry about this. Eddie had his work to do. Helen understood.

'Oh Eddie, I was *so* excited! But I understand. I'll go and see Martha. It's probably just as well. I'll call you again in a couple of hours. I love you.'

Being in love gave Helen a sense of empathy now rarely evident in her relationship with Flack. Again all too aware of the relative merits of the two men in her life, she reflected on her new-found capability for compassion as she dialled Martha's number. Flack annoyed her more than anything; Eddie – her Eddie – could do just about anything and she'd forgive him. Flack's foibles were excruciating; Eddie's were fun and forgivable. Flack's problems – to the extent that he had any, which was doubtful – were an irritant; Eddie's were challenging, a part of his life that she wanted to make better. In short, if Flack had a cold, Helen couldn't give a damn; if Eddie was under the weather, Helen would gladly be his nurse.

Martha answered the phone sounding in diametrically the opposite state to Conrad. She was bright and lively, as if she'd been up since seven, had done a five-mile run and then, at the finishing line, just received some wonderful news. The first two elements of this trinity were true, but such was Martha's disquietude about Helen's personal life that the news that she was coming round hardly qualified as wondrous. Nevertheless, mused Martha, it would make for a change to see her old friend for Saturday lunch.

Martha's home was a Victorian three-up, three-down in Clapham which she had been able to buy thanks to an inheritance. Close to the park, it was the envy of friends like Helen, who although in ostensibly better jobs – the law trumping publishing hands down, at least in terms of remuneration – were yet to climb onto the property ladder. 'You're *so* lucky!' exclaimed Helen, when she swept through Martha's porch (the house even had a porch) and into its neat, tidy and book-lined sitting room. 'It never ceases to amaze me! You, of all people, managed to find a place like this! You! I mean, you're just *so* jammy!'

Once upon a time, Martha might have pointed out that having her sole remaining parent – her father – die of cancer when she was in her late teens might be construed as bad luck, but she had given up making this point. She was lucky, she supposed; after a fashion, anyway, for who among her contemporaries owned their own house, so young? And besides, Helen had never been known for her tact. Better to let her get her gauche declarations out of her system. She was always quick to change the subject, anyway, and lost no time in plunging into the story of her latest encounter with Conrad.

'I saw him two nights ago. It was as lovely as ever. But Martha, you'd like him if you got to know him. He's writing a novel, you know.'

'Really?' asked Martha.

'Yes, really. He's really bookish. He's always reading me poems and quoting his favourite lines. Even you would be impressed.'

Martha wasn't convinced. 'Why, if he's so literary, does he work as a tabloid journalist?'

'Oh Martha! Don't be so precious. I know what you're thinking –

that he's sold out. But he hasn't. He's always learning so much in his job and it's all material for his novel. Eddie will get there. I'm convinced of it. One day he'll be the editor of one of the nationals and he'll also publish a great novel. I know he will. And besides, you shouldn't be so snobbish. The tabloids are just as good as the broadsheets. It takes just as much skill to write for them as it does for the papers you read. It's just a different kind of writing, that's all.'

'Perhaps,' murmured Martha. She then changed the debate to that which always concerned her most in these discussions about Conrad. 'Isn't it about time you did the right thing and broke off your engagement to Harry? I'm sorry, Helen, but carrying on like this is wrong. I don't agree with it. No one does – none of your friends. They just don't have the nerve to tell you. It's such an insult to poor Harry.'

Helen groaned. 'Yes, Martha, my friend and my conscience, my old, old friend from school, yes you're right. It's wrong. I know it is. I'm just waiting for Eddie to tell me when.'

'Why is doing the right thing dependent on him?'

'Oh Martha! Stop it! It's a difficult situation. You wouldn't understand.'

At this, Martha agreed. Affairs were not something she understood. She did not feel inclined to find out more about them, either. The bits and pieces she knew about Helen's affair was more than enough. Just as she was wondering how to divert Helen away from further eulogies about Conrad, her phone went. To the surprise of both women, Flack was on the other end of the line. Martha asked if he was ringing in search of Helen, adding, to her immediate regret (not because she almost betrayed her friend, but because she might hurt Flack), that 'for once she's actually here'. There was a pause, but it transpired that Flack had not called to speak to the woman he would be marrying. He merely wanted Martha to pass on a message.

'Please just tell Helen that I'm going out,' he said. 'Something's come up. I'll be back early in the evening.'

Martha relayed the news. Helen's eyes lit up. She made her excuses, rushed from Martha's house and found the nearest phone box. This time, she met with a rather more enthusiastic Eddie Conrad. He was clear of work and would love to see Helen; the problem was that his flat was out of bounds – the builders needed access, apparently.

'Eddie, Harry's not around,' said Helen.

'Really? Are you sure? He's definitely going out for the day?'

'Yes, I'm sure. We'll have the place to ourselves. The bed, especially,' replied Helen.

*

Later, when he looked back on what had happened, Flack couldn't remember what made him return earlier than he'd planned to the flat. He remembered that at about 10.30am he and Helen had exchanged harsh words; he recalled that Helen had gone out, saying something about staying at Martha's for the night; he knew that initially sitting quietly and reading the papers had taken his mind off things. So, too, could he remember why he'd decided to go out: he'd chanced upon a small piece in one of the Saturday supplements about an auction of cricket memorabilia, taking place in Bermondsey. All this, Flack knew – but what had made him stop his journey half way across London and return, empty-handed, to Fulham? He had no idea.

As he went to unlock the door Flack noticed its paintwork. It was gleaming. Painting the door had been a job well done – and one that he'd enjoyed, too. He knew the value of simple tasks, which sustain one's sense of pride and order, though on closer inspection there was a scuff mark at the bottom of the door, as if someone had pushed it open with a boot. It wasn't him, and the mark couldn't have been made by one of the pairs of high heels Helen had taken to wearing lately. How had it got there? As he entered the flat Flack met another unexpected sight. A pair of shoes was in the hall. They weren't Helen's, they weren't Flack's, and they were a man's.

Flack stood still, studying the shoes, a pair of brown brogues. A little beyond them was a jacket; beyond it, a pair of trousers. Flack crept along the corridor, past the shoes, past the jacket, past the trousers. The further he went, the more he could hear sounds from the bedroom. Eventually, he stood at its doorway. The door was ajar. He could hear Helen alternately moaning and saying things, words of endearment, words of sex, he wasn't sure. He pushed the door further open, until he could see the bed and on it a man, naked, on top of his fiancée.

Flack stood as if paralyzed. He was unable to take his eyes off the couple. The man's buttocks rose and fell, the woman's hands clasped him ever more frenziedly, until finally it was over.

Still Flack stood in the doorway. His gaze was riveted to the man's buttocks as he slumped on top of Helen. Flack thought of an infamous libel trial, in which a Neo-Nazi South African sometime-poet's behind, glimpsed through a keyhole, had been the focus of courtroom mirth. Unaccountably, he wondered if Eugène Terre'Blanche's arse looked like the one he was staring at, he thought of how it had presented itself, and been presented, in the evidence in the Jani Allen trial, as if to think about libel would save him from what was before his eyes. No one moved. No one said anything. Flack was alone, looking on. Silence, but then the man rose above Helen and holding himself with his back arched, as if about to do a press up, looked tenderly down at her. They giggled.

'God, that was *so* good!' said Helen.

'Yes, it was. It was amazing. You're amazing. And beautiful.'

'I love you, Eddie.'

'I love you too. But we'd better get cleaned up. Won't your faithful husband-to-be be coming home soon?'

Helen groaned. 'Kiss me so I can forget him. I wish I'd never met him. I wish I'd only ever known you.'

The man laughed. He lowered his face to Helen's. They kissed.

Silently, Flack turned away. Not even a lost libel trial could help him now. He walked down the corridor, past the trousers, past the jacket, past the brown brogues. He opened the front door, glanced at the scuff mark that he would never repair, and left.

CHAPTER 9

Goodbye, Dr Tax

Dr Tax was not in a mellow mood. Summoned to the senior partner's office, Flack barely had time to sit down before Bowles & Parkes' leader was bellowing at him.

'And what, pray tell, is the meaning of this?'

Dr Tax waved a letter in Flack's direction.

'It's my resignation letter,' said Flack.

'I know it's a bloody resignation letter. I am not a fool, and, even better, I know how to read. If I was a fool I wouldn't be the senior partner, even if I could read, would I, Mr Flack? But I can read, so that takes care of that. Now, as I say, what is the meaning of this?'

Despite the letter being flung about in the air again, and for all the agitation so palpable in the senior partner, Flack had nothing to say. Confronted by an unconcerned, almost embarrassed shrug of the young solicitor's shoulders, Dr Tax persisted.

'It's a bloody outrage, that's what it is. That's what it means. It's an offence to me, to my colleagues, to your colleagues, to the firm. It's an affront to the notion and principles of Bowles & Parkes. We train you up, pay you good money, give you a future and then, like some will-o'-the-wisp without a care in the world, you decide to leave.'

'I'm sorry, sir,' said Flack. As usual, he quickly regretted calling Dr Tax 'sir'. Worse, the appellation did not appear to quell the noted tax expert's irascibility.

'But why? I thought you liked life with Melanie. I've given you scope to work on your bloody libel cases and build up something good with her. You're making a name for yourselves. What was it *The Lawyer* said the other day? "With yet another victory in Court 13 under their belts, Melanie Masters and Harry Flack are rapidly emerging as the two brightest prospects in defamation law in London." Something like that. Apparently the *Gazette* said the same thing and so did the other legal rags. And let's face it, there are worse women to work with. If *The Lawyer* had also said. "One of the key reasons for Masters' rise to the top are her fantastic tits and arse" they wouldn't have been wrong, now would they, young Flack?'

Flack hesitated, then disagreed. 'I don't think you should speak about Melanie, or women generally, like that.'

'Oh for God's sake, Flack! Don't go all PC on me. That's not what's ailing you. It can't be. You're a red-blooded young man, not some daft pseudo-feminist who pushes prams, says women can have it all and won't say boo to a goose. Aren't you?'

'I am a man, and I am young,' replied Flack. 'And if I had a child, I'd be happy to push its pram.'

'Don't be so bloody impertinent!'

'With respect, I don't think I was, sir.'

'That's for me to decide. But anyway, we're straying off track. You can push all the prams in the world for all I care, so long as you do so outside work. But after everything we've done for you, you go and bloody resign!'

'I'm sorry,' said Flack. Inwardly, he congratulated himself on not adding a 'sir'.

'Sorry! You're bloody sorry! Well, I'm sorry too, not least because I note, Flack, young Flack not from Bristol but from Oxford, young Flack with empathy, bills to pay and a fiancée, I note, Flack, that I was not a 'sir' to you then. No matter! Your boldness merely adds to my belief that no one will be as sorry as you if you go through with this ridiculous idea. You have security and prospects here. You have a congenial working relationship with a woman whose intellect is second to none, a woman who is brighter than all the men in her department put together, a woman whose physical charms – lest you find yourself confused – are wholly irrelevant to her ability to do the job. You have a pension, private health care and luncheon vouchers, partnership prospects and, thanks to a new initiative that I am shortly to announce, use of the firm's car park on weekends which, Mr Flack, is a perk of no small import given the disgraceful cost of parking in central London these days. What on earth has possessed you to give all this up?'

'I'm going to be a night lawyer,' said Flack.

Dr Tax choked.

'A night lawyer!' he boomed, crumpling Flack's resignation letter into a ball and hurling it at the young solicitor. 'You're going to be a night lawyer! One of those incompetents who can't hold down a proper job! A bloody night lawyer! One of those fools who hasn't got the wherewithal to do proper fee earning! Good grief, Flack, have you gone mad? I have never heard of anyone resigning from any firm anywhere, let alone one with the prestige of Bowles & Parkes, to go off and work as a night lawyer. You must be even more of an idiot than I thought.'

'Then you won't mind me leaving, will you? All I ask for is a decent reference. After all, as you say, I've worked hard here and built up a good practice with Melanie.'

Dr Tax grunted. It seemed that his strategy of bombast and bluster would not make Flack change his mind. Perhaps he should try a different tack. He took a few steps towards Flack and stooped to pick up the letter, which had ended up on the floor next to the brightly polished shoes of the man whose inveterate modesty meant that he never mentioned that Oxford was his alma mater. Then he made his way back to his chair and sat down. For a few seconds he adjusted his tie, then he let half a minute go by in silence, during which time he appeared to busy himself with some correspondence. Eventually, Dr Tax spoke.

'Look here, Flack, I'm sorry if I sounded a bit heated just then. Sometimes I let myself get a bit carried away. It's just that I don't like to lose good people. We've treated you well here. You're bright. You're talented. You're one of us, a perfect Bowles man. You get on well with Melanie – and by the way, I apologise unreservedly for my crass comments about her finer features. I didn't realise you were so sensitive, what with you getting married and all that. Everyone likes you, even if you are a bit of a quiet old cove. The libel work the pair of you like so much is booming – you'll remember what *The Lawyer* said better than me, but, damn it, the praise was well-deserved. You're on the up, and what is it they say – that London is the libel capital of the world? Well, why not stay and make Bowles & Parkes the legal capital of the libel capital? Come on, old chap, how about it?'

Flack maintained a steady eye on Dr Tax throughout this speech, but found himself unable to say anything, positive, negative or indifferent. His silence prompted a thought in Dr Tax's anxious mind.

'If it's a question of money, Harry, I can always find a bit more in the pot.'

This time, Flack found some words. He said that no, it wasn't down to money, though he thanked the senior partner for his generosity. And yes, London was the libel capital of the world, though he doubted that he was as talented as the plaudits *The Lawyer* had been kind enough to bestow and which, he noted with gratitude, the senior partner had been decent enough to endorse. 'Thank you, sir, you're very kind,' concluded Flack. 'But my mind is made up. I am leaving. I feel that I need to make a change.'

'Partnership, would that make a difference?'

Flack did not bat an eye. Even so, Dr Tax fleshed out the thought.

'There's that chap at Carter-Ruck, you know the one, you and Melanie are bound to have come across him. Tait, yes Tait, that's it. Old Carter-Ruck made him a partner when he'd been qualified for barely a minute. I could do the same with you. Yes, why not! Tait went on to be one of the best libel lawyers in London. What do you say? Partnership so early, your name on the headed paper, a stake in B&P – not a massive one, mind you, but a stake all the same. Imagine it, Harry! Partnership! What would *The Lawyer* say then?!'

Flack regretted that even this very generous offer could not make him change his mind.

Dr Tax would not give up. Continuing with his kindly manner, he said: 'But Harry, young Harry, what about that girl of yours? If I remember correctly she was quite something at the last Christmas party. You're marrying her soon, aren't you? I know she's got a job with one of the big boys but you mark my words, she'll want to jack it in and have junior Flacks soon. First she'll be at home, on maternity leave, costing her magic circle firm a magical amount of money, then before you know it she'll decide she doesn't want to go back to work after all. She'll decide her destiny is at home, in charge of your child, Harry. Quite right too, in my view, though from an employer's perspective it is very, very annoying when women go off and have babies. I know I shouldn't say that but you can see how galling it is for chaps like me to pilot a business to the heights and, in this era of equal opportunity, to be good enough to take on women, only for them to bugger off and have kids. It's a blasted nuisance. No, you listen to the old man. I've seen it all before. That pretty lady of yours will be putting her feet up at home before you know it. And you'll wish you were still here, with a good wage and joint responsibility with Melanie for the media department. Think of it, Harry – your own department much, much earlier than you'd planned. More money! Real responsibility! As much coverage in the trade press as you like. Why, the nationals will start quoting you, too. And the wife and kids will be happy as Larry and secure as Shirley. Won't you reconsider?'

Flack was not a man to share confidences. The fact that he had found

Helen in his bed with another man just a few days ago was the kind of thing he would never tell even his closest friends or family, let alone the likes of Dr Tax. And albeit that Flack's friends tended to remain on a hinterland of amiable acquaintanceship rather than dine at the table of confidence and intimacy, still less, in the ordinary course of things, would he tell anyone that he had left Helen, and that their engagement was off. But when he answered the senior partner Flack decided to depart from the norm.

'I found the pretty lady in my bed, fucking another man, about a week ago,' he said. 'They didn't even realise I was there, watching them finish, an eye-witness to their contempt as they soiled the sheets of the bed that belonged to us – me and Helen. So I left the flat we shared, me and Helen, the pretty lady, and wrote to her a day later telling her the marriage was off. Perhaps it would have been more accurate to say that the engagement was off, but you get the point. I didn't tell her why. I just said it was over. So you see, sir, that I feel I need a new life. One without prospects. One without a career path. One that won't net me a fortune, to be spent by the woman I was supposed to marry and the children we were supposed to have. I'd like a life that isn't as secure as Shirley, though if you don't mind me asking, is that your own expression, or is it common usage? It's just that I've never heard it before.'

For once, the senior partner was tongue-tied. He struggled to mutter that 'as secure as Shirley' was a phrase his wife tended to use, and that he had no idea of its origin beyond that, then heard a strained 'good luck' issuing from his lips as Flack got up and left his office.

After Flack had gone, Dr Tax reflected that perhaps he'd got the young man from Oxford wrong. Was there more to him than met the eye? That was a feisty and confrontational little speech just then. Good grief – Flack had even sworn too, which really wasn't the done thing, save by the Dr Taxes of this world. Flack's blood must have been up. Did he have some fire in that careful, measured and ascetic lawyer's belly, was it just as well that he was going? Dr Tax was clear: the last thing Bowles & Parkes needed was a nonconformist who might, for reasons too complex to fathom, do as he pleased from time to time. Was Flack one of them? Had his sense of the man been wrong? But no. Flack was as predictable as his cricket, with its summer rain, white flannels and evenly mowed wickets. It was a shame that he was determined to go, for men like Flack – those who follow life's rules – are useful in every walk of life but especially the law, where without protocol and order there is nothing. The loss of Flack's very equanimity, his obeisance to life's strictures and rituals, was understandable given its spur but it was a regret, rather than good riddance, that he was going.

Equally, however, the senior partner was well aware that there were plenty more fish in the sea. The wellbeing of a firm like Bowles & Parkes was not dependent on Harry Flack, for the very reason that there were so many Flacks around. Dependable cogs like him were ten a penny and as for Flack's future, Dr Tax gave it not a moment's thought, though he did allow that the quiet old cove had had a raw deal in coming home to find his fiancée being rogered by another man.

'Would have infuriated me, too,' said Dr Tax to himself. 'Mind you, I think I'd have done something about it. I'd have given the pair of them a good slap, for starters. I wouldn't have just stood there. That's Flack, though, that's the man all over. A man on the sidelines. A man who looks on, and says nothing.'

*

Dear Mr Madison,

I write with regard to the possibility of joining the night lawyer rota at The Record.

I qualified with Bowles & Parkes two years ago. I spent much of my articles working on libel cases and then concentrated exclusively in this area with the well-known plaintiff solicitor, Melanie Masters. However, I believe I am better suited to defendant work, given an abiding belief in freedom of expression. I want to help journalists publish stories; I abhor the notion of censorship. I have therefore resigned from the firm with a view to building up a portfolio of work for the national newspapers on their night lawyer rotas.

While there is no doubt I will be able to learn much from your long-standing night lawyers, I can offer a sound knowledge of libel law, so that they need not feel they are nursing an innocent amid the complexities of this fraught arena. Since being at Bowles & Parkes I have also become familiar with the laws of contempt, various reporting restrictions and confidence. I believe my skills would be an asset and, given that I live in central London, would easily be able to attend The Record *for shifts. I am also happy to work weekend shifts, including Sunday evenings.*

Please find attached my CV. I hope that it may be possible to join the rota and look forward to hearing from you in due course. Meanwhile, if there is anything you would like to discuss, please do not hesitate to contact me.

Yours sincerely,

Harry Flack

Flack felt satisfied with his letter. It was polite and yet confident. Writing it was the last thing he did within the offices of Bowles & Parkes, for this was not the era of the ubiquitous home computer and besides, having moved out of the flat he shared with Helen, Flack did not have access to the glamorous young couple's reasonably advanced PC, this acquired thanks to Helen's magical salary. No, he knew that he had to take advantage of the firm's equipment, and this he did on the same day that he handed his resignation letter to Dr Tax's secretary. He wrote identical letters to several heads of legal at newspapers in London, and printed them out along with copies of his CV. Then he placed them in a file, and then he placed the file in his briefcase. Briefcase in hand, and his meeting with the senior partner behind him, he left Bowles & Parkes' offices without looking back. The following morning he posted his letters.

Each received a reply.

Three newspapers had no vacancies on their rotas, one expected a vacancy to arise and would keep his details on file, while four others invited him in for an interview. James Madison, the head of legal at *The Record* – the paper Flack most admired, if he had to pick one, though this was difficult for all had their merits – wryly pointed out an error in Flack's CV, but did not hold it against him. He was invited in for an interview which, should it go well, would lead to him joining within a matter of days for, as it turned out, two night lawyers had just resigned from the rota. It seemed that Flack had a future, albeit not one of the law's more obvious ones.

The interview went well. Madison and Flack were cut from the same cloth. Both were restrained and careful men, discreet and temperate, in some ways more akin to the dry corporate lawyers of cliché than the supposedly more thrusting and zestful types attracted to media law, those who wore pink shirts with their smart suits, eschewed ties and joined raffish clubs in Soho. But Madison and Flack were not united merely by what both, if pushed, would admit was genteel liberal conservatism. They also shared an undying love of print media, a love which was happy to speak its name and which would withstand all, even the internet. And so, having spent a few minutes on the usual stuff of interviews – where are you from, which university did you attend, why did you choose the law, why do you now want to work as a night lawyer? – they gravitated to a clubby chat about newspapers, press freedom and the role of lawyers. For all the world, or a vigilant fly which was honoured with a place on the wall of Madison's office, they were two old friends, catching up after a month or so apart, cutting straight to the quick of what mattered to them most. Needless to say, they agreed that an unregulated press was a vital part of any thriving democracy ('How could it not be?' said Madison); they regretted the way the law of confidence was going ('People will be suing for privacy in a few years if we're not careful,' said Flack); they bemoaned the exorbitant costs of plaintiff libel lawyers ('I don't know how they sleep at night,' said Madison); and they wondered whether, when all was said and done, journalism was an honourable profession or a necessary evil.

'There is still honour in it,' said Madison. 'There are those who go too far but their actions are dwarfed by the sensible conduct of most hacks. They do a good job, day in, day out – a job the great British public takes for granted. Don't you think?'

Flack agreed. And it seemed to him – from afar, of course, for he had not yet been lucky enough to work shoulder to shoulder with journalists – that ethics were alive and well, if occasionally elastic, in the Fourth Estate. The exposure of iniquity, especially by those in positions of power and trust, was also, suggested Flack, a valid reason for investigative methods that might not always conform to the letter of the law.

'Quite so,' said Madison. 'And what are your thoughts on the PCC?'

Flack said that the Press Complaints Commission had a worthy aim but struck him as a fairly redundant body.

'I think you're right,' said Madison. 'But more to the point, I fail to comprehend how it can be of any meaningful import, being overseen by the very editors whose papers it seeks to police.'

Flack not only agreed but asked if, for this very reason, it was true to say that newspapers cared not a jot for a rap on the knuckles by the PCC?

'That is true,' said Madison. 'They say they care, but they don't. It's a wonder the public even bother to make complaints, but they do.'

'But if it's fundamentally toothless, do we, as lawyers, need to worry about it?'

'Appearances count, Mr Flack,' replied Madison. 'You will recall that justice must not only be done, but be seen to be done. For this reason even though the PCC is pointless, we, *The Record's* lawyers, are not in a position to treat it with the derision that it deserves. We must take it as seriously as a claim for libel. Or pretend to, at least.'

Discussion of the PCC was followed by an unexpected question.

'Are you a sportsman?' asked Madison.

'Not especially,' said Flack. 'I love cricket but haven't played it for a few years.'

'Excellent,' said Madison. 'The Queen's own game. We have a team here at *The Record* that you might care to join. *Wisden* is one of life's great pleasures, don't you think?'

'It is perhaps the most perfect publication on earth,' said Flack.

'I rather hope it goes on as it is, forever,' replied Madison. 'And I think it will. I think it'll survive the digital age that seems to be swooping down upon us, destroying everything that once was certain.'

The two men were quiet for half a minute, as they mused over *Wisden's* ability to withstand the coming twenty-first century. Madison broke the peaceful silence.

'Did you say you were free to start immediately?'

Flack said he was. Madison shook his hand and told him to come in and go through the ritual of a few training shifts.

'I can tell they're not necessary in your case, but we have to keep to the form. You need to be seen to earn your flying colours, even if you're already airborne,' he said.

*

Neither Flack nor Martha had ever been to the Witterings. Their decision to leave London one balmy Saturday morning was not motivated by a long-standing but unfulfilled urge to experience them, either. Rather, having bumped into each other early on a Friday evening, they had conceived of a trip to the south coast simply by way of something to do.

'What have you got planned for the weekend?' asked Martha, after she and Flack had exchanged the pleasantries to be expected when two people meet accidently in London, or, for that matter, anywhere (*My* word, what are you doing in this neck of the woods? Well, I'm on my way to see a film, what about you? Me? I've nipped over to see a friend. What a coincidence that we're both here at the same time! Yes, isn't it? What a small world! Shall we have a drink? What a good idea.).

'Nothing,' said Flack. 'Nothing at all. I shall read the papers but that's about it.'

'Aren't you watching the cricket? Isn't that what you usually do?'

'Yes, it is, but there's no game this weekend. I'm going to be awfully quiet. It's a trait of mine that used to drive Helen mad. But I don't mind. I rather like being quiet.'

'Harry,' said Martha, 'I was so sorry about what happened.'

'Don't be,' said Flack, with faux jauntiness. 'It was for the best. I imagine she's gone on to get engaged now. They're probably making plans for their honeymoon as we stand here chatting. As for me, I've never been happier.'

Martha wasn't able to summon a response. She was ill at ease with irony, and disturbed by sarcasm. She could only look up at Flack – he was a good foot taller than her – with a pained and solemn expression.

'Really,' said Flack, suddenly desperate to put her at ease. 'It's fine. I've barely thought about Helen these past six months. I've moved on. I know she has too. It was for the best.'

An idea came to Martha.

Timidly, tiptoeing an inch forward, then rocking backwards a fraction, she said 'Harry?', leaving Flack's first name hanging amid the scurrying end-of-week commuters.

'Yes Martha, what is it?'

Martha took the plunge.

'I'm not doing anything either. Would you like to go somewhere tomorrow, for the day? With me?'

'Of course,' said Flack. 'But where?'

Martha was so surprised by the alacrity of Flack's assent that she couldn't think of a destination. She began to mumble something about the fine weather they'd been having, and how London's parks were at their best in late spring, and even spluttered the word 'picnic', but her sentences were muted and confused. Flack came to her rescue.

'Shall we go to the sea?'

Martha was delighted. Her invitation to Flack was borne of chance, whimsy and impetuosity, but here he was, saying yes and suggesting a trip to the coast. Self-aware as she was, Martha registered the feeling of joy she felt upon Flack's agreement, so too its intensification when he came up with an outing which a great many people would regard as romantic. Only then did she allow that, for all these years, she had feelings for the diffident young lawyer that were more than merely Platonic.

'That sounds lovely,' she said, beaming. 'But where?'

'I have no idea,' said Flack. 'But you're right, we've had some wonderful weather and the evening paper says it's set to continue. Why don't I pick you up at 9.30, at your house, and then we'll just point the car to the south and drive? Camber Sands is supposed to be lovely. I think they play a cricket tournament there, once a year. I don't suppose it'll be happening tomorrow, but we could go all the same.'

'Or Brighton,' offered Martha. 'It's closer, I think, and I love the pier.'

'Camber Sands, or Brighton – what does it matter? I'll look at my map when I get home. There's always Bognor Regis, as well. I've heard it's quite a contender.'

'Harry, we can't go to Bognor Regis!' said Martha, coquettishly. 'It's all dirty weekends and rude postcards!'

'So much the better!' said Flack. 'But I mustn't keep you. Enjoy your film. I'll see you tomorrow at 9.30.'

*

As they drove south, not to Brighton, still less to Camber Sands, but in a more south-westerly direction with Chichester as their first stop, Flack revisited the previous evening's conversation. Had they been flirting, he and Martha? He felt as if he'd known her all his life, but as a sisterly presence, not one to provoke sexual desire. And yet, as they stood on a warm and busy London street, people swarming around them, endlessly, purposefully and pointlessly moving, something had happened – hadn't it? Martha's eyes; her body – inclined towards his; her words; her shyness – all spoke of emotional interest, not to say intent, which he had never once discerned – or did they? Had he got it wrong? What was it that Helen used to say, that he was 'about as perceptive when it came to women as a cricket bat'? Yes, that was it. He was a blunt instrument, a man of lacking emotional refinement, a man for whom the feminine psyche would always be a mystery. He would be well advised to abandon this excursion into the meaning of last night's conversation. Besides, everyone knew that Bognor Regis was associated with smutty postcards and dirty weekends. The conjunction was doubtless unjust, for surely there was more to the place, but to infer that there was an innuendo meaning in this part of his exchange with Martha was foolish.

'An innuendo meaning indeed,' said Flack to himself, as they drove through the pretty market town of Midhurst. Imperceptibly, he shook his head. 'Why do I always have to think of everything in legal terms? What is wrong with me? Any normal person would have wondered if there was more than meets the eye to Martha's mention of dirty weekends and rude postcards. Not me. I have to process what she said in libel law terms.'

'It's such a lovely day,' said Martha, as they emerged from Midhurst into the West Sussex countryside. 'What a place to live. People must have an awful lot of money round here, don't you think, Harry?'

Flack did not reply. His mind had wandered into the alleyways of innuendo, as libel lawyers understand them. Before reaching this unnerving place, there was the natural and ordinary meaning of words, a clearing in which the ordinary, reasonable reader could make sensible conclusions as to what the words meant, but beyond, even at the outer reaches of this dangerous labyrinth, there was a slippery thing, the innuendo meaning, which itself morphed into true innuendo and false innuendo. The true innuendo arose when words seem innocent, and yet, because the person happening upon them has some special knowledge, they carry a malignant additional meaning. 'The classic example,' thought Flack, 'is of the ostensibly anodyne account of X and Y getting married. It is anodyne and libel-free, to all but the person who knows that X is already married, and not divorced. He is thus a bigamist according to this, a true innuendo.' But if this wasn't perilous enough the law also carved out space for the false innuendo, an alternative meaning which could be inferred from reading between the lines. Flack was just about to test himself by coming up an example when Martha managed to bring him back to earth.

'Harry, you seem awfully distracted. Is something on your mind?'

'No, no, not at all,' said Flack hurriedly. 'Sorry. What were you saying?'

Martha said again that the day was lovely. Flack nodded vigorously, as if she had said something daringly insightful but a little extravagant, something that needed excessive endorsement. His response was the same when, passing yet another grand home amid fields and greenery, she observed that this was a moneyed area, the place, perhaps, to which rich lawyers retired. To this, Flack added a thought.

'They don't just retire here. A lot of them make enough money to move down here midway through their careers, sometimes even earlier. They commute to London, and commute back again, and their weekends are spent in this bucolic idyll. Not a bad life. A couple of the partners at my old firm lived round here somewhere.'

To this, Martha decided to chance a question about Flack's career.

'You could have had this, Harry, if you'd stayed at the firm, couldn't you?'

'Yes, I could've,' replied Flack. 'It's what Helen and I used to talk about. When we talked, that is. We'd work hard, rise through our firms, she'd go on maternity leave, return to work for a bit, then go off again, and then, with a couple of kids, we'd settle in the country. I'd commute to town and she'd bring up the kids until school age, then, depending on how she felt, she might go back to the law. Or she might buy a delicatessen and run it in a little village. That was the plan. It proved to be of the best-laid variety.'

Not for the first time, Martha could think of nothing to say. They sat in a silence that teetered between uneasiness and companionability, as Flack drove south. Arriving in the village of East Lavant Flack stopped the car, declaring it was such a gorgeous day that it was time to put the roof down. He owned a white 1975 MG B Roadster with a soft-top and chrome bumpers, a car which he kept in immaculate condition. As Flack took the roof down, Martha stood by the car and enjoyed the glow of the sun on her face. It was a windless day, absurdly warm for the time of year; already, in the middle of the morning, the temperature was in the early twenties. Martha wondered if it would be warm enough to swim once they reached a beach – she had packed a swimsuit, just in case – and resolved to go for a paddle, at the very least.

'That's better,' said Flack, as he turned the ignition. 'I love the feeling of the wind in my hair as I'm driving. Do you?'

'I don't know, Harry, I've never been in a sports car before.'

'Helen used to love it,' said Flack.

In silence, they entered Chichester. Its cathedral was unremarked. In silence, they emerged from Chichester. Beyond were East and West Wittering. To Martha's surprise, Flack suggested they buy some provisions for a picnic. He parked in a car park near some shops, and disappeared into a supermarket. He seemed happy, or happy enough, but Martha was not sure where the day was going. Somehow she had assumed they would eat lunch in a pub; there was a lassitude about having a picnic that she couldn't equate to Flack. On impulse, as Flack bought some French bread, cold meats and salad, she rushed to a shop selling tourist tat and bought two bats and a ball. Flack looked at them quizzically when he returned to his MG.

'I love bat and ball,' said Martha.

Flack laughed. Martha could tell that he had never played bat and ball before.

*

On the beach, under the sun, Flack and Martha did well to find a space of their own. The fine weather had inspired the hordes, both on land and at sea. Everywhere they looked, there were families picnicking, young men and boys playing football or cricket or throwing Frisbees, children swimming in the shallows and teenage sweethearts slyly courting. On the water, a parade of yachts meandered back and forth on the Solent, joined by the occasional windsurfer. Martha was tickled by the latter breed.

'I don't understand the appeal,' she said, laughing. 'Look! All that bloke has done so far is fall off.'

'It's better if it's windy,' suggested Flack.

'Really?' said Martha.

'Yes,' said Flack. 'I'm sure of it. I've read about windsurfing. You have to learn in a slight breeze but when you get good you can whizz along in strong winds.'

'So we're watching a learner?'

'Maybe, I'm not sure. The trouble is that there's virtually no wind. Look at the yachts. They're not exactly flying.'

As they watched the small, near-shore water craft a larger vessel bisected the sun, further out to sea. It was an old sailing ship, doubtless restored and most probably – thought Flack – being crewed by some hearty young outward-bound types, under the benign and watchful eye of an old sea dog, the kind of man who, unlike Flack, wouldn't think twice about using the words 'outward-bound', in contrast to the young libel lawyer who couldn't help himself from wondering if someone, somewhere, now owned the words 'outward-bound' or, at least, had got them trade marked, meaning, in theory, that everyone else had to be careful when using them but then again, it would depend on the context in which the words were used and – of course – the exact form of the trade mark, whether the words were separate, conjoined, capitalized, perhaps italicized or even deliberately misspelt, as seemed to be the way with brand names these days. Martha observed the tall ship, too. It reminded her of a painting by Albert Marquet, the name of which she couldn't remember. She thought of mentioning this to Flack but, again seeing a look of remoteness on his face, decided against it.

'How about a game of bat and ball?' said Martha. 'Come on, it's great fun! We can play over there.'

She gestured to some firm sand just a few yards from where they were standing. Flack did not, initially, do or say anything. But then, holding out his hand for a bat, he said, 'Why not? But you will tell me how to play, won't you?'

They stood facing each other, near their towels – non-descript dark blue for Flack, a mosaic of Moroccan hues for Martha. Suddenly, they laughed, perhaps with embarrassment, perhaps with simple pleasure.

'Let's play,' said Martha. She skipped off and stood, ball in her left hand, bat in her right, ready for action. She was wearing a short green dress, the sides of which she hitched up to tuck into the elastic of her knickers. Her legs were slender and toned, her bare arms were modestly tanned, her entire being spoke of healthiness, athleticism and zest for life.

'It's strange, I always thought she was such a bookworm,' said Flack to himself, as he took up a position some ten feet opposite Martha. 'I never would have thought she was so, well, *free.*'

Suddenly, a ball flew past Flack's head.

'Pay attention, Harry!,' said Martha, chiding him girlishly.

Flack stooped to pick up the ball. For a second, Martha expected him to ask her what to do next. 'How does he ever manage to play cricket?' she wondered. 'Then again, maybe he just watches the game. I've never met anyone quite so disconnected.'

But then Flack hit the ball towards her. Twisting lightly to her left, Martha returned the ball with her backhand. She hit it accurately, and at just the right pace. Somehow, Flack missed it. The ball landed on the sand, at his feet.

'I'm sorry,' said Flack. 'I wasn't concentrating.'

He served the ball to Martha again. This time, remarkably, they managed a rally of some ten or twelve shots, before Flack overhit the ball. Martha skipped a few paces to retrieve it, laughing. 'It's as if she hasn't got a care in the world,' thought Flack.

Later, as they sat on their towels having played bat and ball for almost an hour, it dawned on Flack that he was happy. It dawned on him that Martha was happy. People around them were happy. It was a beautiful, tranquil day; he readily agreed with Martha's suggestion that they go for a swim. The water was warm; in the shallows, they paddled and splashed and swam. Children ran back and forth on the sand; a little out to sea, in a better breeze, the windsurfer was having more luck. Flack caught Martha's eye, as she swam, doing breaststroke, towards him. They smiled. Neither said a word.

*

Their return drive to London was cheery and relaxed. Any silences were easy and companionable; for the most part, they talked about everything and anything, favourite books, music, how pleasant the sea had been at The Witterings, what a find this stretch of the south coast was, how funny it was that they thought it was a find when the droves on the beach were ample proof that place was far from undiscovered. But as they entered the suburbs of south London, Martha took the conversation into more delicate territory.

'Harry,' she began, with her voice sounding as it did when she'd asked if Flack wanted to spend the day with her.

'Yes, Martha, what is it?'

'I am sorry about what happened. With Helen, I mean.'

Flack said nothing.

'I mean,' pressed Martha, 'I have to say I think she treated you very badly. I didn't condone anything she did. I used to tell her what I thought.'

Abruptly, Martha stopped. She sighed, but then started again.

'I'm sorry. It's all coming out now. Maybe I shouldn't say anything. I'm sorry. I really think she behaved very badly. I don't blame you for wanting to have nothing to do with her.'

This time, Flack chose to speak.

'Thanks, Martha,' he said. 'I did find what happened very painful. To an extent, I understand – now – Helen's frustration with me. I am too serious. I'm a bore. I don't have anything racy about me. But I think having an affair was wrong. Very wrong. And sleeping with him in our bed was a terrible thing to do.'

'Oh, Harry, you're not a bore. Serious, yes. But I think you're lovely.'

Martha turned to Flack as she said this. The car was stationary, at traffic lights, enabling Flack to turn to the woman with whom he just spent a blissful day. He wanted to say something. He wanted to reply in kind. As he searched for the right words the horn of the car behind sounded; the lights had turned green. Flack put his MG into first gear and drove on.

After a few minutes' silence – this time, not so comfortable – Flack spoke.

'What is Helen doing now? Do you know?'

Martha seemed relieved to talk again. 'I do,' she said, swiftly. 'Things didn't go well for her. It's sad, actually. She made a fool of herself over that man. I think he was just using her. He never struck me as serious. Eddie Conrad, he was called. He strung her along but not long after you found them together he ended it. Said he wasn't ready for commitment. She took it very badly. She was obsessed with him. I'm sorry, but she was. Her behaviour got worse and worse and eventually she got the sack. Trouble is that by then she was pregnant. I don't know if she got pregnant by Conrad deliberately, to snare him, or whether it was an accident. But she left the law in disgrace, heavily pregnant, drinking too much despite having a baby on the way, shrieking about Conrad and how he'd ruined her life. He didn't want anything to do with her, or the child. I tried to talk to her but the truth is that we were never that close. She knew that I disapproved of the whole thing anyway, so didn't talk to me at the best of times. But then she disappeared. No one has heard from her for ages. One or two of her friends from work tried to get in touch; no joy. If you ask me, I think she moved abroad. Didn't her parents live overseas? I think she just wanted out. She must have felt utterly humiliated by everything.'

Flack was quiet for a few moments before he asked Martha another question.

'Did she have the child?'

'I don't know, Harry. No one does. She was binge-drinking so much that I wouldn't be surprised if things didn't work out.'

'You mean the child might have had a problem?'

'Yes. Or it was stillborn, or she miscarried. I just can't see that she had a perfect baby and everything worked out. And if she had it, what then? No dad, no 'thrusting young Eddie' to be by her side. I'm sorry. I know this is difficult for you. You must still care for her.'

'Not really,' said Flack. 'Though I wouldn't wish misfortune on her, still less on a child she had, even if it was by him. I'm pretty amazed, though, that all these months later – what is it, nearly a year since I walked out? – no one knows what's become of her.'

'People can disappear when they want to,' said Martha. 'One of the authors I used to deal with vanished without trace when his marriage broke up. We couldn't find him anywhere. Still don't know where on earth he is. Just send his royalty cheques to a PO box.'

'I suppose so,' said Flack.

A few minutes later they found themselves in Martha's road. Something about the turn the conversation had taken dissuaded Martha from suggesting Flack come in, and he did not ask.

CHAPTER 10

Noon, Day Lawyers' Offices

Flack was alone.

'Isn't that right, Mr Lawyer?'

The words obsessed him. Flack sat alone in Patricia Phillips's office, nursing them like a hangover. They hurt and tormented him; they were a cause of regret; they made him yearn to feel better. How patronizing, how contemptuous; how in keeping with the essence of Eddie Conrad. The man had stolen his fiancée, all those years ago; he'd led her up the garden path, then dumped her; he'd had the gall to have sex with Helen in Flack's flat... And the words he'd said, the words she'd said, after the act; their clinical contempt for him... A child, too, somewhere – or not. The vileness of it all. The disregard. Everything came flooding back. Years of careful repression crumbled in the face of a torrent he was powerless to resist. He could see Conrad's bare legs and buttocks, on top of Helen, as if they were in front of his very eyes but now, as much as the words the couple exchanged then, he also heard the snarling mirth of Conrad's mock-question, at the end of the morning's editorial conference.

'Isn't that right, Mr Lawyer?'

The words mingled and spun around, echoing in his mind and ricocheting off the walls of Phillips's office, but more livid still was the memory of Conrad that day, in the Fulham flat. He'd trampled all over Flack's home and treated him as an object of ridicule – and yet Flack had done nothing. He'd merely stood there, unseen and unheard, and watched, and listened. How Flack wished he had walked into the bedroom, grabbed Conrad by the neck with both hands and snapped his cervical spine. How he wished he'd shouted at him, that he'd screamed at Helen, that he'd smashed the room up, that he'd done something – anything, just one small act to show that he existed, and that they were wrong. But he had done nothing. He had been weak and pathetic. Perhaps he had deserved their contempt. And now, after all these years – years in which Flack had worked with tireless commitment to erect walls and barriers, behind which he was impregnable – now here was Conrad, as mirthful, as mocking and as merciless as he'd been when he courted Helen and cuckolded Flack.

But why had he been so naive to think that somehow he could avoid Conrad all this time? He'd watched his career, noting, without emotion, his arrival at the helm of other newspapers. In later years Flack had abandoned night lawyering at two titles, precisely because he got wind of Conrad's imminent arrival. As his retirement approached he confined himself solely to *The Record*, blind to the possibility that Conrad might end up as its editor. Perhaps it was the nature of *The Record* itself that caused what Flack now cursed as gross negligence. It was the most august of all newspapers, the longest-running, the most prestigious in the land. Surely *The Record* would never open its doors to a shady operator like Conrad, a man known, if Flack's memory served, as 'The Collector' not merely because of his indifference to the receipt of a libel writ but also, if the rumours were true, thanks to his vast collection of illegally tape-recorded phone conversations.

'Isn't that right, Mr Lawyer?' Yes, yes it was; Conrad's unscrupulousness knew no bounds, he'd paid thousands of pounds to private detectives over the course of his career, brooking at nothing to secure voicemail messages left by the rich, famous and unworthy, transcripts of rows among lovers, illicit or otherwise, recordings of royals and their paramours and taped confessions of politicians on the make. All reputedly formed a compendium whose criminality Conrad rejoiced in, to the horror of most journalists but also their sneaking admiration. Conrad didn't care what it took to outsell his rivals. The law was there merely to be broken.

But Flack had been wrong. *The Record* had seen fit to employ the editor known as The Collector. Perhaps it was because of the digital age, the way in which boundaries were merging, shrinking even. It wasn't so long ago that *The Record* had been resolutely broadsheet but now look at it – a broadsheet in tabloid form whose style and ethics were increasingly low-brow too. The media was changing, of course it was; perhaps it was more accurate to say that it was dying, at least in its traditional print form. Flack knew this as well as anyone. And in its attempt to survive, Flack should have anticipated that even the most prestigious title of them all, *The Record*, would turn to a man like Conrad. Here he was, then, in the building, alive and kicking and in charge. On this, Flack's last shift.

Flack tried to gather his thoughts. In his disarray he realised that his life had been a mistake. His inaction in the face of Helen's infidelity summed it all up. Flack was a good lawyer, yes, but he *didn't do anything.* Even the most cynical hack, jovially able to destroy someone's reputation and yet sanguine about the ephemera of his output, was more creative than Flack. He was a man who stood on the side, watching. He was a man who chose to bury himself among newspapers, to read the news rather than dare to make it, to watch cricket rather than play it. How many times had he turned out for *The Record's* cricket team? A paltry three. At university, he had played cricket for the third eleven. This was not a spectacular achievement, but it was something. In his working life, Flack had avoided any sports at Bowles & Parkes (despite the firm's bustling after-work scene of five-a-side football and, from spring to summer, its round of cricket matches), and once at *The Record* it had been all but impossible to cajole him into playing the game he loved. Each of the three times he'd played, over the course of twenty-five years, he had acquitted himself well. His colleagues had praised his skill as a batsman and the nous he displayed as a bowler. He was good in the field, too. And yet, try as they might, they almost always failed to induce Flack to play again.

I'm some sort of Bartleby, paralyzed, stuck, alone. I prefer not to.

Of a sudden, it seemed to Flack that his very professionalism was a disguise. It was a cover for his inadequacies. He had lost Helen, because he deserved to lose her. No wonder she'd had an affair – a bright, vivacious young women like her needed more than what Flack had to offer. He could have been happy with Martha, but failed, as usual, to act (they met again, some months after the trip to The Witterings, this time with Brighton as their destination. The moment had gone and the day was excruciating.). He was liked by colleagues, and even had one or two friends, but he was alone and had nothing to show for his life. Nothing at all. Just a good reputation. A reputation as *a true professional, a man of dignity and wise judgement, an unflappable man, a man you can trust.*

'Isn't that right, Mr Lawyer?' Conrad's insouciant smile as he mocked Flack hovered in the room. Why, oh why had Flack not shot something back at him? He felt like a young articled clerk, at the mercy of Dr Tax's mercurial barbs, tongue-tied and thwarted. He might as well have called Conrad 'sir'.

But then again, what could he have said?

'Yes, that is correct, Mr Editor', or, 'A magnificent observation, in keeping with your munificence, Mr Editor', or perhaps, 'That's right, yes, but if you will allow me to make an observation, Mr Eddie 'The Cunt' Conrad, it is this: you are a disgrace to journalism'?

His head in his hands, Flack despaired as never before. There was nothing to do. His had been a pathetic attempt at a life. It was his last shift and he was an esteemed and respected night lawyer at the glorious, serially award-winning *Record* – but so what? Conrad would endure, Conrad would have the last laugh, a laugh that had always been coming, a laugh Flack tried not to hear as he reviewed his life of passivity and torpor.

Lifting his head, he caught sight of *Unreliable Evidence: Life As A Lawyer Among Fleet Street's Finest*, a book written by James Madison. Hugely respected by both journalists and lawyers alike, Madison had retired a decade earlier. His book had been a bestseller, both because of its curious, almost Victorian sense of propriety and many louche or, at least, outré stories.

Madison had not pulled his punches, but as a veteran libel lawyer he knew exactly what he could get away with. He had also been a gentleman to the last, not only paying homage to Flack but also to Phillips, a lawyer he described as 'undoubtedly the best media lawyer at work in London today'. Hence, a signed copy of *Unreliable Evidence* stood proudly on the middle shelf of Phillips's bookcase, alone, well-thumbed and justly cherished.

Flack could recall every sentence that Madison had written about him. He had a knack with words, something akin to a photographic memory. Once they were on a page, he never forgot them; all the more so, the few times when words had had a direct bearing on his life. Was he one of the best night lawyers in London? Or rather, to be precise, *the* best night lawyer in London? That's what Madison had written, at the close of one of his anecdotes, when yet again Flack had dropped what he'd been doing to spend a night at *The Record*.

I would go so far as to say that if Patricia Phillips is the best in-house media lawyer working daylight hours in London, wrote Madison, *Harry Flack is her nocturnal equivalent. The mystery, to me, is why he didn't pursue a more lucrative career in the conventional arenas provided by the law. He could have made a fortune, but why he chose not to is both beyond the parameters of this book and, indeed, another story. With due allowance for a degree of selfishness, for without Flack my newspaper's trips to the Royal Courts of Justice would have been much more frequent, I am convinced that the mainstream legal profession's loss was Fleet Street's gain.*

Flack didn't need to open the book to recall this passage. But now, it came back as a taunt, not a complement. What would Madison say to him, if he were to walk into Phillips's office and behold so meagre a man? 'Harry, I am disappointed. You are a man who could have done more. I don't take back everything I ever wrote or said about you but I do now offer it with qualifications. I can only hope that one day you find it in you to do something. Perhaps, in your retirement, you might actually contribute to life. Maybe you'll even find the wherewithal to commit to a woman. Your affairs of the heart, such as they are to date, amount to precious little. There is still time, so I hope you take what I'm saying on board. In the meantime, you might as well finish your last shift in the spirit of all those that came before. Assess the problems put before you, assess the evidence, assess what's right, and advise accordingly. You have been a good night lawyer; you remain arguably the best of your brethren to have worked in Fleet Street. There is nothing to do now but see out your last few hours here. Walk out of here with your head held high but then for God's sake make something of the next twenty years.'

Madison's imaginary words were, of course, correct. Everything about Madison was correct, even words he hadn't said. For a moment, Flack objected to his former boss's probity, but he quickly reined in this emotion. It was his fault, and his alone, that when it came to his affairs of the heart, there was very little to report.

Steeling himself, Flack sat upright in Phillips's chair. He must do what was expected of him. He must hold the fort for the absent day lawyers, and then, come the night shift, he must prove himself once more, though for the last time, the most capable night lawyer in London. And then – only then – he could go home, and, if he so wished, confront in despair the loneliness of his life.

*

'Harry! How lovely to see you!'

Mary was a tall, slim and stylish woman from the East End whose youthful beauty must, so Flack had often conjectured, have turned just about every head in Whitechapel. With long, flowing hair, a sassy smile and, despite a chronic flirtatiousness, a sensibility that was both wise and wholly committed to just one man – Michael, her husband of over forty years – Mary was still, in her early sixties, every inch the blonde bombshell. She and Flack had always liked each other. Mary's affection for the veteran night lawyer (or 'NL', as she liked to call *The Record's* night lawyers) arose from a simple premise: she believed him to be a good man. Likewise, Flack's views of Mary. Flack believed her to be a good woman, though every time he saw the long-standing PA to Evan Brooke (who had also worked for James Madison) he was aware that something else kindled his affection for Mary. The mere sight of her would make him smile, not simply because of her good looks but because she radiated decency. 'She's the kind of woman who'd always look out for her friends and family, who'd never let anything happen to them, and yet who is tough enough to look after herself too. And she's always got a nice word to say, whatever's been going on in her life.' Fresh from the torment of his encounter with Eddie Conrad, Mary was even more of a welcome sight than usual.

'Mary!' exclaimed Flack, rising from the chair behind Phillips's desk. He kissed Mary on each cheek, a ritual she insisted upon though reciprocated without ever quite brushing her lips against Flack's skin. Standing back a pace, the two members of *The Record's* legal department smiled comfortably, and for perhaps longer than was necessary, before Mary asked a question.

'So, Mr Flack, Mr NL, our venerable Harry, it's your last shift. Your *last ever* shift at *The Record*! And you're looking as dapper as ever. How do you feel?'

As usual, the words were accompanied by a coquettish laugh. Confronted by this – or rather, by Mary being Mary – Flack's angst evaporated. Instantaneously, Mary was having her usual effect. Life was good. Life was gentle. Life was fun and free and perhaps even a little bit saucy on the side. Life was full of laughter and forgetting and there was no need to dwell on the Eddie Conrads of this world, still less the notion of failure.

'Oh, I feel terribly sad, Mary,' replied Flack, inadvertently stumbling over his words, before rallying. 'After all, I won't see so much of you any more!'

This was the reply that Mary had been hoping for. Ordinarily, it would be the cue for a few more sentences of mock-amorous banter. This time, though, Mary checked herself. She beheld in Flack, with his ruffled hair and anxious eyes, a troubled man, a man who was, she assumed, feeling genuinely sad and who probably wasn't really in the mood for larking about. Switching, as only Mary could, from banter to concern, she changed tack.

'Harry, are you all right? You don't seem yourself. Are you sure everything is OK?'

Flack decided to do what he had done all his life, and offer the reassurance that all was as it should be.

'Of course it is Mary, why wouldn't it be? I'm a little tired, that's all. Yes, of course I'm also a little sad. Twenty-five years is a long time. But all good things come to an end, even the great joy of working in this madhouse. Then again, from tomorrow I won't have to work here anymore. That can't be bad, can it?'

Mary eyed Flack carefully.

'If you say so, Harry, if you say so,' she said. 'Are you still planning on moving to the country, of getting away from all of us?'

'I think so. I think I've done my time in London. I'll still come back and see my old friends every now and then, but it's time for a change.'

Mary sighed.

'Whenever I go to the country I like it for half a day, then I can't think of anything to do. I've always been a high heels and pavements girl.'

'I know Mary, I know. But you and Mike will come and see me, won't you?'

'That depends. Where is it that you're going again? Someone told me you were going to go and live in Dorset. Is that true?'

'Not quite,' said Flack. 'But you're heading in the right direction.'

'Not further west? Harry, I couldn't possibly travel beyond Bath. I went there once, mind you. It was a long time ago. I seem to remember it being very elegant with lots of art galleries.'

'That's a fine and accurate description. You might add Roman baths as well.'

'Roman baths! How quaint! But it's not London, is it? I bet you'll disappear to Bath or Weymouth or wherever you're going and forget all about us up here. We'll just be little flickers in your memory.'

Flack laughed. 'Not at all,' he said. 'I've had the happiest working years of my life here. All twenty-five of them. I'll be back so often you'll think I haven't left. You'll be calling security to chuck me out.'

Mary tutted, unconvinced, and Flack did not try to persuade her otherwise. He had plans for his retirement, and though they would entail the occasional trip to London they didn't involve returning to *The Record*. Not least, now that Eddie Conrad was its editor.

Conrad. There he was again. Why did he have to arrive as the editor on the day of Flack's last shift? Why couldn't he have turned up the following month, or week, or even the next day? But Conrad hadn't respected Flack's sensibilities all those years ago. Why would he start now? 'But hang on,' cautioned Flack inwardly, 'he can't possibly have turned up today to make your last working day hell. To think that he's timed it like this is ridiculous. Worse, it dignifies the bastard. No, he's here by coincidence. It's just a really bad coincidence.'

His mind had drifted. It took Mary two attempts to bring him back to 'Planet Legal Department', as she called it. Once she had Flack's attention, Mary again asked if he was all right. Flack said he was, and for the second time, Mary tutted, though this time as if she was genuinely vexed, before saying that she ought to grapple with the eternal mess of Evan Brooke's office. She added that neither Donna nor Sarah, the legal department's other PAs, would be coming in: Donna had taken a holiday to play in a five-a-side football tournament (much to Mary's bemusement; she was not an enthusiast for women playing what were traditionally male sports), while Sarah was on one of her legal executive courses. 'It's just me and you, Harry, here in the legal department. I hope you cheer up. You don't seem yourself. Oh, by the way, I'm off at 4pm today.' Such statements, by any other PA or secretary, would have been met with consternation, but Mary carried them off. If she declared she was going home early, she was going home early. This was even true when she arrived late, as was the case on this occasion. Mary's hours were a matter for her and her alone. Flack didn't even bat an eyelid at the news of her early departure.

She made another statement, though, that Flack found more difficult to stomach.

'Of course, it's all change for another reason today, isn't it? We've got a new editor.'

Dismayed, Flack said nothing for a few seconds, before replying: 'Yes, Mary, we have.'

He said this in so flat a fashion that Mary couldn't but question it.

'What's the matter?' she enquired. 'Do you know him?'

'In a way, I suppose I do,' said Flack. 'At least, I know of him, and I have seen him before, or a bit, or bits, of him. And heard him, too,' he added, before gazing blankly at a money tree which, despite the absence of natural light in Phillips's office, seemed to be flourishing.

'Harry, you're really not yourself,' said Mary, putting an arm around the night lawyer's shoulder. 'How about a coffee? Sit down and I'll go and get you one.'

Muttering quietly, Flack tried to protest that he was feeling fine, really, and had to get on with the day's work. Mary would have none of it. She almost pushed him into Phillips's chair before quickly taking her coat off and hanging it up in the large adjoining office, which she shared with Donna and Sarah. Popping her head back into Phillips's office, she told Flack to sit still and wait. 'I'll be back in two shakes,' she said. 'I'll have a nice strong cup of black coffee for you, just the way you like it.' She then sped off down the corridor towards *The Record's* canteen, leaving Flack staring at the money tree.

When she returned, with an almond croissant (for which her colleague had a penchant) as well as an Americano coffee, Flack was nowhere to be seen.

CHAPTER 11

Execution Dock

It was lunchtime and the day was grey and dry. Instead of taking himself to his favourite bench in St Katharine Docks, Flack felt compelled to vary his routine. Though he could not say why, he took himself to Execution Dock. On the way there, he tried to think straight. There were various cherished mechanisms he could deploy, quirks and tricks that would bring order to his mind if ever it became disheveled. They included mentally replaying a series of great innings in cricket – for example, Graham Gooch's 154 for England against the West Indies in 1991, or Ian Botham's 149 against Australia a decade earlier. Flack had watched replays of these performances (both of which, he knew well, took place at Leeds) hundreds of times, and to imagine them in his mind's eye usually had a soothing effect. So, too, did taking himself through the sinuous rhythm and melody of 'All Blues', the Miles Davis track he had first heard when he was thirteen. He had found it by accident. It was late on a Sunday night and the pubescent, jazz-innocent Flack had turned on the radio expecting to hear an interview with a cricketer, only, because he had got his schedules mixed up, to find a presenter introducing the Spartan piano solo on the fourth piece of the *Kind of Blue* album, this by way of a tribute to the pianist, Bill Evans, who at the time was battling his addiction to heroin. Not that the presenter mentioned this; that would not have been the form. No, Flack only learned of this facet of Evans's life later, in his late teens (or perhaps his early twenties), by which time he had become a jazz buff. Perhaps, he had since reflected, the presenter knew Evans, was aware of his struggles and was trying to help him. Certainly, Flack couldn't remember a precise peg for the tribute, in contrast to that which was broadcast by Peter Clayton on *Sounds of Jazz* shortly after Evans's death in September 1980, and which also reprised Evans's solo in 'All Blues'. Astonished, the day after fate first led him to the Evans solo Flack had sought out a vinyl recording of *Kind of Blue*, and then discovered, on 'All Blues', the solos by Davis, Julian 'Cannonball' Adderley and John

Coltrane which precede Evans's work. Ever since, Flack was heedless of the curse of *Kind of Blue's* worldwide popularity, which lent the album the twin unwanted badges of lift music and cliché. For Flack, who also became dedicated to *Sounds of Jazz* every Sunday night and the broadcasting skills of the self-effacing, effortlessly professional Clayton, what Davis had created was quite simply the most glorious music on earth. And of its glories, 'All Blues' was the greatest.

Flack was not overtly musical, in the sense that he could sing well or play an instrument, but, as with words, he had a knack of being able to recall the entirety of a piece in his mind. Of all those that he could recite inwardly (and there were many), 'All Blues' was his favourite. It almost invariably brought calm and tranquility, but if, for some reason, it failed, there was the simple expedient of counting steps between destinations, a far better system than avoiding cracks in paving slabs, which was far too onerous and, besides, tended to make Flack wonder if it was true, had swathes of the population of Liverpool issued claims against the city council for tripping over as they walked along pavements? Was the dread 'compensation culture' really as alive and well as this? This, in turn, would put him in mind of the famous Winnebago case, the story of the driver of a motor home who had departed the driver's seat – having put the vehicle on cruise control – to make a cup of coffee. The Winnebago had crashed, and the driver had sued for millions. The manufacturers paid out, and rewrote their instruction manual to make it crystal clear, for the avoidance of all possible doubt and just in case an idiot was at the wheel, that on no account should drivers let go of the steering wheel when the vehicle was subject to the cruise control facility, or, indeed, at any other time, unless, of course, it was stationary. Crashes might result, for which the manufacturers excluded all liability. This tale of absurdity would make Flack chuckle, but it would not assist in levelling his thoughts, for at its core was an insuperable problem, as revealed in August 2005 by *The LA Times*: it was a complete fiction. Flack struggled with fabrications of all kinds, and so, re-imaginings of cricket's greatest batsmen and their heroics having failed, and Miles Davis, unaccountably, not even getting a look in, he forced himself to pretend that there were no cracks in the paving slabs and to focus solely on the task in hand: the counting of the steps from *The Record* to Execution Dock.

Once there, he encountered a problem. The truth was that the precise location of the dock was not known. All that Flack, and anyone else for that matter, could say for certain was that it was somewhere on the Thames foreshore in Wapping, in the vicinity of The Prospect of Whitby, The Town of Ramsgate and The Captain Kidd, public houses which were today as full of tourists as Eastenders. But how, if neither he nor anyone else, tourists especially, knew exactly where it was, could Flack be sure of how many steps it took to reach it?

The decision to abandon Mary and her kindness had backfired. Alone, looking over the murky waters of the Thames, Flack's confusion was complete. He was bereft and pathetic. He didn't even know how many steps it had taken to reach his destination, and what was it anyway? It was here that pirates and brigands were hung for their crimes – but where was 'here'? Where had Captain Kidd been executed? Where, precisely, did George Davis and William Watts – the last men to be hung at the dock, on 16 December, 1830 – take their final breaths? Could he even be sure of the date of their execution? Nothing was certain but that his life had been a failure. Under the cloak of professionalism, itself a fabric of a far greater edifice, he had been content to hide, and why? Because one man had entered his life, his home and his fiancée, unbidden by him but invited by Helen; a man, a journalist who went on to become an editor of renown (though not always for the right reasons), because of this, because of lust and carnality and betrayal, Flack had annulled his prospects of a happy life, he'd opted to trundle along invisibly, on the margins, or in the shadows, but in any event unseen, and now, during the lunch break of his last shift, when he ought to have organised a trip to a pub, perhaps even The Captain Kidd, with long-standing colleagues, here he was, confronting the irreducible obscurity of his life and its failure to engage, a failure which meant that he was childless and alone, a man with a tidy sum in his bank account but otherwise with nothing of real value, nothing to show for all the years he'd watched cricket and listened to jazz and read the papers and immersed himself in the rectitude of being a lawyer.

'But was it my fault?'

Flack, standing above a flight of steps that led down to the mucky, litter-strewn and uninviting foreshore, spoke the words aloud. Unbeknown to him, a young woman was at that point standing just behind him. Suddenly becoming aware of her presence, he swivelled round. She eyed him with concern which only grew as Flack announced that it was here, or nearby, that criminals were hung, back in the days when hanging was too good for a certain kind of man; yes, it was here, or perhaps over there, that the illustrious malefactor Captain Kidd was executed; it was here, definitely not anywhere else, and between 1735 and 1830, that seventy-eight murderers and mutineers were hung from a gallows, their deaths often watched by crowds on land and on sea, for yes, people would not only line the streets but also hire boats when they knew a good hanging was in the offing, they'd take a picnic along and watch from the water as Captain James Lowry, or John Tune, or James Sweetman and other men who'd ill-advisedly served on French privateers, or killed their comrades, or betrayed the Crown, they'd gawp as these rogues – who were often drunk, having been served a last quart of ale at The Turk's Head, then a pub, now a café, which lay on the route from the courts, or was it the prison, to Execution Dock – they'd look on as these men, 'stupidly intoxicated, and scarcely awake', as *The Gentleman's Magazine* had put it, at least Flack remembered something along those lines, anyway the crowds would watch as the inebriated criminals were killed and who knew what they made of what they saw, perhaps they enjoyed it – entertainment back then was not as it is today, people had to make do with actual death rather than Facebook or whatever it is that you call it – or maybe they made the sign of the cross and prayed for the salvation of the souls of the dead, and their own redemption into the bargain, but if all this is so much conjecture we can nevertheless only imagine their faces when, yet worse, the court ordered that their bodies be gibbeted, covered in pitch and left further down the Thames on the Isle of Dogs, or at Bugsby's Hole, there to admonish the devilish urges of passing pirates or anyone else who might do wrong, though mercifully, for it was not especially hygienic, gibbeting is thought to have ceased in 1834.

Yes, said Flack, at Execution Dock, criminals were hung from a gibbet which was built close to the low water mark – can you imagine it? Flack told the woman about the fate of Captain Kidd, who, having been convicted of piracy and murder, was taken from Newgate Prison and executed at the dock in 1701. It's extraordinary to think that pirates like Kidd were hung by a shortened rope, making for a slow death by asphyxiation; a longer rope, once their footing on the scaffold was taken away, would have broken their necks. 'The law moves in mysterious ways, as does life,' declared Flack, blind to the look of terror on the woman's face. 'And as if this wasn't bad enough such men were thrice more humiliated, their corpses left to moulder in the mud as three tides washed over them. George Davis and William Watts were the last men to be hung at the dock, on 16 December, 1830. At least, that's what I read somewhere but accuracy is one of those strange things, too often out of reach and maybe not all it's cracked up to be. But anyway – just imagine what the world would be like if not only hanging was still practised but gibbeting, too. Would it be a better place, if we could look on at the decay of those who've done us wrong? I wonder.'

This speech met with stupefaction. The young woman fled.

'What is happening to me?'

Again Flack spoke aloud. Again he looked down the steps, to the Thames and its ever-grey waters. Perhaps the answer to his life was obvious. Perhaps he should descend the steps, walk into the water and let the current take him.

But I detest suicide. As a solution, I abhor it.' And he told himself he had never entertained a suicidal thought in his life.

Yet again, Flack took no care over whether anyone was listening. He spoke clearly, as clearly as a barrister in court, presenting an argument, or maybe a plea in mitigation.

His immobility, though, was just as pronounced. His stasis seemed eternal. He would never move again, he would never do anything again, he would stand stock still and continue to breathe until, to the amazement of journalists dispatched to chronicle this most curious of last days, he would draw his last breath and crumple to the ground. This was his fate, this was what would happen, this was how the man of inaction would end his persecution. As he stood stock still, a scarcely conscious prisoner awaiting his hangman, he felt something tug at his jacket. Turning, he saw a young boy.

'Mister, have you got a light?'

How old was the boy? Flack was not experienced in dealing with children. He had none of his own, and as an only child there had never been a possibility that he might become an uncle. Nor had anyone ever asked him to be a godfather. Flack's knowledge of children was largely confined to what he read about them in the papers. Ageing the specimen now standing before him was impossible, but there was no doubt that he was under the legal age for smoking.

'I haven't,' replied Flack.

The boy greeted this news evenly.

'Can you give me a pound, then?' he asked, eyes unblinking.

'What for?' asked Flack.

'So I can buy a lighter.'

'But surely you're not old enough to smoke. And why aren't you in school?'

Again, the boy took Flack's words in his stride.

'School is for losers,' he said. 'There's no point in it.' This wasn't said stridently, or with any sense of resentment. Rather, it came in lacklustre, bored tones, as if it were a statement of the most obvious truth imaginable.

'Perhaps,' said Flack. 'But you're still too young to be smoking.'

The boy laughed. 'Bollocks, mister. That's bollocks. If I want to smoke, I can smoke. We're all going to die one day, anyway. So what if I get a head start with a bit of lung cancer?'

'You seem to have thought deeply about some profound issues,' said Flack, after a pause. 'Tell me, what do you think of this place?'

'What place?'

'This place, here, where we're standing. It's called Execution Dock. Murderers and pirates used to be hung here. Gibbeted, too. I don't suppose you know what gibbeting is. Or was.'

The boy, who Flack had by now hazarded as being thirteen or fourteen, peered down the steps and beyond, over the river. Then he turned and looked up and down the nearby streets. Eventually, his gaze settled again on Flack.

'Have you got a quid, or not?' he said.

'I have,' said Flack. 'But I want to know what you think of this place. Do you live here?'

'Not far from here. I don't think anything about this place, one way or the other. It's just a place. What happened in the past has got nothing to do with my life now, and what happens round here now.'

'What would you think if I were to walk down these steps and into the river, and then sink, because I made no effort to swim and survive?'

The boy's dark eyes flickered. 'Is that why you're here? Because you're going to top yourself?'

'I don't know,' said Flack. 'But it's an option.'

'I think you'd be a loser if you did that,' announced the boy.

'But we're all going to die one day, aren't we? That's what you just said. Why shouldn't my day be today, if I want it to be? I'd simply be accelerating what you're intent upon achieving by smoking.'

'I still think you'd be a loser.'

'But why? This place offers you nothing. It offers me nothing. Your life is desperate and pointless. Mine is even more so. Why not just end it now? Why not be brave and confront the stupidity of your life? You can do it – you know you can. You're tough enough to ask a stranger for a light, you're big enough to miss school and smoke cigarettes and get up to who knows what else. You're a big boy. So come on, take my hand – let's walk down the steps together. The water will be cold but what's that to us, when we've decided to die?'

The boy stepped away from Flack. A shadow crossed his eyes. He began to fidget. His hands disappeared into the pockets of his scruffy, worn jeans, then came out, then disappeared again, then returned to the fresh air and adjusted his dirty parka. He looked down at his shoes, tattered and with different-coloured laces. His patina of world-weary confidence evaporated. Flack looked down upon a child, small and scared and vulnerable.

He reached into the inside left pocket of his black suit and found his wallet. In it, he always kept some small change. He opened the wallet and took out a pound coin. As he was about to give it to the boy he changed his mind. Instead, he gave the boy a ten-pound note.

'Forgive me,' said Flack. 'I didn't mean to scare you.'

The boy took the money with a rapidity that Flack had been expecting, but which nevertheless impressed him. Instinctively, Flack put out a hand. He wanted to ruffle the boy's hair, to say something kind and positive and optimistic, something to redeem the past ten minutes of fear and doubt. But the boy flinched, and stepped out of reach, leaving Flack's hand hanging palm down in the air. Then he spoke.

'Mister, I don't know what's wrong with you, but something's up. I reckon you need a head doctor. Thanks for the tenner.'

With that, the boy was gone. As he watched him scurry off, Flack felt that his failure was complete. With a final look at the steps leading down to the Thames he trudged back to *The Record* like an automaton, his mind a void save for one thought: in all these years he'd had barely any interaction with children, and now, on the day of his last shift, one had come along out of the blue.

But he'd scared the boy, unnerved and maybe even terrified him with his talk of Execution Dock and his invitation to descend the steps and enter the freezing river.

The donation of a ten-pound note was nowhere near enough to salve his conscience. Flack's life was a charade. It was a lie. The farce began when Eddie Conrad cuckolded him, and Flack had acquiesced in its continuance. How on earth, though, to end it? He didn't know, but he thanked God that tonight was his last shift.

*

Despite already being a qualified barrister, whose precocious intellect and fine, instinctual judgement had been noted by her superiors in chambers, Maya Berlin was nervous. No matter that she had acquitted herself admirably during her pupilage, so much so that her being offered a tenancy at 9BR was inevitable; no matter that in just one year at the leading media set she had achieved standards of excellence that all but the senior QCs found inspiring and threatening in equal measure. This, her first training shift at a national newspaper, was sure to be of a different order to the work she had undertaken so far in her short but glistening career. She knew, from colleagues who had done their time as night lawyers, that while some shifts were quiet and congenial, the majority was chock-full of stress and conflict. Niceties were discarded as journalists sought answers – which they needed immediately, without the luxury of consulting precedents or discussing with other lawyers – to one plain but frequently fraught question: can we publish? The typical shift sent adrenaline levels sky-high, with everything conducted at breakneck speed and then, at the end, not so much as a thank-you from anyone in the building.

One of Berlin's fellow barristers had given her a tip. 'Don't take your work home with you. That's the joy of night lawyering. It's over when the shift is over, unless, of course, they call you with a query for a later edition. But even then, don't, whatever you do, worry about the calls you've made. It's too late to change anything and what will be, will be.'

Sensible advice, but would Berlin be able to heed it? Did she, in the first place, have what it took to work as a night lawyer? Could she cope with the pressure, pressure which was ever greater given the intense scrutiny on the media thanks to the Leveson Inquiry rumbling along in the background? Perhaps, though, Leveson would make journalists more amenable, more willing to listen to a night lawyer's advice, less likely to reject changes to copy in the way narrated by Berlin's colleague: 'There's a well-known story of a night editor telling a night lawyer to fuck off,' she mused. 'He said he didn't trust the lawyer's judgement, thanked him for his time and told him to go home. Said he'd take it from here. The lawyer protested, courteously, I believe, but then the editor said, "Look, just fuck off. Fuck right off. Fuck off out of this building and don't come back". Granted, the lawyer in question was very green, but he was doing his best.' To Berlin's irresistible question – who was the night lawyer who'd been so poorly treated – her colleague said she couldn't possibly comment.

The stakes are high. I hope I don't mess up. Berlin's anxiety returned, unbidden and without warning, at regular intervals in the hours before she set off for her first shift. She had taken the day off work, believing that to do so would give her time to prepare, but now regretted this decision. *It would have been better if I'd gone into chambers. I'd have been distracted by people and cases, by the hubbub of work.* So went her thoughts over lunch, a moderate affair of sliced avocado, a few cherry tomatoes and baby spinach. Then it was time to dress, for Berlin had spent the morning in her dressing gown, reading the papers – two broadsheets, and two tabloids, of which *The Record* was, of course, one. She did not know exactly what was in store for the evening, but she did know that to turn up without knowing what was in the day's paper, or knowing the news at all, would be a grave error.

Having contemplated wearing a trouser suit Berlin opted instead for a black suede skirt and a light cashmere jumper. The outfit was conservative and yet elegant; pleasingly, it required little thought. Her choice of shoes, a mid-heeled leather pair that she wore often, left her feeling confident of her appearance, at least, as she stood before the mirror of her two-bedroom Clapham flat. There, looking for a few seconds at her reflection, she uttered beneath her breath: *You look demure. Which is just right, all told.*

It was just gone 2pm. Berlin would allow a good hour for the journey from Clapham to Wapping, and soon, therefore, it would be time to leave. She rifled through the pages of that day's *Record* one more time. Its coverage of the so-called 'Murder of the Century' trial was, she noted, scrupulously fair and accurate. She felt sure that *The Record's* lawyers had had a hand in it, perhaps also its night lawyers, maybe even Harry Flack, their doyen, the man she would be learning from in just a few hours. What would he be like, this famous Fleet Street lawyer? Berlin wondered. Flack was not well known for his strength of personality, or notable victories in court, or powers of persuasion, still less for remarkable pastimes pursued beyond *The Record's* doors. He was well known, feted and revered, even, for qualities which were quite the opposite of celebrity: his unflappability, his measured good sense, his steadiness of character. Naturally, Berlin had read *Unreliable Evidence*; she was familiar with the plaudits bestowed upon Flack by James Madison, whom she had met at one or two lawyers' parties. What the legendary Madison said was endorsed by everyone who was anyone in media law. Flack might, if you probed his life, be a quirky old cove, but he was unquestionably one of the very best night lawyers in London.

Berlin had done more than talk to colleagues and read Madison's book by way of preparation for meeting Flack. Those who worked with her, or who grew up with her and saw her excel in every subject at school and then in her law degree, would not have been surprised. She was diligence itself, ever ready to go the extra mile, or through the hoops, or even the whole nine yards, if success, academic or otherwise, was contingent on her efforts. Not for her the arrogance that can come with intellectual excellence, the disdain for hard work and application, as if all the gifted among us have to do is turn up, sign their names, proffer a smile and pocket a fortune. No, this was not Berlin's style. If she was ever asked how she had managed to stroll through all her various exams and emerge with the best grades for miles around – and Berlin was asked this question, often – she unhesitatingly quoted Edison and his ratio of perspiration and inspiration, albeit that she was at pains to stress that no, she was certainly not a genius, she was simply a hard worker who enjoyed her studies and was more than happy to put in the hours, as many as were needed until the job was done.

Many hours had been allocated to Flack, to finding out about him, talking to her mother about him, to trying to understand him, to wondering what kind of man he was, whether he would be easy to work with, whether he would blanch at a woman like Berlin, young, polished, intelligent, attractive, and yet an innocent when it came to working with journalists, a woman who knew nothing of the rigours of toiling by night at the coalface of libel law and associated all-but-immovable objects like contempt and copyright. It is fair to say that Berlin agonised over their impending encounter in a way that Flack, had he been aware of it, could safely have said had not been evident in a single would-be night lawyer who preceded her. Most had been nervous, to a degree; if they weren't nervous, felt Flack – and, for that matter, Dixon and O'Donoghue – they had little chance of cutting it as a night lawyer for *The Record*, for the fundamental reason that *The Record*, and every other newspaper, is not the place for an excess of confidence, least of all when it is going to press. Even if the process of what is quaintly still called 'going off stone' seems to happen without human agency, men and women are involved, their tempers fray, and anyone who fails to understand the seriousness of a newspaper's nightly birth may as well sign up to career suicide.

Berlin understood what was before her very well. Nevertheless, she was riddled with anxiety, so much so that the night before her first shift she barely slept. Even a tried and trusted routine – the counting of sheep – failed to see her slip into unconsciousness. Usually, Berlin would imagine sheep jumping over a fence, and count them as they did so. Often enough, she got no further than the fifth or sixth sheep before this ancient remedy had worked its magic. But last night, awash with worry, sheep and fences posed more problems than they solved. No sooner had the first of the many willing ruminants cleared the fence than a question formed. Was the fence too high? Troubled by this thought, the next sheep in line took a run at the fence, only to hit it and bleat its frustration. This was no good. Berlin made it return to the back of the queue, only to be met with yet another problem. Surely, sheep did not form orderly queues? They congregated in flocks, did they not? How could she have been so negligent of the ways of sheep? No wonder the counting of sheep, which were jumping a fence, was failing. To counter the mercurial tendencies of the sheep Berlin introduced a sheepdog, a black collie with flecks of white. It was a bright dog, and had been trained to command the sheep to jump by a bark. Soon enough, three sheep had jumped the fence, eager to escape their fate if the dog decided to follow up the implicit threat of its bark. But then, disaster. The third sheep landed on the other side of the fence, there was grass all around, and, in the distance, the blue of the sea. There was a tree, too, an old oak, but wait, what was it that lurked behind its gnarled trunk? Why, yes, a fox! Berlin at once took precautionary steps. She built a fence around the field – yes, it was a field, not unfenced pasture land – and introduced a shepherdess, too. She was willowy and ethereal and clasped a staff in her right hand. The sheep were surely safe now, but how many had successfully reached this haven? Perhaps ten? Berlin couldn't be sure. But wasn't this the point of the exercise, anyway – to lose count of the sheep, and, in the process, fall asleep?

As she got ready, combing her hair one last time at 2.45pm precisely, Berlin grimaced as she recalled the problems caused by simply counting sheep. 'Why did I do that?' she asked herself, speaking aloud as she gathered her things. Needless to say, no one answered, for there was no one in Berlin's flat, even at the best of times. She was single, and rarely got involved with men, not because she didn't enjoy sex but because she was at a point in her life when it was a secondary concern. Her career, for now, was what mattered – that and her imminent meeting with Harry Flack. 'Speaking of which,' she said, 'it won't do to turn up at *The Record* like a bag of nerves. You've got to pull yourself together. It'll be all right. You'll be all right. And Flack will be all right.'

Berlin hoped that what she was feeling was just a temporary weakness, an aberration. Certainly, it was uncharacteristic – unprecedented, even. She told herself that it would surely melt away within minutes of meeting Flack and getting into the swing of things. She was a rising star of the libel bar, wasn't she? At the very least the venerable night lawyer would respect her legal knowledge. He might even like her; perhaps they would form a bond and become friends.

Suitably girded, Berlin set off for her first shift as a night lawyer at *The Record*.

CHAPTER 12

3.15pm, at *The Record*

Mary was worried. Flack was not himself. It wasn't just that the coffee she'd brought him had gone cold, or that he hadn't been around to drink it, still less to savour the almond croissant she'd dashed off to buy in a vain attempt to cheer him up. It wasn't even the fact that he'd failed to turn up to lunch at The Rose, where a number of people had been expecting him, herself among them: a casual get-together had been in the diary for weeks, albeit that the legal department would be taking Flack for a formal farewell lunch in the weeks to come. Even Flack's non-appearance at the pub was half-expected: everyone knew that he didn't like a fuss, and more than a few of his longstanding colleagues put their money on Flack not materialising.

'He won't show,' said Archie Lewis, the man who headed up the obituary department, when he'd bumped into Mary earlier in the week. 'Harry can't bear being in the limelight. He'll go and sit on his bench in St Katharine Docks, with a copy of *Wisden*.'

Mary wanted to disagree, but couldn't. 'You're probably right,' she'd said. 'Still, we can all have a drink in his nib's honour, can't we?'

And so it had proved.

But if Flack's no-show was predictable, his disarray, as he sat at Patricia Phillips's desk, wasn't. Mary had popped in twice – once, when she'd returned from The Rose, at about 2.30pm, then again half an hour later. Each time she'd been typically jolly; each time, Flack had barely registered her presence. Slumped in Phillips's chair, her copy of Madison's book open in front of him on the desk, Flack was so preoccupied that a thunderclap could have burst above his head and he wouldn't have noticed. But there was more. Mary would go further: he looked forlorn, as desolate as a man who has just been sentenced to life imprisonment, or – she shuddered at the thought – death. No matter what she said, Flack was alone in his despair, able only to mumble in response. Mary joked and teased, then tried being attentive and serious (she even, to her mild horror, thought about giving him a kiss, full on the lips), until finally Flack said: 'It's no use, Mary. I have nothing to say.'

Alone in the office she shared with Donna and Sarah, Mary wondered what on earth had become of the steadfast, likeable and phlegmatic man she'd known for the past twenty-five years. Was there a personal tragedy that he'd just heard about? Everyone knew that Harry kept his cards close to his chest, but perhaps he did have a family, after all – maybe an estranged brother or sister, or perhaps his parents were still alive. The received wisdom was that Flack was a man apart, an island who took such solace as he needed in the anonymity of jazz clubs, but maybe people were wrong, maybe he was close to someone, a relative or otherwise, and maybe whoever it was had just died, or been diagnosed with a terrible disease. *One thing's for sure,* said Mary to herself, *Harry isn't in this state just because tonight's his last shift here. A job is just a job, even when you've been doing it for twenty-five years.* But what ailed him? Why did he look as abject as an orphan?

The phone rang. It was an internal number. Mary answered it, and found herself talking to Eddie Conrad, *The Record's* new editor. Yes, she said, the lawyer is here. Yes, he's in his office. Well, it's not his office, it's Patricia Phillips's office, but neither she nor any of the day lawyers are here. Yes, you're right, the lawyer who's here is deputising for them for the day – and the evening, too. Yes, he's the same one who was at morning conference. Of course he'll have time to talk to you. Do you know where the legal department is?

As soon as she put down the phone Mary rushed to see Flack.

'Harry!' she said, 'You've got to pull yourself together. The editor is coming to see you. He wants to talk about the coverage of that murder trial. Come on – chop chop! Don't let him see you sitting here looking as miserable as sin.'

Scooping up the untouched cup of coffee and the plastic plate with its equally undisturbed almond croissant, Mary rushed from the room. Within seconds she was back. She picked up *Unreliable Evidence*, closed it and put it back on the shelf in Phillips's office. Then, as miraculously as she had somehow managed not to spill a drop of the coffee, she produced a comb. 'Come on, smarten yourself up, Harry! You look like you've been dragged through a hedge backwards.'

Not before time, Mary's urgency infected Flack. He sat bolt upright, combed his hair and adjusted his tie.

'That's better,' said Mary. 'You look almost human again.'

'I'm sorry,' said Flack. 'I don't know what's wrong with me. Or rather, I do, but I don't know what to do about it. When's he getting here?'

'Any minute now. Have you got the latest court orders on the trial?'

Flack said he'd seen them earlier, but didn't know where he'd put them.

'Oh Harry!' exclaimed Mary. 'You're impossible today! He's going to want to go through them, isn't he? I imagine that's what he wants to do. You need to look as if you know at least the basics of the case. I'll go and get the file.'

Mary departed in search of the legal department's file of court orders, injunctions and warnings. Or rather, the latest file, for the whole was contained in lever arch files that stretched back over the years and filled two walls of bookshelves. Flack had often thought, whenever he went to look something up, that the effort deployed by the legal profession in ensuring that only certain things are said, and that certain things remain unsaid, was worthy of some kind of award, though for precisely what – effort in the face of futility, the embrace of the absurd, a dedication to Ozymandias? – he remained unsure. Mary, though, had no truck with any such musings, least of all today with Eddie Conrad about to arrive. Swiftly locating the correct file, she ran the few steps back to Flack.

'Here it is,' she said, noting, to her relief, that Flack seemed to have got his act together. 'At least if he asks you something about the reporting restrictions you've got everything in front of you.'

'Thank you, Mary,' said Flack. 'And Mary – I'm sorry.'

Mary looked tenderly at Flack. 'It's OK, Harry. I know it can't be easy.' She was about to say something else when the pair heard footsteps in the corridor. She winked at Flack, and scurried off.

*

Conrad stood in the threshold of Phillips's office. Tall, and with a waistline that was developing into a tribute to the Fleet Street lunches of a bygone era, he dominated the space. In earlier years, his physical appearance would have been characterised as similar to Flack's, but now, where once both men were dark-haired, lofty and lean, there was another difference besides Conrad's more expansive belly: unlike Flack, he had not gone grey. He retained a full head of hair so effulgent that there were rumours it was dyed.

'So this is your lair,' said Conrad.

Flack stood up to greet *The Record's* new editor.

'Yes,' he said. 'Yes, it is. Or rather, it's my temporary lair.'

'Yes, that's what I've been told. You're here for the day while the other lawyers are all out, isn't that right?'

Flack nodded. As he did so, it struck him that Conrad's hair was unnaturally black for a man of his age.

'Where are they, then, these colleagues of yours?'

Flack explained the whereabouts of each of the legal department's day lawyers. 'I often come in as a locum,' he added. 'It's quite normal.'

'No one is saying it's not normal,' replied Conrad.

Silence fell. The two men stared at each other until Conrad spoke again.

'So you were at morning conference not as an imposter but, at the very least, as an interloper, rather than the paper's employed lawyer?' There was an unpleasant tone in Conrad's question, as if no good could possibly come of its answer, whatever the answer might be.

Flack chose not to answer. Instead, he offered Conrad a seat, and asked what he could do to help.

'I'd rather stand,' replied Conrad. 'I'm sure you are aware that we have a newspaper to get off stone. No offence, but I don't like hanging about at the best of times, and as for hanging about with lawyers, forget it. Nothing personal, you understand. I've come up here to double-check something with you.'

'Of course,' said Flack. 'As you wish. You won't mind if I sit down.' Once seated, he asked: 'Now, what would you like to know?'

'The jury went out in the Peter Terry trial just before lunch,' said Conrad. 'Their verdict should be in any moment now. They'll find him guilty, so we can publish everything we've got. Correct?'

Flack shrugged his shoulders. 'To a point,' he said. 'It depends what 'everything' is. I'd need to see exactly what you've got in mind.'

'Typical lawyer. It always 'depends' on something, doesn't it? You lot can never give a straight answer to anything. But tell me this – and try and be straight: what if the jury don't come back in with their verdict today, but a little bird tells us that they're going to convict on Monday morning?'

Flack said that he didn't quite understand what Conrad was getting at.

'It's exactly as I just put it,' said Conrad, looking as vexed as he sounded. 'Honestly, why are lawyers always so bloody obtuse?'

Flack said that he didn't know.

'What I mean is obvious. Think about it.'

Conrad let the words hang theatrically. The penny dropped.

Flack looked aghast. 'You don't mean to tell me that one of the jurors is talking to you?'

'You don't need to know exactly what I know, or who's talking to me, or if anyone is. But let's just say that little birds can fly unexpectedly into people's rooms. Once they're there, they flutter about and see a lot. So just suppose this little bird is bang on the money, what then?'

'You mean, what if the jury deliberately refrains from returning a guilty verdict today, in favour of doing so on Monday, at your behest?'

Conrad sneered at Flack; in his sneer, there was something that came close to malevolent glee, as if what was happening was a strange kind of sport, not a dialogue between an editor and his lawyer. 'That's not what I said. I wouldn't stoop to doing deals with jurors. Of course I wouldn't. There are standards. And they're not all to be broken.'

'Not to mention the question of contempt, if you tamper with the jury's deliberations in any way, or even publish them,' interrupted Flack.

'I know the law as well as you do,' spat Conrad. 'What I'm getting at is risk assessment. That's what I want from my lawyers. Risk assessment.'

'Assessment of precisely what risk?' asked Flack.

'I want to publish all of Terry's previous convictions in tomorrow's paper. It's a Saturday and the readers will love it. And I want to run the story from the woman who escaped his clutches.'

'But that's absurd,' said Flack. 'It'd be the most clear-cut case of contempt in years. You mustn't publish. It'd be a disaster. You'd destroy yourself and *The Record's* reputation would be mud.'

Conrad took a step forward, placed his hands on the edge of Phillips's desk, and stooped down to stare into Flack's eyes. He held his gaze for a minute, before stepping back and bursting into unrestrained laughter.

'Bloody hell, you lawyers crack me up!' he exclaimed. 'You believed me then! As if I'd ever authorise anything so insane!'

Flack tried to keep his dignity, but he could feel his lower lip trembling involuntarily. He felt like a small child, humiliated by his own actions, but worse was to come.

'I know who you are,' said Conrad, the staged mirth gone from his voice. 'I know exactly who you are. You're a prick from the past who has no business in a newspaper of mine. You were pathetic all those years ago, and you're still pathetic now. Helen used to tell me all about you. Yes, your beloved fiancée. You know, if you want to know about contempt, you should think back to how she treated you. The things she used to tell me. You and your stupid routines, your cricket and jazz, and worse, your doomed integrity – they used to drive her mad. The look on your face then was a picture. You actually believed me! You seriously thought I was going to run all of Terry's convictions and God knows what else! Never mind having a mole on the jury, I could go to prison for that sort of thing!'

Conrad paused, before speaking his last words to Flack.

'It's your last shift here. Don't even think about coming back. I don't want you, and I'll make sure the legal department know what I think. See today and tonight through. After that, you're fired.'

He turned on his heel and left. Seeing Conrad's departure, Mary hurried to see Flack. She had heard every word, and was incensed. But what she beheld flummoxed her even more than her colleague's catatonic self of earlier.

Flack was smiling. He was happy. He looked benign and beatific.

Mary shook her head. *What a day*, she said to herself. She concluded that it takes all sorts, and left Flack sitting contentedly at Phillips's desk, grinning, she thought, like a Cheshire cat.

What Mary could not know was that Flack had made a decision. It was one that would avenge the event of twenty-five years ago that had ruined his life. It was one that would avenge the mockery and insults he had experienced on this, his last shift at *The Record*. It was one that would put Eddie Conrad in his place.

On his last shift Flack would introduce rather than eliminate legal risk. Wherever possible, he would ensure that copyright was infringed and trademarks ignored. He would breach as many reporting restrictions as was possible and tell the journalists that copy was libel-free when it was anything but. He would make the first edition of *The Record* under Eddie Conrad look foolish and laughable.

It would fly in the face of the discretion adopted by newspapers throughout the land as Lord Justice Leveson deliberated on the future of the media. And, thanks to the Murder of the Century trial, Flack would see that *The Record* published the most heinous contempt of court imaginable, a disregard for the law so profound that only a custodial sentence would serve to make certain that other newspapers never dreamt of following suit.

On Flack's last shift, London's most reliable night lawyer would be the architect of Eddie Conrad's imprisonment. He didn't care what this plot meant for him; all that mattered was that it succeeded, and that Conrad never worked on Fleet Street again.

Part 2

CHAPTER 13

4.10pm, Night Lawyer's Office

Dixon raised his eyebrows and looked quizzically at O'Donoghue. The pair had worked together for so long that both men would joke they were like a married couple. In contrast, however, to many married couples, they never argued. The absence of any discord in their relationship was not because they were immune from experiencing moments of profound irritation with one another, but because their mutual sense of professionalism prohibited anything other than a respectful and courteous devotion to the tasks at hand. Perhaps, if they were conducted in a similar spirit of diplomacy, many marriages would survive, instead of collapsing to the dismay of just about everyone involved save for the spouse who wants out and the ever-watchful legal profession. Indeed, it is even possible that such restraint is what makes a marriage, but leaving this thorny issue aside one thing, so far as these two seasoned journalists were concerned, was undeniable: the job was all. Their commitment to the cause meant that neither Dixon nor O'Donoghue would allow, even *in extremis*, more than a weary sigh.

Flack's rapid exit from their office, so soon after he'd arrived, would not normally have been a cause for concern. The newspaper's night lawyers shared an office with Dixon and O'Donoghue, who were used to the sight of their transient colleagues hurtling out of the small, artificially lit room to deal with one crisis or another. Dixon, as the chief revise editor, and O'Donoghue, his assistant, had seen it all before. They would have been alarmed if a night lawyer did *not* appear capable of moving at the speed of light every now and then. No, it wasn't Flack's swift disappearance that provoked a look of mild consternation on Dixon's face. It was what he'd said. O'Donoghue anticipated precisely what his colleague was thinking.

'Has Harry been on the Scotch over lunch, do you think?' he asked.

'Do you know, I was just thinking the same thing myself,' replied Dixon. 'That little incident was most unusual.'

With that, the two men turned back to their computers. O'Donoghue absorbed himself in the howlers perpetrated by *The Record's* business journalists, while Dixon pulled up the middle leader on screen. After perhaps two minutes, as if suddenly aware of Berlin's presence, the pair simultaneously stopped in their tracks and turned to face the young barrister. If they had been capable of telepathic communication, they would have agreed that of all the night lawyers, trainee and otherwise, who had shared their office over the years, Maya Berlin was easily the most beautiful. Regardless, neither express nor telepathically engendered agreement was required for the pair to rally to Flack's defence, without even formally introducing themselves to Berlin.

'It's not that Harry did anything wrong then,' said Dixon.

This time it was Berlin's turn to look perplexed. Dixon continued.

'It's just that, well, he isn't normally quite so ...'

'Effusive,' interjected O'Donoghue.

'Quite right,' said the chief revise editor. 'The thing about Harry is that he's not a man to waste energy on words. He gets on with the job, diligently and effectively. It's not his style to ...'

'Exclaim,' said O'Donoghue.

'Yes, perhaps that's the right word. *Exclaim.*'

'I'm sorry, but I'm a little confused,' said Berlin.

The two men, chief revise editor and his assistant, looked at each other. Perhaps at that moment one, or even both, of them had thoughts about Berlin that were not purely professional. However, their very professionalism would never, in a thousand night shifts, allow them to do anything other than behave with the utmost courtesy. Dixon took it upon himself to elaborate further, but felt it wise first to assess exactly how much, or little, Berlin knew about the night lawyer with whom she was conducting her first training shift.

'Well, it's like this,' he began tentatively. 'Harry Flack is the longest-serving night lawyer this newspaper has ever had. In fact, he's probably the longest-serving night lawyer in London. He's a real, living and breathing Fleet Street legend. It's no accident that he's been here so long; it's because he's so good at what he does, even if he does it in a quiet and modest way – an unheralded way, to be fair. But that aside, the point is that we're used to him. He's been with us so long that he's part of the furniture. However, we can appreciate that, to outsiders, the manner of his exit just then might have seemed a little ...'

'Eccentric,' said O'Donoghue.

'Exactly,' said Dixon. 'Eccentric. Of course, the irony is that Harry's not really all that eccentric. Or rather, that his ways here, with us, aren't particularly eccentric.'

Dixon paused. No sooner had he begun than he felt he was floundering. He wanted to find out whether Berlin knew Flack, whether an existing relationship – familial, probably – between the pair had meant that *The Record's* most venerable lawyer had arranged a series of training shifts for her. This was often the way with night lawyers, for among them, as much as in so many other walks of life, it is often not what you know, but who you know. Momentarily sidetracked by this rumination, Dixon found himself stuck and, to his surprise, a little flushed. There was something about this woman – her ingenuousness, perhaps, combined with her beauty – which was enough to make a man of even Dixon's calibre, not to say *modus operandi*, stop short. O'Donoghue also seemed tongue-tied; certainly, Dixon noted that he was again immersed in the havoc wreaked by the paper's business writers, tutting and muttering as if this was all that had ever mattered to him, and all that could ever matter to anyone, anywhere. How, at this rate, would Dixon find out if Berlin already knew Flack? As for the young woman provoking this disequilibrium, she merely sat on the chair which Flack had earlier found for her, a look of patient curiosity on her features. *She really is very good looking,* thought Dixon, but even as he indulged this reflection he knew that he had to say something, and say it fast. And so he found himself blurting out an atypically unsubtle, not to say blunt question:

'Do you know Harry?'

Berlin smiled. Dixon was aware that O'Donoghue had torn himself away from an error-strewn story about an errant Wall Street hedge fund to see how the young lawyer answered.

'No, I don't,' she replied.

There was a pause as the two men readjusted their posture and absorbed this news. O'Donoghue broke the silence.

'So you don't know him!' he said jovially. 'That's OK, not a problem. So what brings you to this madhouse, if not an introduction from his nibs?'

Berlin looked at him quizzically.

'Introductions by night lawyers happen all the time,' explained Dixon. 'They're always getting relatives or family friends in to sample the, ahem, atmosphere.'

'Not in my case,' said Berlin. 'I wrote a letter to the legal department asking if I could do some training shifts, with a view to joining the rota. They wrote back saying fine, and suggested I do my first shift with Harry Flack. They said he was the most experienced night lawyer in London and that after the first shift with him I'd shadow other night lawyers. "Harry Flack will look after you on your first night. You couldn't be in better hands." I think that's what the letter said.'

Dixon sat back in his chair. In an ideal world, Berlin would have been related to Flack. Even if only a distant relative, she would at least know something of him and his character, and would therefore probably ignore his exclamatory exit from the office he had inhabited, with Dixon and O'Donoghue, on and off for a quarter of a century. *After all, blood is thicker than water,* thought Dixon to himself, *it's always the way, blood is thicker than water.* However, he rallied himself. *No matter. So she's not related – fine. She doesn't seem unduly fussed. Equanimity is her middle name. What is the reason for you, a man old enough to be her uncle, or maybe even her father, to feel otherwise? Yes, she's pretty, but come on, get a grip! You can't let her think that Flack is some sort of excitable maverick on this, his swansong shift, and especially when the truth is so very different.*

Steeled by these thoughts, Dixon once more stepped into the breach.

'The legal department is right,' he announced. 'Harry Flack is the night lawyer of night lawyers.'

'That's true,' agreed O'Donoghue. 'There's not a finer, more reliable night lawyer in London.'

'Absolutely,' said Dixon. 'And you must understand that when he rushed off just now, exclaiming that he was a night lawyer, he was just having a little joke.'

Berlin was studious and attentive as the two men raved about Flack, but with the information that he had apparently been joking in some fashion, the look of confusion returned to her face. 'Joking?' she said. 'Do you mean he was being ironic?'

Once again, the two revise editors, men in their late fifties who knew every nuance of their newspaper, felt strangely discombobulated. Not, it must be said, because of the injunctions against the misuse of 'ironic' contained in *The Record's Style & Usage Guide*, one whose author cautioned that journalists should remember that 'ironic' 'means using or displaying irony, or in the nature of irony; it does not mean strange or paradoxical.' No, it was because there was something about Berlin which spoke of knowledge beyond her years – as if it were she, and no one else, who was being ironic, because only she was *capable* of being ironic. Once again, Dixon regretted his decision to illumine Flack's words of a few minutes ago, but fortunately his colleague seemed to have acquired a second wind. O'Donoghue, an assiduous devotee of boxing – a sport he insisted was a noble art, rather than a sweet science – stood up, walked to the door, looked out into the newsroom and, apparently satisfied that he was free to do so, turned to talk to Berlin.

'It's like this,' he began, folding his arms and reaching, with the thumb and forefinger of his left hand, to scratch the wispy white hairs of the goatee on his chin. 'Flack is a quiet sort of a chap, the kind of man who lets his actions speak louder than words. You might say that he's the strong and silent type. So when he jumped up and ran off just now, saying, "Leave it to me! I'm a night lawyer!", together with that bit about being experienced and putting things in pipes and smoking them, he was acting a little out of character.'

'Perhaps even a lot out of character,' added Dixon.

'Yes, quite possibly a lot out of character,' agreed O'Donoghue. 'But we wouldn't want you to think that Harry's judgement has gone awry. That's judgement with an "e", of course, not the legal kind, which, in lacking an "e", always reminds me of that novel by Georges Perec, *La Disparition*, do you know the one?' Berlin's blank face could only encourage O'Donoghue to explain that Perec, one of his favourite writers ('as he is for pedants and grammarians everywhere, even those who can't read him in the original French') had, in 1969, succeeded in writing a 300-page novel devoid of the letter 'e'. 'It was translated by Gilbert Adair as *The Void* and is a lipogram, a word game in other words, a sort of self-imposed constraint which prevents an author from using certain words or letters throughout the text.' Again, Berlin appeared nonplussed, leading O'Donoghue to curtail the kind of lexical digression that he, Dixon and Flack had so enjoyed over the years. 'Be that as it may,' said O'Donoghue, clearing his throat, 'a judgment of a court of law doesn't have an "e", while a moral one does. Just as certain is that while we've never known Harry to do anything quite like that, we're sure that his commitment to the cause, and his judgement and ability to do his job, remains second to none. As my colleague says, Harry Flack is the night lawyer of night lawyers.'

O'Donoghue's tone, even as he meandered amid Perec's lipogrammatic byways, was full of paternal patience. Despite his hefty frame – a legacy of many years as an amateur heavyweight boxer – he appeared avuncular and utterly loyal to Flack. With Dixon nodding his head and watching her every move, Berlin felt a flush reach her cheeks. She decided it was best to vacate the room for a few minutes and, with a delicacy that both men regarded as becoming (though neither said as much), made her excuses.

'Saved by the bell,' muttered O'Donoghue, when she had gone.

CHAPTER 14

4.15pm, Legal Department

Evan Brooke's office was strewn with papers. There were court orders, solicitors' letters, claim forms, witness statements, reports from private detectives, notepads and photocopied pages from law books, all jostling for coherence not merely on Brooke's desk but on the surrounding shelves, the spare chair and even, to Flack's horror, the floor. How, he wondered, could anyone make sense of all this? As was his wont when confronted by the habitual disorder of Brooke's office, Flack shook his head and muttered under his breath. 'It's always been a mess. He's never kept things in order, not once in his life. Even when he's not busy it's always like this.'

There were many, however, who sympathised with Brooke's inability to maintain an orderly office. The Record's head of legal affairs was much respected for the crusading zeal he brought to defending the paper, even in the face of litigation it appeared to have little hope of winning, but on top of an unendingly oppressive caseload (sometimes, Brooke was fond of saying, 'The world and his wife want their day in court, not to mention the litigators du jour – Premier League footballers with third-rate morals and second-rate celebrities with third-class ethics') Fleet Street was under scrutiny as never before thanks to a public inquiry into the culture and practices of the British print media. Brooke was old enough to remember the last government-appointed inquiry into newspaper conduct; following a suitable bout of tub-thumping by appalled ministers – and cap-doffing by apologetic editors – it had yielded precisely nothing by way of change. This in itself should not be regarded as a surprise, if the words of one eminent media lawyer, in a book entitled Law and the Media, are accurate: 'For those who believe that media excess is a modern phenomenon, a study of the newspaper industry's regulatory history is an enlightening experience,' wrote the lawyer. 'Outrage at the perceived misbehaviour of the press has been with us as long as the newspapers themselves. At least once a decade since the Second World War parliamentarians have threatened legislative controls and the industry has responded with tightened self-regulation and resolutions of good behaviour.'

But this time, things were different. Revelations of phone hacking by a major newspaper group had resulted in public outrage; a prime minister eager to be seen to make a stand had set up the inquiry; the following wind seemed to grow stronger each day, with seemingly endless revelations of unconscionable conduct by the members of the fourth estate. It was even possible, mused Brooke to anyone who would listen (he was a loquacious man, occasionally prone to indiscretion) that legislation to curb media recklessness might, at last, happen. 'Freedom of expression is under threat as never before,' he would declare. 'This time the bastards have got us on the rack. It's our own bloody fault. You can't expect the government to put up with journalists going round hacking phones and stealing people's mobile phone bills. If we're not bloody careful there'll be a statute telling reporters how to go about their business – on penalty of imprisonment for any failure.' No wonder, then, thought his colleagues, that Brooke's office was in disarray. The inquiry, at which he was often present (whether as an observer or, on one occasion, to give evidence), had effectively doubled his workload.

Moreover, the Old Bailey was presently the scene of what the red-tops were billing as the 'Trial of the Century' – a case involving a man accused of the serial murder, over twenty-five years, of twenty-five women, all of whom were twenty-five at the date of their death. Extreme enough in its own right, there were rumours that the murderer had been aided and abetted by a senior minister. Orders restricting the reporting of this and other aspects of the case emanated from the court office with the relentlessness of winter rain on the Yorkshire moors – but however many there were, it was vital that *The Record* complied with them. The publication of prejudicial material could amount to a contempt of court, wrecking the trial, costing millions in fines and costs and even, conceivably, leading to the imprisonment of the paper's editor.

Brooke had this to contend with too, but at least the backdrop of the Leveson Inquiry – so named after Lord Justice Leveson, the man appointed to conduct it by the Prime Minister – meant that *The Record's* editors were less inclined to take risks than usual. For once, they were happy to take the advice of their lawyers, with few of the usual protests. Brooke insisted, come the start of the Murder of the Century trial, that 'it would be highly unwise to ruffle his Lordship's feathers any more than they may already have been tousled' – and, so far at least, the paper's senior staff had agreed. *The Record's* coverage of the trial was, to date, a textbook an example of fair and accurate reporting.

If Flack objected to untidiness, he liked Brooke as a man and allowed for the stresses to which *The Record's* head of legal was subject. There were plenty of them but, as a freelance night lawyer, the majority were not shared by Flack. Once his shift was over, that was it: job done. Granted, the night desk might ring, once he was home, for advice on a late-breaking story, and if he cast his mind back long enough he had even had one or two injunctions to deal with as the midnight hour approached, but that was the extent of after-hours work. Even if, in his early years as a night lawyer, Flack had agonised over whether stories really had been Legal OK, or whether in letting one through he had presided over an impending catastrophe, he had long since abandoned this habit which had only ever seen him muse over a story for half a day at most. That was the great joy of being a night lawyer: the work could be stressful on the night, but the stress ended with the shift.

Momentarily, as he scrutinised the disarray of Brooke's office, Flack reflected on the pros and cons of his working life, compared with Brooke's and all the other lawyers he knew, but his mind was on other things. He retreated from Brooke's office and walked three steps to the door opposite. He pushed it open. This was where he had spent much of the day.

'Incredible, really,' said Flack to himself. 'All these years go by, and nothing. And then, out of the blue, everything is upside down.' He sat down in Phillips's chair, behind her desk, one whose order pleased him. 'Everything is in its place,' he murmured, scanning the paperwork, the books, the neatly placed stationery and the interloping evidence of a private life: various photographs of Phillips's children, three healthy-looking lads; a card one of them had sent her to brighten another dull day in her office, one which, like so many at *The Record,* was utterly devoid of natural light; and a book positioned alone on the middle of an otherwise empty shelf, as if to be a memento as much as something anyone would want to read.

'Of course,' said Flack, reaching for the book for the second time that day. It was by the man who had been *The Record's* head of legal affairs for a quarter of a century, steering the paper through countless crises and amassing a host of anecdotes, some of the courtroom variety, others of rather more eclectic, not to say downright bizarre, hue, such as the occasion when he was physically assaulted by a plaintiff in a libel case, who had turned up at *The Record* dressed as a druid and wielding a staff.

How Roxanna de la Rue – as she called herself – got past the security on reception has always baffled me, but there was no doubting that she meant business. Clad in a white robe and wearing sandals, she loomed over my desk with a look of outrage and terrifying ferocity. Ms de la Rue was unhappy with a story we had published, doubting that she had psychic powers. In fact, we didn't just doubt her; we described her as a fraud and a charlatan, a shameless woman who sought to profiteer from the gullibility of the recently bereaved with her promises of a direct line to the dead. She had made a small fortune in this way, claiming that, as a descendant of the druids, she possessed unique powers lost to modern society. Astonishingly, Ms de la Rue sued for libel, maintaining in her statement of claim that she was neither a fraud nor a charlatan because she genuinely did have the ability to communicate with the dead. We had just served a robust defence when she breached The Record's ordinarily impregnable security and arrived in my office.

'Can I help you?' I asked politely.

'Yes!' she bellowed. 'You can admit that it's true, that I do have psychic powers. You can confess that your original story and defence are disgusting. Go on, admit it!'

Roxanna de la Rue banged her staff on my desk. I replied, as calmly as I could, that we have to let the matter be decided in a court. After all, I said, this was the inevitable consequence of the issue of a writ for libel.

'You bastard!' shouted the psychic. 'I'll prove it to you! I'll show you!'

I was about to ask whether she intended to subpoena various members of the dead as witnesses, when Ms de la Rue's staff flashed through the air and hit me on the temple. That was the last thing I remembered about our meeting. Next thing I knew I was in hospital, having been knocked unconscious. Roxanna de le Rue dropped her libel action but in subsequent criminal proceedings insisted on going into a trance on a regular basis to take advice from Lord Denning, with whom she said she had a special relationship.

Her insistence on communicating with his Lordship did her no favours: she was found guilty not just of assault occasioning actual bodily harm but also of contempt of court.

No one could have foreseen Roxanna de la Rue's intervention in the legal affairs of The Record *that day, but fortunately she did not have too disastrous an effect. I soon recovered and on the day in question I was able to call upon one of the most reliable men I have ever known, Harry Flack. He arrived promptly and not for the first time, bailed us out, covering me for the rest of the day and continuing on for his night shift. Night lawyers are too often unacknowledged, but Flack is one of the best. As for Roxanna, she received a message from a dead film star to the effect that the dead would, when she regained her freedom, cease communicating with her and anyone else, for that matter. She therefore sought to live quietly and took on occasional work as a gardener. I know this because, naturally enough,* The Record *door-stepped her shortly after her release. We ran a piece headlined 'Psychic druid says she's had it with the dead – and takes up gardening', but what became of Ms de la Rue after this I have no idea.*

Flack smiled. There was something in this, some fun to be had. He read a few more paragraphs:

Ms A – I refrain from giving her full name out of discretion rather than fear of a lawsuit – served proceedings on us through her solicitors, Messrs Barth & Weed, on a Wednesday. Within a very short time the action had been discontinued. It was a remarkable conceit, Barth & Weed contending, via a rather ineptly settled Statement of Claim, that A had been grievously defamed by The Sunday Sun's *front page splash of a few weeks earlier. Granted, it was defamatory, alleging that A had performed oral sex on a film star in a red telephone box outside a nightclub in central London. Few of us would choose so cramped, and public, a venue for an exploit of this nature but passion is a beast that can rarely be quelled, and perhaps A and Mr X (whom again I disguise out of discretion rather than fear) had come to find this inside the febrile air of Club Hydra.*

Be that as it may. And, indeed, as it was. At the time the presses were about to roll, I was absent on leave, but Harry Flack was at the helm, legally speaking, of the paper. He had been through the evidence – CCTV footage, eye witness accounts, even the recollections of a girlfriend A had called once in the phone box, only to neglect to replace the receiver, an omission one hopes was down to her getting carried away and not because she had a yen for an unusual kind of ménage a trois – and was satisfied that we would be in good shape, should anyone decide to sue us. With Flack having assessed the evidence, I didn't stop to think twice about it – his judgement was so sound I'd have trusted him with my life. When a Writ turned up, I think I refused to register that it had arrived, and then, two weeks later when the Statement of Claim appeared, I remained confident that we'd have the wherewithal to see off what was surely a spurious claim.

As it most assuredly was. Before I'd even had a chance to contact Flack and ask him for his thoughts, I took a call from a solicitor at Barth & Weed. 'As a matter of professional courtesy, I'm advising you that we are discontinuing the claim made by A.' I didn't respond, a trick I learned from a lawyer at Carter-Ruck by the name of Pepper. Tall – extremely tall – Pepper's strategy when on the other end of a call is to allow longueurs to flourish. In this way, his adversaries feel compelled to fill the void. 'They say the most remarkable things,' he once told me. And so it was with the lawyer from Barth & Weed. 'Yes, we're dropping the claim,' he repeated. Still I said nothing. 'Excuse me, we're discontinuing the claim – didn't you hear me?'

Yes, I said, I heard you. But I didn't embellish this comment. The Barth & Weed man could take no more. 'Well, wouldn't you like to know why?' he huffed.

Do tell, said I.

'It's because our client came in today and told us we'd forgotten to ask her one simple question.'

Which was?

'Whether the allegation that she'd performed oral sex on X was true.'

And?

'Well, she wanted to point out that it was.'

I see, I said. And then, having thanked him for the flexibility of his sense of professional discretion, I reflected that, as with every walk of life, the law has its incompetents, too.

And then he found again the passage he'd read at lunchtime, that which praised him so effusively and yet suggested that there was more to his life: *He could have made a fortune, but why he chose not to is both beyond the parameters of this book and, indeed, another story.*

'Another story, indeed,' thought Flack, who, while gazing at Maya Berlin and the two sheets of A4 paper whose words had so worried her and yet failed to make any impression on him, had experienced an unaccountable need to isolate himself from the demands of *The Record*. Hence he had fled upstairs, first to Brooke's office, then to Phillips's. But he ought to be downstairs. There was a trainee night lawyer to supervise, there were stories to read, there were journalists waiting for him to make a decision. In fact, hadn't he almost bolted from the office, with some bizarre words?

'"Trust me! I'm a night lawyer!" That's what I said. I even told them I was experienced, too! Or something like that.'

Flack whispered the words and tried to recall why he'd said them. But yet more insistent was the memory of the urge he'd had when Dixon and O'Donoghue had been absent from the office. The urge, whose wellspring came as Conrad turned on his heel, having insulted and then fired him, to subvert and destroy; to be, in short, the antithesis of the professional man he had always been, to introduce rather than eliminate legal risk and create rather than prevent calamity. Now, as he sat at Phillips's desk, alone amid the late afternoon frenzy enacted, every day, at *The Record* and indeed within the walls of every daily newspaper around the world, Flack felt at once terrified and liberated by the compulsion that had gripped him. This wasn't how he'd envisaged ending his career – far from it. At the beginning of the morning, when he left home for the paper, he was contentedly looking forward to retirement, to enjoying a meal with Phillips and other colleagues in a few days or so, to bowing out with grace, distinction and perhaps even, as his last shift ended, to the accompaniment of desks being thumped and with the gift of a mocked up and framed front page devoted to his life and its quiet heroics.

But that, Flack said to himself, *was then*. He eyed the law books lining the bookshelves of Phillips's office and selected *Gatley on Libel and Slander*. It was the authority on all things defamatory, or, at least, the law thereto, a book which Berlin would immediately respect when he reappeared downstairs to proffer it by way of a helpful resource. 'Have a look at chapter five,' Flack would say, 'it's very good on the point you've raised.' Berlin, eager to please, would do just that. And meanwhile Harry Flack would proceed with his plan, something which, had he been religious, might have struck him as an opportunity handed down from God: the chance to destroy Eddie Conrad, *The Record's* new editor, a man he hadn't seen for over twenty-five years and whom he hated with every muscle, every sinew, every blood cell, every bone and every heartbeat in his upright, restrained and oh-so-very-proper body.

CHAPTER 15

4.30pm, Night Lawyer's Office

Just as the length of Flack's absence from the office he shared with Dixon and O'Donoghue was veering towards the unusual, he reappeared. Neither of his colleagues betrayed their relief, but both thought there was something odd about the way Flack rushed off. As for Berlin, despite her lack of familial, or any other, ties with Flack, she too felt relieved at his return. She may have been inexperienced in the ways of night lawyers, but she was sure they didn't tend to jump up, make strange announcements and dash off.

Earlier, Berlin and Flack had met for the first time. It was precisely 3.50pm, the time at which Berlin had, as instructed by Phillips, arrived at the absent day lawyer's office.

'You'll find Harry there,' she'd said, phoning Berlin as soon as she knew Flack was able to cover for her. 'The night lawyers use our offices if they're available and then go down to the newsroom for a 4pm start. I think they like the peace and quiet – they're that little bit further away from the madhouse. Anyway, go and find him in my office. Get there for 3.50pm. Harry will be getting ready to go downstairs then. He's very nice and will take you to the night lawyer's office.'

So it had proved. Flack was scouring one of the financial pages when a knock on Phillips's open door revealed the svelte frame of Maya Berlin. 'Yes?' said Flack.

Berlin replied that she'd been directed to Phillips's office in search of Harry Flack, with whom she was to complete her introductory shift as a night lawyer. 'Are you Harry Flack?' she'd enquired.

'Yes, that's me,' said Flack. 'Welcome to *The Record*.'

He had chosen to say little more, revealing merely that it had been 'a funny old day so far' but that he had better just finish off reading the share price page. Dismissively, he added: 'Not that there's any likelihood we'd ever be sued for anything in it. It's just a list of numbers with a few market tips. They never cause any concern.' Berlin lurked, neither in Phillips's office, into which she felt doubly disinvited, nor in the corridor, retreat to which struck her as signifying defeat, but somewhere between or, if exactitude is required – and it is never a bad thing – on the threshold. Soon enough Flack rose briskly, said 'come on' and strode among *The Record's* maze of corridors until he reached a room comprising several intense-looking journalists, all of whom were hunched over desks, engrossed in the content of PC screens, or newspapers, books and magazines, or sheets of A4 paper. Truly, thought Berlin, are forests felled for our daily press.

'Legal OK,' said Flack, handing an overweight man in his fifties the share price page.

'Thanks Harry,' said the man. 'Drinks later?'

But before he could reply Flack was gone, Berlin trailing in his wake. He swept down a circular staircase, made his way across a foyer – ignoring the chance to buy another coffee from the newly installed kiosk – and pushed open a wooden door. It led to yet another corridor and, immediately on its left, a glass door held open by a strategically placed waste-paper bin.

'This is my lair,' said Flack, ushering Berlin into the office. 'I share it with two old lags or, as they prefer to call themselves, revise editors. But, as you will no doubt have noticed, they're not here at the moment. Must be busy somewhere redeeming the English language, or what passes for it here. Now, pull up that chair and have a read of this story.' Flack had plucked a couple of pieces of A4 paper as if from nowhere and, a little brusquely, placed them in Berlin's hand. But Berlin, as she hung up her coat, excused herself. Could she possibly return to the kiosk and buy a coffee? She felt the need for a boost before starting her debut training shift. And would Mr Flack like one, too?

At the shiny new kiosk that had so improved the lives of *The Record's* employees, Berlin fell into a conversation with a young journalist, a confident individual who bluntly declared that so far as he was concerned, print media was dead. 'It's only a matter of time before this building becomes a museum,' he announced, 'don't you agree?' Berlin, by nature a diplomat, explained that she was on the premises as a trainee night lawyer and, as such, didn't have an opinion either way, although she did wonder, if he felt so strongly, whether he might be better served looking for work elsewhere. 'Feisty!' said the young man, before winking and saying that actually, as it happened, the social media department had some good ideas, it was only a matter of time before they were implemented and when they were, well, the likes of him would be set fair. He then vanished, with a fresh cup of cappuccino, leaving Berlin feeling both mildly amused and slightly taken aback. Just a few minutes later, returning to Flack's office, it seemed – although she couldn't say why – that she'd caught him in the middle of something, or rather, just *after* the middle of something. What was it? Why did she feel disconcerted? It was almost as if, in her brief absence, Flack had surreptitiously tried on her raincoat before quickly putting it back again. She decided to ignore her unease and settle to the task at hand, the story Flack had asked her to consider, only for him to retrieve the two sheets of A4 and flee the room telling her, and Dixon and O'Donoghue, that he was a night lawyer – in other words, exactly what they knew he was.

So far as Dixon and O'Donoghue were concerned, their knowledge of just how uncharacteristic this behaviour was had gnawed away with an insistence that grew more pronounced for every minute that Flack had been idling in the day lawyers' offices. Their disquiet that had no respect for seniority: it was not as if Dixon, as the chief revise editor, shouldered more of a burden than that felt by O'Donoghue, his assistant, or even, to the contrary, that because of his position he was able to delegate his anxiety to the broad shoulders of his Irish deputy. No, the two men felt equally perturbed, although, save for their discussion of the matter with Maya Berlin, neither said another word, preferring instead to immerse themselves in their many jobs. But when Flack ambled back into their room, holding *Gatley on Libel and Slander*, both felt as if order had been restored.

'Ah, Harry,' said Dixon, 'we were beginning to wonder if you'd been spirited away.'

Flack smiled. 'No such luck,' he said, 'I'm here, as always. You gents know as well as I do that there's no escape.'

This was more like it. The three men laughed, a gentle, relaxed laugh, one of years spent working together for a common purpose.

'Well, just a few more hours and then you're free,' said O'Donoghue. 'Unlike us poor sods. Enjoy your retirement on the glistening white sands of a beach in the Caribbean, won't you?'

'And send us a postcard, if you have a moment,' said Dixon.

Flack grinned and promised that he would. But then, just as his colleagues returned to their scrutiny of the copy in front of them, he started, as if remembering a long-forgotten task.

'Where's the girl?' he asked, his brows furrowing.

O'Donoghue did not look up from his work, and so didn't register the look of anxiety on Flack's face, one which was, however, duly noted by Dixon. Instead, he chuckled and said: 'You've noticed her charms, then? Quite a beauty, isn't she? Don't worry, we haven't frightened her off. She'll be back in a minute.'

'Yes, but where is she?'

O'Donoghue glanced at Flack. His taut, usually alert face was haggard and drawn. Clearly there was something wrong with him. Perhaps, thought Dixon, it was the conjunction of this being his last shift and Berlin's all too obvious physical allure. After all, if he was scrupulously honest, Dixon himself found her presence something of a distraction. The chief revise editor took it upon himself to put *The Record's* night lawyer at ease.

'She went to the ladies' room, I believe, old chap. She spoke very highly of you, you know. Do you know each other?'

Flack said that no, they weren't acquainted. In fact, he'd never even heard of her, and he knew most of the up and coming libel barristers. But he needed to find her, and quickly. It was just possible that she would bump into the journalist who'd asked for advice a little earlier, and find herself embarrassed because she didn't have an answer for him. Or, worse, she might give a legal opinion which was flawed.

'I'm going to go and find her,' he announced. 'Don't worry. As you know, I'm a night lawyer. And I'm very experienced, too.'

CHAPTER 16

4.35pm, Meeting Room

The Record's premises were unprovided with greenery. All was bright, bland and man-made, from the revolving doors giving access to the street to the clanking, ancient lift, to the vaults of the dusty underground car park and the unceasing fluorescent strip lights. Even the pot plants in the foyer were artificial, sparing anyone the task of watering them and yet, as Flack sometimes reflected, suggesting that somewhere in the minds of the interior designers responsible for *The Record's* approximation of architectural harmony the bucolic notion, however fanciful, was alive and well.

The nearest *The Record's* employees came to the natural world was during their lunch break, when those with a yen for fresh air would depart the site of the vast publishing enterprise in favour of a walk along the Thames footpath or, perhaps, an idle hour in St Katharine Docks. Some would don shorts, trainers and T-shirts and go running, while others would buy a sandwich and sit on a riverside bench, watching the ebb and flow of the Thames, marvelling at its always ruffled surface and scurrying watercraft.

Whenever he was called in to act as locum lawyer for the day, Flack would take himself, at lunchtime, to a bench in St Katharine Docks. Once upon a time, he had a favourite bench, one that he always headed for, but that was in the days when the dock was undeveloped, or less developed, days when it was empty, or less busy. Now, it was never less than packed over lunch, with employees of *The Record* and other businesses and tourists making pilgrimages to the nearby Tower of London and then taking themselves in a deeper trawl through London's murky history, perhaps even in search of the fabled Execution Dock, their numbers, and need for rest, meaning that Flack had to content himself with any old bench and, on some days, not even finding a place to sit at all.

Alone on a bench, or hovering near one – perhaps even his favourite, waiting for a chance to pounce – Flack rarely enjoyed an undisturbed lunch break. Almost invariably his mobile phone would sound and he would say, 'Yes, Flack here,' and a voice – breathless, frantic, rushed – would quickly regret having interrupted him and yet plead for his urgent legal advice on a most delicate matter, can we or can't we publish, what are the risks if we do, what are the other side's lawyers like, does this particular celebrity or footballer or film star or, once upon a time, at least, politician have a record of suing, is this supermodel especially litigious, is there a trade mark issue in using the word Portakabin, if there is, does it matter, can we get away with it, come on, time is pressing, we're up against it and need to get this page off stone in the next five minutes, where are you anyway, you're not down at bloody St Katharine Docks again are you, I mean we all need a break so don't take this the wrong way but look, wherever you are, Flack, what's the answer, what's the risk, we're sorry to trouble you but after all this is your job, isn't it, and if we were on a lunch break we wouldn't mind being disturbed, and we'd also get back to the office pretty bloody quickly if we were needed, as you are now, so hurry up and get back, please, but meanwhile *what's the bloody answer?*

Berlin had an inkling, but no more, that this might be Flack's life as she strode among *The Record's* corridors looking for the ladies' toilet. Safely inside, she looked at herself in a small mirror above a washbasin. Even she, biased as an observer, felt that she radiated – what? Capability? Curiosity? Self-possession? Or was it worry, even fear? She looked keen and alert. Her eyes shone even in the unnatural light of *The Record.* What was animating her? Why was she so wired? Was it the strange, weirdly dissonant conversation she'd had with Dixon and O'Donoghue? Or rather, the conversation she'd let them have, almost as if she wasn't there? Or was there more? Was it Harry Flack himself who so disorientated the young barrister?

As she exited the ladies' room Berlin bumped straight into Flack. Their collision brought a feeling of relief that was mutual, if articulated only by Flack.

'Ah! So there you are,' said Flack, composing himself quickly enough to smile.

'Yes, here I am', said Berlin, also smiling.

'I was beginning to wonder what might have happened to you,' said Flack. 'You wouldn't be the first night lawyer to go AWOL on a shift, you know.'

'Really?' asked Berlin.

'I never lie,' said Flack. 'Young girl, a bit like you. She disappeared after half an hour of her first shift and never came back, having thrown all the proofs she'd acquired in her brief tenure into the bin.'

Berlin was incredulous. '*Really?*' she said.

Flack laughed. 'I'll tell you about her later. If there's time we'll nip across to the canteen and sample some haute cuisine and I'll tell you all about Jasmine and why she threw her toys out of the pram, or what I know, anyway. And lest you fear that an element of sexism underlies this anecdote I'll also tell you about Hugh, whose stint as a night lawyer was even shorter than Jasmine's. Then there is the infamous case of Giles, who liked to conduct his shifts under the influence of cocaine, a practice that was high-risk and doomed to failure. But look, we'd better not stand here getting in the way. Let's get back to the frontline. I wanted to talk to you about that story. I thought it'd be good experience if you were to deal with it.'

By now Flack was striding along a corridor, heading Berlin knew not where. She followed him automatically, nodding to Flack's half-hearted comments. She realised that, clasped in his left hand, he had with him the two scraps of A4 that he'd given her as soon as she'd arrived.

As they rounded yet another corner in a building whose labyrinth Berlin was convinced she would never, in a thousand night shifts, master, Flack paused. In front of him was a door, left slightly ajar. He pushed at it and looked inside.

'Let's just borrow this room for a minute,' said Flack, turning to Berlin. 'It's quiet in here. We can go through the story in peace.'

Flack held the door open for his new colleague and asked her to take to seat. For a second, his earlier thoughts returned and he wondered whether to sit next to her so that he could inhale her perfume and perhaps place an avuncular hand on hers, but no, that would never do. What was in his mind was bad enough. He told himself to stop all such thoughts, once and for all. *You're old enough to be her father, get a grip and get on with the plan.* He pulled out a chair opposite Berlin and, sitting down, pushed the paper across the table.

'This is a good story for you to think about,' he began. 'It's got one or two banana skins, but you should be able to avoid them, à la Krapp. Did you say you were already qualified?'

Berlin had said no such thing. Her introduction to Flack had been so brief that she assumed he knew next to nothing about her. 'I'm a barrister at 9BR,' she said. 'But what do you mean, "à la Krapp"?'

'Ah! 9BR,' replied Flack. 'Don't worry about Krapp, he's a character in a play who likes bananas too much for his own good. Tell me, do you agree with the trend among law firms and now, so I infer, barristers' chambers to reduce everything to the form of an acronym? In my day Bowles & Parkes was Bowles & Parkes. Now they're probably thinking of becoming BP. Or BAP. Or some other abbreviation, which makes me think that actually, in fact, 9BR isn't an acronym, it's an abbreviation, and it beggars belief that I would make such a mistake after all these years of toil in the company of pedants of the calibre of Richard Dixon and Denis O'Donoghue. Forgive me, an inexcusable lapse, but the point is the same, maybe Bowles & Parkes is now BAP. I don't know. I do my best but don't always keep up with the changes in the profession.'

Berlin laughed nervously. Flack had not expected this. His knowledge of her was scant but their brief dealings had persuaded him that she was made of stern stuff. In teasing her about law firm nomenclature he had anticipated repartee, not the image of the woman opposite him sinking, discountenanced, deeper into her chair.

'Never mind, just one of my hobby-horses,' said Flack jovially. He added that *Tristram Shandy* was full of hobby-horses, or, at least, that they occurred somewhere within its surreal pages – had Berlin read Sterne?

She shook her head.

'Well, anyway, let's forget about literary things and deal with this story,' said Flack, whose composure, not to mention resolve, was no longer quite what it was when the pair had entered the room. But as if he couldn't help himself, far from helping to explain the story's hidden legal intricacies Flack embarked again on a tangent.

'What brings you here, if you don't mind my asking?'

Berlin seemed to welcome the question.

'I've always been fascinated by the media,' she said. 'And it might sound pompous but I believe in freedom of speech. I wanted to see how newspapers work and, with luck, help get stories published.'

'That's very noble. The same, or similar, sentiments made me turn up here, a century ago. But there's no money in being a night lawyer. You know that, I hope.'

'The money's not important.'

'No, but there's *really* no money in it. We get an inflation-based raise every year and it takes our hourly rate to, let's see now, perhaps a tenth of what a partner in a City firm will charge – or a QC at 9BR, for that matter.'

'Yes, I know. I've been told what the rates are.'

'Mind you, if you're at 9BR – a fine chambers, if I may say so – you'll make some money with your day job. Just don't give it up, that's the rule round here. Not if you want to be able to pay the bills.'

'Honestly, the money's not why I'm here. I want to learn.' Berlin fidgeted as she added: 'My colleagues in chambers tell me that you're the best night lawyer in London. It's an honour to meet you.'

Flack laughed. 'No, far from it. I'm just the oldest. There are bright young things like you who know laws I've never heard of. Trade mark law, for example. Have you any idea how easy it is to offend the people who make Portakabins?'

This time, Berlin laughed. 'I imagine they rigorously protect their intellectual property rights,' she hazarded.

'Quite so,' said Flack. 'They write to us all the time telling us about the extraordinary history of the word 'Portakabin'. It is not, as you will readily apprehend, an ordinary word but, in fact, a trade mark, one first used to describe a stand-alone, relocatable building way back in the Forties. Since the auspicious day on which Portakabin's renowned inventor, Donald Shepherd, registered the word as a trade mark only buildings produced by Portakabin can be called a Portakabin building or even, if you will, a Portakabin. It is important that we get this kind of thing right, but sadly we never do. *The Record* seems to have a mental block when it comes to the comprehension of Portakabins. You've no idea how many buildings we have rashly described as having Portakabin capability, when they don't, or, yet worse, of being a Portakabin when they are no such thing.'

The vague sense of unease with which Berlin, at least, had entered the meeting room had vanished. Now, she felt comfortable in Flack's presence, as if she had known him all her life. He was generous and amusing, acerbic only in the gentlest of fashions. Granted, he seemed a bit tense, but surely this came with the territory. For the first time since she'd arrived at *The Record*, Berlin felt relaxed. She was only too pleased to accept Flack's overture regarding the two sheets of A4 which lay in wait in front of her. 'Come on then, what do you make of it? What's the 9BR take on the legal issues here?'

Berlin discoursed succinctly and accurately on the tale of the celebrity who'd had an affair with a teacher. She was rightly concerned not merely with the possibility of a claim for libel by either party, but one for privacy, too. 'Is there a public interest in knowing so much about these people, even what they eat for breakfast?' she asked, not altogether rhetorically. 'I mean, gossip is gossip, but surely there are limits?'

Leaning back in his chair, the room empty save for its eight-seater table and, opposite him, this pretty and earnest would-be night lawyer, Flack was every inch the master of his domain. 'You're quite right to worry about privacy,' he said. 'These days it's all the rage. I'm sure more than a few of your colleagues at 9BR derive a healthy income from settling pleadings whose cause of action is the infringement of some poor soul's private life. Quite right, too. What possible justification is there for the publication of these things? Freedom of expression? Or prurience, pure and simple?'

To this, Berlin said nothing. She held Flack's gaze for a second, before dropping her eyes to the paper in front of her.

'Ah, of course, the story,' said Flack. 'Well, do you know what I think? I think that it's Legal OK.'

Flack couldn't be sure, but later, when he thought back to this moment, he wondered if a pout appeared upon Berlin's lips. Certainly, there was something in her reaction – a subtle sense of play, of mystery – that took him altogether by surprise. It was almost as if her beautiful indifference was a challenge, perhaps even an invitation. Again, she said nothing, choosing instead to nod, ever so slowly, all the while staring into Flack's eyes.

Flack found himself shuffling in his seat. For a second – no more – he even felt a surge of arousal, no more than a flickering of long-forgotten sensuality but a reminder, if there needed to be one, that sexual desire can spring from the most obscure, deeply hidden wells, even those which lurk beneath the offices of a modern newspaper such as *The Record*, springs whose waters you would have thought have long since run dry but then, just as you are surveying the reaction of a journalist to ensure that she has understood the legal issues you have so painstakingly explained, or find yourself in the midst of a disquisition to the night news editor about the law of contempt, or even, as now, when you are alone with an agreeable young barrister from a leading London chambers, a woman who must, if there is any order in the world, have a list of suitors stretching all the way to the Royal Courts of Justice, it is then, at precisely these junctures, that desire arrives, unbidden and not always welcome, not least, in Flack's case, because he had always drawn the line at liaisons with women who were not, give or take a year, his own age. Now here he was, discreetly adjusting the way he was sitting and focusing with atypical intensity on the law, the curvature of the desk, the shape of the door – anything, so long as he could stop himself from thinking just how attractive Maya Berlin was.

But the mixed blessings of his reverie could only interrupt him for the briefest of interludes. Newspapers are not places of idleness, and there was work to be done. And the very looks that he found so alluring in Berlin could not but make her an ideal, if unwitting, accomplice in his plan.

'It's Legal OK,' said Flack. 'That's the term we use round here. Look, you see – I've signed it off.'

Berlin watched as Flack scrawled *Legal OK, Harry Flack* on the first page of the print-out before ticking it and the second page. Then, as he pushed back his chair and stood up, he said: 'Why don't you go and find the journalist who gave it to us? If you can't find him, give it to the chief sub.'

'What if they have any questions?' she asked.

'They won't,' said Flack. 'So long as they see the words "Legal OK", they're happy.'

CHAPTER 17

4.40pm, Night Lawyer's Office

As Flack entered the cramped office in which he had plied his trade for so long Dixon rose to greet him.

'Everything all right, Harry?' he said, his unruly hair for once mirroring the unrest in his mind. Dixon's flowing curls were the source of an evergreen if not especially funny joke among Dixon, O'Donoghue and Flack, as well as many other journalists at *The Record*, and Flack lost no time in resorting to a favoured, if sometimes uninspired, routine.

'Yes, of course, Richard. Anyone would think that hair of yours was getting in the way of your ability to think. Why wouldn't everything be all right?'

'Oh, no particular reason,' replied Dixon, unflappably. Then, drily, though not caustically, he added: 'It's just that even through this hair of mine I have a nose for, how shall I put it?'

'Trouble?' suggested O'Donoghue.

'No, I wouldn't go that far. Perhaps "the distracting properties of a gorgeous young woman" would be more apposite?'

O'Donoghue smiled. Flack, loitering next to his desk, was aware that the eyes of his colleagues were fixed upon him.

'I can assure you, gentlemen, that the charms of this evening's debutante have not swayed me in the slightest. She is diverting, though, I give you that.'

'Diverting? I'll say!' With that, O'Donoghue returned to a story about the indiscretions of a British diplomat in Belize. Dixon contented himself with a look that began with complicity but ended with a sigh. 'Back to the grindstone, then, chaps,' he said, sitting down at his desk though not without wondering where the attractive trainee night lawyer had got to. 'They're like yo-yos tonight, the pair of them,' he said to himself. 'What's it all about?'

Soon, though, the three men were absorbed in their work. O'Donoghue's story about the diplomat was, he noted under his breath, 'not bad, in fact a pretty good effort,' this a tribute to the quality of its grammar and spelling, as well as a laudable allegiance to the ideal of factual accuracy, rather than a judgement on whether it was in any way interesting. Dixon's labours were concentrated, again, on the leader page. 'I wonder if they'll ever remember anything I tell them?' he murmured, as he removed a hyphen from 'copycat', changed 'consortia' to consortiums and gave 'government' an initial cap.

Flack, meanwhile, was busy at his computer terminal reading a series of e-mails alerting the night lawyers to court orders that might have a bearing on *The Record's* stories. They were circulated during the week by the PAs in the Legal Department whose job it was to digest and disseminate court documents which, if scrutiny were ever to be given to them from a philosophical point of view, were as profoundly negative as it were possible for any document, anywhere in the world, to be, save for a piece of paper on which the only word is 'No'. Time and again a court, whether criminal or civil, had devoted itself to the assertions of lawyers representing the two sides of an argument but, it struck Flack, whatever the result the decision was almost always couched in prohibitive terms. In front of him, on the computer screen, was a classic example:

THE QUEEN

V

DAVIS ANTHONY HARRIS

ORDER PURSUANT TO SECTION 4 (2) OF THE CONTEMPT OF COURT ACT 1981

1. There should be no further publication or broadcast of any matter contained within the headlines or the body of an article which appeared on pages 8 and 9 of the *Morning Sun* on 8 April 2001.

2. There should be no further references in any publication or broadcast to the said article of headline, save for reference to the fact that this jury was discharged as a result of an article in the *Morning Sun*.

3. No publication or broadcast should make reference to racism or

racist motivation in relation to the above proceedings.

4. For the avoidance of doubt, the above Order does not preclude
    publication or broadcast of any material relating to, or comment
    upon, the McPherson Report, or issues of racism generally,
    provided that no reference in such publications or broadcasts is
    made to these proceedings.

5. This Order is effective forthwith.

'A series of peremptory injunctions *not* to do things,' thought Flack.
'Even the last line sounds like an order saying 'no'. Then again, that's
what this is – a court order arising from a serious criminal trial. Of
course it has to be expressed with due weight.'

It would be wrong to say that Flack had never entertained subversive
thoughts about the law. He was well aware that his very role as a night
lawyer was, in a small way, a gesture against the straightjacket of
conventional legal practice. Night lawyers have to think creatively, on
their feet; they have to be articulate and authoritative; and they need
a flexible relationship with academic legal analysis. They were not
expected to wear suits, though most, including Flack, did, and many
did ostensibly outlandish things with their spare, daylight time, like
write, or pursue businesses, or even, in one remarkable case, work as
an actor in soft-porn films. But if the job had a sense of freedom so
often absent from mainstream legal practice, a night lawyer like Flack
was not the out-and-out maverick described, in his tender days in the
law, by Dr Tax. Flack, especially among night lawyers, had secured so
estimable a reputation through qualities of reliability, acumen, speed
of thought and, when all was said and done, an abiding respect for the
law. How else could he perform his duties so well?

But tonight, as he read the latest court orders and legal warnings,
Flack did not feel in thrall to the law. Quite the opposite. He was
gripped by an unprecedented desire to misuse the law for his own ends,
as became clear to him when Maya Berlin returned to the office.

'Did you find the sub?' said Flack, as Berlin pulled up the chair next
to him and sat down.

'Yes,' she replied.

'Any problems?'

'No, he was happy.'

'They always are if you clear their stories,' said O'Donoghue, who, like Dixon, had noted, with pleasure, Berlin's return.

'Do you know,' continued the Irishman, 'I don't think we've been formally introduced. Our colleague seems to have forgotten his manners.'

'I think you're right,' said Dixon. 'It must be the excitement of knowing that this is his last night of toil. Come on, Harry, do the right thing.'

Flack turned to face his colleagues, and, with exaggerated ponderousness, rose from his chair. 'Gentlemen,' he said, 'forgive me. May I formally introduce you to Maya Berlin, a barrister with 9BR and, for reasons she has yet to reveal, a young lady who is keen to join *The Record's* rota of night lawyers.' With that, he bowed.

Berlin continued to sit in her chair, unsure what to make of this latest quirky turn. In her contemplation of what life would be like as a night lawyer for a national newspaper, the last thing she imagined was that anyone would have the time, let alone the inclination, to introduce her with a bow. But if Dixon and O'Donoghue were also surprised by Flack's excessive courtesy, they did not show it.

'That's better,' said Dixon.

'Much better,' added O'Donoghue. 'Now we know who we're sharing our office with.'

'I am delighted to set the record straight,' said Flack, returning to his seat. Then, as his colleagues set about the correcting of copy, he took Berlin through the early evening drill at *The Record*. The night lawyers arrive at 4pm, said Flack, and their first task is to make themselves known to the Legal Department. Berlin had, he felt, ably completed this admittedly undemanding job. Then they make their way here, to the night lawyer's office, or, as it might better be described, the revise editors' office, the pedants having the upper hand when it came to time spent in the building. No surprise there, said Flack, for they are full-time, while we are mere part-timers, here not at our whim, as it were, but every now and then and only ever in accordance with that most hallowed of documents, The Rota. The first thing we do, when we get here, is read the letters page. It is always the first on the pile, and, with practice, can be completed blindfold. There might be one or two news stories here, too; if there are, they'll always be on A4 paper rather than in proof form. Sometimes they'll be marked 'urgent' but even if they're not it pays to knuckle down to them straightaway. That way if a journalist turns up demanding answers, you're on the case. If no one comes, you take the copy either to the journalist in question, if he or she favoured us with a name, and go through any legal issues you've identified, or you ring his number. I use 'he' here as shorthand, denoting both sexes, in case you were wondering. Once you've done that, or if there are no stories requiring attention, you check e-mails. Here, on the screen – you see? There might be one or two attaching a piece, but more likely than not you're doing this to bring yourself up to speed with court orders and injunctions. Look at this one, for example, banning the mention of racism in a case involving some footballers. Make sure, once you've got your flying colours, that you keep tabs on these things. I needn't tell you, as a barrister at 9BR, that the consequences of breaching an order or an injunction are severe. But don't be unduly worried by the responsibility. The journalists will also have a working knowledge of these things; often your job is to interpret the minutiae of an order about which everyone is well aware, making a call as to whether, for example, a child can be identified in family or criminal proceedings. And anyway, if it all sounds a bit too serious, there are always my colleague Mr Dixon's e-mails to read.

At this juncture Flack paused. He was impressed to note that Berlin had been listening attentively, and a little touched, too. Perhaps he shouldn't deploy her in his scheme? She was an innocent, a young woman who had done nothing to deserve being cynically manipulated by a tired old night lawyer with a score to settle. 'That's what I am,' said Flack to himself. 'Tired and old, working my last shift, scheming for belated revenge.' But then again, if he were successful no harm would come to Berlin. People would realise that it had been Flack, all along. Her career would survive. People might even feel sorry for her.

'Is this one of them?'

It was Berlin. She accompanied her question with a gesture to Flack's computer screen, pointing out an e-mail from Dixon.

'Yes, it is,' said Flack. He manoeuvred the cursor over the e-mail and opened it. Entitled *Style: Leaders' Debates*, it read as follows:

Hi,
For the debates involving the party leaders, on balance it would be better to write an apostrophe.
   Always trying to float your vote,
   Richard

'You see?' said Flack. 'Quite entertaining. More fun than the law on elections, that's for sure. I do find all that nonsense in the Representation of the People Act very tiresome, don't you?'

Berlin said she wasn't sure.

'All the rubbish about not reporting exit polls! You know, the ban on revealing how people have voted. There's our man, standing in the rain in some desolate town, notebook in hand, or is it a tablet or some other digital device, I don't know, but there he is, or there she is, soaked through to the skin, and along comes a noble voter, a member of this country's glorious citizenry who's only too happy to say that he plumped for the idiot who wants to ban immigration and send homosexuals to Scandinavia. He's not just happy to say how he voted, he's proud, and why? Because this country isn't glorious but is, in fact, going to the dogs. And our tired and sodden reporter, what can he do with this information? Nothing. Nothing until the polls have closed. A stupid law if ever there was one.'

Berlin felt she had to say something. 'But isn't it based on not unduly influencing the outcome? On the media being seen to be as objective as possible throughout?'

'Yes, but how likely is that? I mean, let's be honest – in today's world, where people put what they had for breakfast on Facebook and Twitter before they've even had it, do we really think that revealing who John Bigot voted for will make a blind bit of difference? And while I'm at it, do you know what else that ridiculous statute says? We can't make any false statements of fact about candidates during an election. Now I know what you'll tell me – they teach you well at 9BR, I know – you'll tell me this is meant to catch dirty tricks among rival candidates, when they slag each other off. But we, the media, are caught by this bit of the law, section 106 I think it is, and a very annoying and stupid section it is too.'

Having delivered this speech Flack sighed so conclusively that it was clear there would be no further discussion. After a minute or two, he returned to his PC, then found another e-mail and opened it, gesturing to Berlin to lean over and read it too.

Hi,
From the Style Guide:
    Always check the spelling of MPs and their constituencies if not entirely familiar. For the names of parliamentary constituencies

generally, follow the format of place name first and then compass point, area etc, eg, Ilford South (not South Ilford), Sheffield Hallam (no comma). Where several place names occur in a constituency name, use an ampersand, e.g., Poplar & Canning Town.
  Yours, lurking in the marginals,
  Fine, Tune, Nit & Pick Central

Flack watched Berlin as she read Dixon's advice to *The Record's* journalists. She chuckled at its close, prompting Flack to make another comment.

'More on elections – and again, much more fun than the bloody law. You won't always have time to read Mr Dixon's stylistic decrees, but, as you can see, they brighten up the evening. Let's have a look at another.'

But just as Flack and Berlin – for all the world looking as if they were father and daughter hunched over some homework – were learning that the American spelling of Pearl Harbor was permissible, they were interrupted by the arrival of Lucy Lousada, one of *The Record's* senior reporters. As was her wont, Lousada was wearing a large amount of very expensive perfume. Not for nothing had Flack, Dixon and O'Donoghue often joked that she was smelt before she was heard, or even seen. Not that they objected. She was a bubbly woman and her appearance always brought a cheer to the trio's room.

'*Hello,* Harry!' said Lousada, whose speech, like her perfume, had a tendency to ostentation. 'How *are* you? I haven't seen you in *ages.*'

'You'd better make the most of him while you can,' said O'Donoghue, looking up from his work. 'Tonight is Flack's last shift.'

'*Really?*' gasped Lousada.

'I'm afraid so,' said Flack. 'All good things come to an end.'

'They *do*, you're right. But *really*? Will I *never* see you here again?'

'Not unless you have another story for me to look at later. Talking of which, is there something I can do?'

As he asked this question Flack glanced at three sheaves of paper in Lousada's left hand.

'Ah, *yes.* If you don't mind, that is. I'm sure it's fine but if you wouldn't mind taking a look ...'

Lousada gave Flack a story about a music promoter who, it was alleged, had received a painting by a Renaissance master by way of compensation for a botched shooting. 'Imagine it,' she explained, 'you're lying in your hospital bed the morning after you've been shot by a thug who's been hired to *kill* you. The idiot got it wrong, and you're alive, Harry, *alive*. But as the night becomes morning the man who wanted you dead starts to worry. He knows you're *very, very* well connected. He suspects you'll want vengeance. You'll want to get even. You'll want *to kill him!* But he's not *quite* such a fool as the incompetent assassin. And he knows that you *positively love* Renaissance paintings. It so happens that his fence is at that moment in possession of a famous Titian, stolen *to order* just a few weeks ago. So he calls the fence and *bingo!* He arranges for the painting to be delivered to your hospital, to *your very room*. Imagine it! You wake up and there, staring at you, is a Titian worth at least £10m. Hanging off its sumptuous frame is a note; you reach forward – crying out with pain, for you were shot in the shoulder – and pull it towards you. The note says: "Broken knee caps for the idiot who failed to kill you and a Titian. Quits?" You sit back on your pillow and gaze at the Titian. It's *gorgeous* but what a shame! You can't ever *show* it to anyone. It'll just have to remain your little secret – a nice one, that is, one that you'll enjoy to your dying day. Only a couple of trusty lieutenants will ever know about it; you call one of them and put wheels in motion. After all, you *can't possibly* leave a Titian lying around in a hospital, even a private one! But then, of course, your lieutenant sees a chance for an easy fee, and tells me – *me, Harry!* – all about it. And Bob's your uncle – a great story, don't you think?'

It was, reflected Flack, a good story. The stylish René Gimpel, whose *Diary of an Art Dealer* Flack had read while on holiday in Cornwall, would have approved. But it was also one so full of legal risk as to be virtually unpublishable. What evidence to substantiate any of Lousada's narrative could ever be adduced in court? Just about none. Would her source ever testify? Not in a million years. He'd deny he even knew Lousada. Would the promoter happily confirm that yes, of course, he'd accepted a Titian by way of apology? That he habitually consorts with fences and criminals? As for the rival music mogul, the man who'd ordered the killing, the idea that he would enjoy his portrayal, merely chortling amiably when he read it, was risible. Flack harrumphed as Lousada's speech ended, a noise of disapproval which was familiar to Dixon and O'Donoghue, who caught each other's eye at the sound. 'Business as usual, thank the Lord,' thought Dixon, while what was in O'Donoghue's mind was similar: 'His nibs is going to squash this one, that's for sure.' Neither said a word, but, for just a second, there was a hush of expectancy in the room.

Flack eyed the pieces of paper given to him by Lousada. Her story made no effort to disguise the identity of any of its protagonists. All were named, all were portrayed in a defamatory manner, one which would either make 'ordinary right-thinking people', whoever they were, think the less of them or even expose them to ridicule and contempt, so much so, indeed, that they were shunned and avoided. Not a shred of admissible evidence existed and the meaning was clear: the promoter, his putative killer and the man who'd ordered his death were all criminals, men likely to stop at nothing if murder and the theft of prized Renaissance paintings was their game. 'Even assuming that the fragrant Lucy has not been sold a pup,' thought Flack, 'this is the classic case of the story which is known to be true, but which cannot be published owing to the complete and utter absence of admissible evidence.' There was but one solution if the story was to see the light of day: a wholesale rewrite, entailing the obliteration of their identities. Even then tell-tale identifying signs would have to be removed; it would, for example, be wise not to describe the Titian recipient's occupation but rather cast him as a man 'in the entertainment industry'.

'Legal OK,' said Flack.

Even Lousada seemed to hesitate. '*Really?*' she cried. 'Are you sure?'

'Quite sure,' replied Flack.

Lousada decided to quit while she was ahead.

'*Thank you*, Harry!' she said. 'I knew you'd be the man to help me out!' And, taking the paper from Flack and declaring that they really must go for a drink after work, if time allowed, she rushed out of the office.

Dixon and O'Donoghue said nothing. It was impossible, though, not to note their furrowed brows. Berlin saw them exchange a glance of profound concern, perhaps not so much for their colleague as for the status of his advice.

That Flack's judgement was being tacitly questioned was undeniable. The levity of Dixon's e-mail sign-offs seemed an age away and anxiety permeated the tiny room with the rapaciousness of Lousada's scent. It lingered still, but was expunged when Flack, rising from his chair, said: 'I don't understand some journalists. Why do they bother me with such ridiculous queries? Do they think I'm some sort of experienced night lawyer, or something else entirely? After all these years, too. What, really, is their problem?'

And with that, he left.

CHAPTER 18

5.00pm, Day Lawyers' Offices

Flack sat at Phillips's desk with his head in his hands. It wasn't too late to stop in his tracks. His plan wasn't set in stone, and still less was Flack prey to the kind of compulsive urges that had motivated the killer in the Murder of the Century trial. Yes, he had experienced a revival of rage which he'd assumed had long since abated but the girl was too innocent and besides, what of Dixon and O'Donoghue? Even if his scheme did not have a direct bearing on them, could he really bow out on his last shift and engineer the kind of mayhem that the trio had fought against all their professional lives? For often enough, Dixon and O'Donoghue were astute to legal risks and, on a busy night, would alert Flack (or whichever night lawyer happened to be in the office) to any that they felt might be about to slip through the net. Flack always returned the favour, highlighting solecisms from errant apostrophes to unintended double-entendres.

Even as he sat, tortured, at Phillips's desk – his professional identity ebbing away just as, downstairs in the night lawyer's office, legal issues were incoming – he smiled as he recalled something he'd once said to O'Donoghue: 'Did you catch that stray apostrophe?' The Irishman had indeed deleted an apostrophe appended to a possessive 'its', but he'd chortled at Flack's question. For a few shifts thereafter, Flack was known as 'Mr Stray Apostrophe', a nickname commuted to M'lord Stray, then Mr Stray, before it fell into disuse.

Flack had taken the gentle ribbing in good spirit. Alone at Phillips's desk, it seemed to epitomise the camaraderie of a working life spent on the twin frontiers of the legally acceptable and the linguistically permissible. Now, though, he had conceived of a plan which would, in exacting long-deferred revenge, take casualties. The two revise editors, men he liked as much as respected, would be among them.

Lifting his head from his hands Flack caught sight of the letters tray on Phillips's desk. It was full to brimming but orderly, and on top was a letter which, Flack could easily see, was from Maya Berlin. He pulled it towards him and read:

Dear Ms Phillips,

I write with regard to the possibility of joining the night lawyer rota at The Record.

I am a barrister at 9BR. I was called to the bar a year ago and have since specialised in libel law. As you know, 9BR is a specialist libel chambers, many of whose occupants have spent time at newspapers such as The Record. *Indeed, from speaking with colleagues I am aware that experience 'at the coal face' of pre-publication law is best gained via a spell on a national paper's night lawyer rota. I am very keen to broaden my knowledge in this way.*

While there is no doubt much I will be able to learn from your long-standing night lawyers, I can offer a sound knowledge of libel law, so that they need not feel they are having to explain things to a novice. Since being at 9BR I have also become familiar with the law of contempt, reporting restrictions and privacy. I believe my skills would be an asset and, given that I live as well as work in central London, would easily be able to attend The Record *for shifts. I am also happy to work weekend shifts, including Sunday evenings.*

Please find attached my CV. I hope that it may be possible to join the rota and look forward to hearing from you in due course. Meanwhile, if there is anything you would like to discuss, please do not hesitate to contact me.

Yours sincerely,
Maya Berlin

Flack noted that Berlin's address was in Bloomsbury, and skim-read her CV. It was impressive, if conventional. She'd gained a first in law at Oxford, having been educated abroad, and had breezed through Bar College. She listed tennis as a hobby and had travelled to all the usual places. She liked reading and going to the cinema. She was single. She was, as Phillips had scrawled in an attendance note annexed to the letter: 'A good bet for the rota. Spoke with MB on Monday and arranged for her to come in for her first training shift with HF on Friday night. Further shifts, to a maximum of six, to be arranged.' Phillips had also written an unexpected aide memoire: 'It's Flack's last shift. Oh no! What are we going to do without him?! NB: get his card signed and finish mock-up.'

Flack returned the letter and Berlin's CV to the tray. He remembered writing one in similar terms just over twenty-five years ago. His had gone to various newspaper lawyers, including James Madison, then the second-in-command of *The Record's* legal department. Like Berlin, he'd made a virtue of his belief in freedom of expression. That was what it was all about –helping editors, helping journalists, helping Fleet Street survive even as it changed out of all recognition.

'Quite right,' said Flack to himself. 'The night lawyer's *raison d'être* is to steer a story into print, not unthinkingly to let it be spiked and still less to make it a tissue of legal howlers. That's what I've been doing for these past twenty-five years – helping. Helping my colleagues and helping something much bigger than me.'

With fresh resolve, he stood up and set off to return to the night lawyer's office.

CHAPTER 19

5.20pm, Night Lawyer's Office

Flack was all ebullience when he returned to his colleagues.

'Do you know,' he said, 'I've just been thinking of the letter I sent to James Madison all those years ago, asking for work on the night rota.'

Dixon, O'Donoghue and Berlin stopped in their tracks. Rather than taking his seat again Flack had chosen to stand in the doorway of the office, from which he made this unexpected announcement. Berlin caught a glance between the two revise editors, one which said, 'Now what?' before focusing her attention exclusively on Flack. She noticed that his eyes were aglow.

'Yes,' said Flack, although no one had accepted his overture, whether by a mumbled 'Really? Do tell more' or merely by an encouraging nod. 'Yes, I was just thinking about it. Madison was in charge of the rota all those years ago, though the top man in the legal department then was Thomas Garfit. Does anyone remember him?'

Dixon and O'Donoghue nodded. Flack continued: 'A throwback, was Garfit. One of the old school. So was Madison, for that matter. I miss him. I think he lives in Dorset now. As for Garfit, he's long gone.'

Again, Berlin saw a furtive look pass between Dixon and O'Donoghue. She wondered if Flack saw it, too. If he did, it appeared to make no difference. Flack's eyes had lost a little of their lustre but he remained in thrall to a conceit that had meaning only for him, and which, it was clear, had little or no relevance to the work to be done on the night of this, his last shift.

'Yes, Garfit was a good man. An excellent lawyer, too. You knew where you were with him. *Dura lex, sed lex*, that was one of his sayings. Well, not his exactly, but one he was fond of. 'The law is hard, but it is the law.' You can't argue with that, can you?'

'Er, no, I don't suppose you can,' agreed Dixon.

'Not really,' said O'Donoghue. 'Facts are facts and the law is the law.' Affably, he added: 'And let's face it, if it wasn't, the learned among us wouldn't have been in clover all these years.'

'Quite so,' said Flack, 'though speaking personally, being covered in clover never quite happened. It did for many lawyers, you're right, not least Madison, whose house in Cerne Abbas is, so I'm told, the envy of even the inhabitants of the phallic giant's village, one which could hardly be said to be down at heel.'

'No,' said Dixon.

'Not at all,' said O'Donoghue. 'I was there for a walk with the missus a few weeks ago. The scruffiest house we saw was still worth at least half a million.'

'Extraordinary to think that a chalk giant sporting a huge erection can give a place such cachet, don't you think?' said Flack rhetorically, though he then asked Berlin if she was familiar with Cerne Abbas and, in particular, its peerless giant. No, she wasn't, she said – but it sounded interesting. And who or what was this giant?

'He was carved in the chalk downs above the village a few hundred years ago,' said Flack. 'At least, that's what I've read somewhere, I can't recall where. My friends here would know – it's this sort of thing that falls squarely within their domain.'

Rather than clarify the historical origins of the Cerne Abbas giant, Dixon and O'Donoghue had resumed peering at their computers. Flack, though, was on a roll. Still standing in the doorway, he informed his uneasy audience that the giant's feet faced away from the village, symbolising the fact that he was a lustful abbot who had been driven from polite society, while his gnarled club, held in his right hand, revealed the conflict which had dominated his life. This, too, pointed away from the village, though his phallus, as tumescent as any ever seen, real or imagined, pointed only one way, as was to be expected in the circumstances – up. What, Flack wondered, did Berlin make of that?

She, too, said nothing, though she did, with a bashful half-smile, shrug her shoulders.

'I wonder if it's a pagan gesture of defiance, a statement that, despite everything, life goes on, or perhaps more accurately, that sex still happens.' Flack spoke in an almost wistful manner, and, thought Berlin, seemed to compromise himself further when he added: 'Which is true, of course. Sex still happens. The world must go on. The procreative urge exists even among the lonely and the bereft. Perhaps even more among the lonely and the bereft.' But before the meaning of these words could be absorbed – assuming, that is, that they had any meaning – Flack regrouped. 'But never mind the Cerne Abbas giant. He is not important. Fanciful, yes, but not important. What I wanted to say was that in my letter to Madison I made a gross factual error.'

Dixon and O'Donoghue were by now sufficiently taken aback to abandon what was proving a vain attempt to carry on working.

'You?' said Dixon.

'Make a factual error?' said O'Donoghue.

'Impossible.'

'Yes, I find that very hard to believe.'

'Gentlemen, I'm heartened by your faith in me,' said Flack, 'but it's true. On my CV, a document not dissimilar to that which this young lady would have sent to the legal department in her quest to join the rota, I stated my date of birth. The trouble is that while I was correct with the day and month, a typo rendered the year of my birth at a date in the future, one that hasn't, even to this day, occurred yet.'

Flack's listeners eyed him with perplexity. Surely, thought Berlin, he is aware of the degree of discomfort in his colleagues?

'Yes, it was a silly mistake. Do you know what Madison wrote about it?'

No one had any idea.

'His letter said that I was by all means to come in and try and get my flying colours, working with the existing night lawyers for six training shifts. He said we'd need to have a chat but that, all being well, I'd join the rota. He didn't expect any problems, given my background, but in a handwritten PS he scribbled: "I note from your CV that you are not yet born." Remarkable, don't you think?'

Berlin joined Dixon and O'Donoghue in awkward laughter. Such mirth as they achieved was annulled by Flack's last, flippantly enunciated comment from the doorway before he sat down at his desk.

'To think I could have been guilty of so stupid a mistake in the first place. As for the dear old *Record* and all who toil within its corridors, who knows what will have happened by the time the year of my birth, on my CV to Madison, comes round. It was 2956, if I recall correctly. I put a 2 instead of a 1. How stupid! It's a wonder they ever took me on.'

*

It was Berlin who broke the silence that fell upon the room. She had time enough to observe Flack as he continued scrolling through e-mails, muttering, huffing and puffing, and deleting them if they were requests for legal advice, but before her lay a pile of proofs – obituaries, left on Flack's desk by an unknown messenger during one of his absences. Berlin coughed almost inaudibly before asking if Flack would like her to read them.

Flack accepted Berlin's kind offer, and explained that the obits were always among the first pages to be found on the night lawyer's desk. He said that they invariably presented nothing by way of legal risk, for the simple reason that the dead cannot sue for libel. This, he said, was one small mercy among our otherwise nonsensical system of libel laws. Imagine if, on top of a system which favours the corrupt, the dead could sue too! It would be intolerable. Not, of course, that they would literally sue – being dead, this would be beyond them. Even the late Sir James Goldsmith, a man who enjoyed suing for libel so much that he established a foundation by which to assist others who wished to do likewise, but lacked the means – even Sir James, wealthy as he was, couldn't have brought a libel action once he was dead. No, what Flack meant was that it was a damn good thing that the *estates* of the dead couldn't bring libel claims on their behalf. Yes, London had long been the libel capital of the world, so much so that one could even argue that its allure for wealthy forum-shopping foreigners contributed to the economic prosperity of the nation or, to be precise, a select few lawyers, but at least this was not permissible. Then, deviating radically from the legalistic nature of this speech, Flack asked if Berlin had seen a play called *Closer*?

'Yes, I have,' said Berlin, in a tone that revealed her failure to see the relevance of the question.

'Good,' said Flack. 'Then you'll know that the obituaries, which we habitually call the "obits", are written months, even years, in advance. There is a vast library of them upstairs, ready to go, with just a bit of updating, at a moment's notice. It's an extraordinary thought, don't you think?'

Berlin said that yes, it was. Flack turned her attention to the pages before her. 'Look at this one,' he said, pointing at the obituary of a celebrity chef who had died a *bon viveur's* death. 'This would have been written ages ago because everyone knew he was an old soak. They'd have been waiting for him to pop his clogs. The same with this one.' The second example to which Flack gestured was the obituary of a notable, but very old, British scientist. 'His card would have been marked about fifteen years ago,' said Flack. 'Let's see, how old was he when he died? My word, he was ninety-eight! Good on the old bugger for hanging on as long as he did.' He then picked up a red pen and scrawled through each column of text on all the four proofs, adding 'Legal OK' at the top of each page. At this, Berlin could not contain herself.

'How can they be Legal OK if you haven't read them?' she asked. 'Surely it's as well to read them – what if they make a defamatory reference to a living person?'

'They never do,' said Flack. 'Trust me, I'm a night lawyer – but you know that, don't you? These pages are Legal OK tonight, just as they always are, every night. But you know what's just occurred to me? They might have written the obit for that bastard editor. I'm going upstairs to have a look. Hold the fort, won't you, while I'm gone?'

Moments after he had once again left the room, Dixon and O'Donoghue looked at one another and shook their heads.

'Something's up,' said Dixon.

'I know,' said O'Donoghue.

Berlin busied herself with the obituaries Flack had just marked 'Legal OK' without even reading them. Before long she found precisely the problem she had feared. In an obit about a man who had invented a revolutionary form of rubber, disparaging reference was made to his siblings. 'None of X's brothers and sisters came close to emulating his success, preferring instead to idle their lives away. Y, especially, became known throughout London for his drinking, gambling and womanising.' If Y was still alive, could this allegation safely be made? Perhaps, but surely it needed checking? Berlin ringed it with her red pen, and made a note to discuss it with Flack when he returned.

CHAPTER 20

Among The Obituaries

'Harry Flack! To what do I owe this rare and fine pleasure?'

Flack stood on the threshold of the office which belonged to Archie Lewis, the long-serving head of *The Record's* obituary section, peering at his interrogator as if he had momentarily gone deaf. Such was the intensity of his gaze, not to mention the look of confusion on his face, that Lewis threw another conversational gambit in the night lawyer's direction.

'You all right, Harry? Cat got your tongue? Or is tonight simply so exciting, so blessed with the most thrilling of legal intricacies, that you have become catatonic in the face of their onslaught?'

The words appeared to have no effect on Flack, who, as if to vindicate Lewis's hypothesis, continued to stand stock still, saying nothing, squinting into the gloom of the obit office, itself a throwback to the Fleet Street of old in that far from being an open-plan affair with rows of gleaming computers it was a small, L-shaped room with three desks, one for Lewis and two for his deputies, Jessica Steidl and Alan Shay, a pair almost as ancient as their boss, a man fond of comparing himself to Charon, the ferryman of the Styx: 'It is my role to see the dead to the next realm,' he would say, over a pint of bitter in The Rose, the public house of choice for most of *The Record's* staff. 'I am the keeper of their souls for so long as they hover between their death and deification. Once immortalised in an obituary in *The Record,* they are free. And I can take my pound of flesh.'

There was something in the conceit. Despite its size, the obit office was crammed with filing cabinet upon filing cabinet, inside which, in pale yellow folders, hung A4 print-outs of obituaries written by Lewis, Steidl and Shay, all neatly catalogued in alphabetical order. Lewis was fond of telling Flack, and anyone else who would listen, that there were thousands at any one time, ranging from obits about politicians, film stars and sportsmen to those covering the lives of eminent scientists, lawyers, teachers and aviators, all of which were ready for publication with but the swiftest of updates. 'It's not easy, Harry, keeping on top of who's about to die,' said Lewis, one evening in The Rose, 'but years in the job have given me the knack. Sometimes I know who's about to go six foot under even before their doctors. I feel a shudder, as if a dark cloud has lifted, and then lo and behold, George Harrison has died. If only he'd asked me I could have told him to enjoy life a bit more, told him to give up the Buddhist chanting and watch the football, talking of which, did you see the game last night? United were awfully good, you know.' Flack would say that no, football didn't interest him, well, not as much as cricket anyway, so he hadn't seen the game and wouldn't be likely to either, but surely the health and welfare of the obit section was not wholly dependent on Lewis and his allegedly preternatural ability to predict the fall of the scythe? No, of course not, would be Lewis's reply, that would be foolish, though I do like the way you lawyers use the word 'allegedly', it's as if you can't help yourselves, as if nothing is ever true unless it's been proved by a barrage of legal arguments, but going back to your question, no, good though my sixth sense is I also rely on a network of contacts, one which has been established over the years, a sort of informal death watch organisation whose members are alert to any impending demise, so long, that is, that it's not of the local newsagent, or dustbin man, or road sweeper, for noble though such men are one would hardly expect to pick up *The Record* or any other paper of repute and find their lives catalogued therein, now would one, Mr Flack? But sometimes, for all its intricacy, the system failed: a famous person would die, sans pre-written obit or, as Lewis put it, 'off radar'. This was the kind of death he most feared, for it meant a frantic scrabbling to assess and determine facts and might even, horror of horrors, entail commissioning a freelance to write the obit. 'Never like to do that,' said Lewis. 'Prefer to have the obits done in-house. That way we keep the right tone and the right voice, and I know the facts have all been checked properly. I always worry with freelancers. I mean, if they're that good, why aren't they on staff?'

On the evening of Flack's last shift Lewis, normally as bombastic as his cheeks were pink, found himself running low on bonhomie as Flack continued to linger, soundless, in his doorway. He tried again to coax a word from the paper's night lawyer, a man he had known for a quarter of a century, asking him, this time in a serious fashion, how the night's stories were panning out. 'Anything especially problematic?' he enquired. 'I hear that Murder of the Century trial is throwing up a few issues. I hear the accused has got some pretty serious prior form, but of course we can't publish any of it, can we?'

Still Flack said nothing. By now Lewis was beginning to feel thoroughly ill at ease. It wasn't that Flack was staring menacingly at him, but he was, decidedly, possessed by an air of menace. The question, it struck Lewis, was what might become of it.

Suddenly, Flack moved. Elegantly and determinedly, he took a step into the obit office. 'Good evening, Archie,' he said. 'Do please accept my apologies. I wasn't myself for a minute back then. That damn murder trial is putting me through my paces. You wouldn't believe the number of court orders there are in its wake. It's an effort to remember whether we can even mention it, let alone any of the factual stuff. And on my last shift, too. Not what the doctor ordered, I can tell you. I signed up for a nice, quiet evening followed by a pint in The Rose.'

Lewis found himself experiencing the same kind of relief already felt by Dixon and O'Donoghue: his old colleague, and sometime drinking partner, Harry Flack, had returned. It was a pleasure to have him back. 'I can imagine, Harry,' he said. 'Not at all what you want on your last night. But it's true. It really *is* your last shift, isn't it?'

Flack confirmed that it was, though Lewis would have known anyway. As one of Flack's old muckers, he was invited to lunch the following week, a celebration of Flack's unstinting service convened by Phillips of the legal department, her rationale for a post-event get together being that a night lawyer's farewell on the evening of his or her last shift is, by definition, barely registered, both because night lawyers are, in almost all cases, invisible, hardly known to each other let alone to journalists on the newspaper for which they ply their trade, and because even when, as in Flack's case, they have become a known quantity, part of a newspaper's furniture, by the time their shift has finished almost everyone else has gone home, certainly the day lawyers, anyway, not to mention a great many of the paper's principal journalists, men like Dixon, O'Donoghue and Lewis, the kind who would insist on being present and whom someone like Flack would wish to be present, a set of facts which makes for limited value in official farewells and send-offs on the night of a lawyer's last shift, even if it is one by so respected a figure as Flack.

'You are coming next week, aren't you?' asked Flack.

Lewis replied that he wouldn't dream of missing Flack's farewell do.

'Excellent,' said Flack. 'But tell me one thing. A favour, if you will.'

'Anything you like, Harry. What is it?'

'Do you have an obit already written for Eddie Conrad?'

Lewis paused, then said: 'You mean Eddie Conrad, the editor? *Our* editor, as of this morning?'

'The very same,' replied Flack.

'That's an interesting question, Harry. A very interesting question. I suspect mine is not to reason why, but yes, there is one on him. I had Jessica write it after his skirmish with the Attorney-General. Something made me think it would be wise to get things down, whether on paper, digitally stored, saved on a hard drive somewhere, I didn't care so long as they were recorded. You know what I mean? Mind you, now that he's our leader perhaps I'd better take a fresh look at it.'

'Can I see it, please, Archie?'

Lewis hesitated, then walked along the rows of filing cabinets behind his desk, thumbing their drawers until he reached one marked 'C'. He pulled it open, delved momentarily inside and produced a single page of A4. 'You're not thinking of bumping him off, are you?' he said, as he gave Flack the piece of paper.

Flack chuckled. 'Nothing could be further from my mind. I just wanted to remind myself about him. Didn't he have a nickname – "The Collector" – or something like that?'

'He did, Harry, you're right. If you want to know why, read on.'

Flack read on.

Eddie Conrad, who has died aged [ ], epitomised the fearless, old-school and sometimes unscrupulous Fleet Street editor in the uneasy days when Fleet Street was making its transition from reality to metaphor. His was an era which spanned the heyday of the libel laws, the advent of the internet, the rise of privacy as a cause of action and televisual and online convergence. Ultimately, this was also the time of the death of the newspaper as Conrad, for one, knew and loved it.

Conrad edited three national newspapers: The Star, The Echo, and The Record. In his first two hot seats, he acquired the not wholly complimentary nickname of 'The Collector'. This was because of his knack of collecting writs from the major libel law firms of the day, the likes of Carter-Ruck, Schillings and David Price & Co. To his staff, that he did so was a badge of courage, a statement of his refusal to be cowed by the technical and arcane laws of libel; to his bosses, and detractors, Conrad was reckless, a man who evinced little more than a cavalier disregard for truth and accuracy. But either way, there was no doubting his success: for each of The Star, The Echo *and* The Record *[note: check], Conrad arrested what appeared to be an endemic decline in sales and, in his enthusiastic declaration that 'the modern editor is not just a wordsmith; he is a brand champion', put tangible profits on the bottom line.*

Tall, black-haired and handsome, Conrad was born in Plaistow, East London, the son of a tax lawyer father and accountant mother. He read English at Exeter before studying law via the Common Professional Examination. However, he eschewed the opportunity to go into the law, opting to fulfil what he once described as 'my destiny – words'. Harbouring dreams of becoming a writer, Conrad took a lowly desk boy's job on the Tower Hamlets Herald, but before long had caught the eye of the sports editor of The Star, *Jim Bruce. Under Bruce's tutelage Conrad rose swiftly, working his way first through sport and then the features and news sections of the paper with scoop after scoop. Before long he was news editor, then deputy editor, and then, inevitably, editor.*

Among Conrad's many triumphs at The Star *were the cash for questions story, the MPs' expenses saga and the exposure of systemic racism in the Metropolitan police in the wake of the famous Jones shooting. But at* The Echo, *his knack for being sued reached new highs. For reasons that he never explained, Conrad decided to ride roughshod over the contempt of court laws in publishing details of an accused's alleged sex offences in an especially ghastly sex killing trial. To do so was to fly in the face of the law and sundry court orders; it meant, too, the inevitable collapse of the trial and a substantial fine by the Attorney-General.*

But, as so often, Conrad's flair saw him through. He was appointed editor of The Record, *the longest-running newspaper in the world, in [ ]. His inaugural editorial conference saw the man on typical form. 'I want to nail the bastard,' he said, of the accused in the notorious 'Murder of the Century' trial, which was then drawing to a close.*

A great raconteur, Conrad delighted in being known as a ladies' man. He never married but was rumoured to have fathered a daughter, although, as he put it, somewhat shamelessly for modern

tastes: 'No one ever proved it.' Having edited The Record *for [ ]*
years, he retired to [ ]. He died of [ ] in [ ].

Flack had sat down at Jessica Steidl's desk to read the obit. He suggested,
when he had finished, that Jessica must have had another look at it only
that very morning. Lewis took the piece of A4 and, having read his
colleague's obituary himself, tutted in agreement. 'Yes, very proactive
of her,' he declared. 'No sooner had Jess heard of Mr Conrad's elevation
to the summit of *The Record* than she had updated his obit. More to
the point, she's obviously asked around and got a bit of gossip from
morning conference. Excellent. That's the kind of staff I like. However,
somewhat inevitably, given that Mr Conrad is still alive, it peters out a
bit at the end.'

'True,' said Flack. 'And I'm sure that a man like Conrad will die with
a two-page obit to his name, too. A single page of A4 makes for barely
half a page of newsprint – that could never be enough for him.'

'You're absolutely right, Harry. By the time our man is in the morgue
I'll have made sure that Jess has filed another 500 words. Anything less
would be a travesty.'

'Well, I should hope she does your bidding – she's been working for
you for long enough,' said Flack.

'Yes, I know. Couldn't do without her. But tell me, Harry, why did
you want to read our new editor's obit?'

By now, Archie Lewis, self-proclaimed keeper of the souls of the dead,
or, at least, those favoured enough by *The Record* to be immortalised in
its newsprint, had returned Conrad's obituary to its rightful place amid
his dusty filing cabinets. Flack remained sitting at Steidl's desk, and, to
Lewis's dismay, it seemed that his eyes had reacquired the vacant, yet
threatening, stare with which they had scrutinised the inner sanctum
of the obituary department only a few minutes ago.

Eventually, after a frozen few minutes in which Lewis attempted to
busy himself with mundane tasks, Flack spoke.

'Archie, you've been a good friend. Do come next week. Everything
will make sense then. It's just that I'm a bit fraught now. Just one
question, if I may.'

Lewis said of course, Harry could ask ten questions if he wanted.

'That shudder of yours, the one you feel when people are about to
snuff it. Have you felt it in connection with Conrad?'

This, though, proved a question too far.

'Harry, what on earth has got into you?' exclaimed Lewis. 'I'm sorry old fellow, but that was in very poor taste.'

Flack's disinterested stare disappeared. Touched at once by Lewis's embarrassment, he apologised profusely, before saying:

'Maybe it's last-night nerves? I don't know. Tonight feels strange, and today was stranger still. But I just felt it necessary to check – you know, to *check*, to verify, to ascertain the nature of the man through the facts appended to his life. And to see where he stood, where he's going. You know what I mean, don't you?'

Archie Lewis, keeper of the souls of the dead, nodded.

Part 3

CHAPTER 21

Flack's Last Shift

Flack's return to Dixon and O'Donoghue passed without comment. It was approaching 6pm, and despite their concern at Flack's erratic behaviour the revise editors could ill afford to engage in small talk every time he reappeared. Neither man looked up as Flack sat down at his desk, but Berlin did greet the veteran night lawyer, albeit with a slight frown rather than a smile.

'I must admit that I advised making a change to one of the obits,' she said, tentatively. 'Here, take a look. Did I do the right thing?'

Berlin placed a print-out of Sion Macfarlane's obituary in front of Flack. Halfway down the third column of an otherwise uncontroversial 800-word piece, in which Macfarlane's revolutionary ways with rubber were recounted, a passage had been ringed in red. Flack quickly read it, at the same time noting that he'd scrawled 'Legal OK' on the right-hand side of the proof. Then he pushed the page along the desk, back to Berlin.

'Very good,' he said. 'You passed my little test.'

The sense that Flack's words lacked conviction was accentuated by the absence of any elaboration, as well as the anaemic, sallow hue of his features. He simply sat still, staring at his PC, for perhaps thirty seconds, without even registering that Berlin had spoken. But then his face creased as if an idea had suddenly formed.

'Tell me,' he said, looking earnestly at Berlin, his cheeks filling with colour, 'when you said just now that you'd "advised" making a change, does that mean that you have been and seen someone about this change? And, moreover, that you have dispensed your legal advice, and that someone has gone and made the change you'd advised?'

'Yes,' said Berlin. 'You were away for quite a while, so I thought you must have been waylaid somewhere. Richard told me where to find Archie Lewis, so I went and saw him. He was happy to make the change. He said he had his doubts about that bit and was expecting to hear from you.'

'But I've just been with Archie myself,' said Flack. 'I wonder, why didn't he ask me about this himself? And how did we miss each other?'

Berlin said she didn't know. She added that she hoped Flack didn't mind her going ahead in this way.

'Not at all,' replied Flack, now agreeability itself. 'Initiative is a good thing. It's an essential thing. It's the *sine qua non*, as we Latinists like to say, of night lawyering. And of a great many other things too, not least the work of the good people who toil in this building to produce *The Record*. And let's face it, we can't go round publishing unsubstantiated allegations of sibling rivalry and base rumours of drinking, gambling and womanising among the heirs of Sion Macfarlane. We'd get a writ before we knew what day it was. No, you did absolutely the right thing. I marked the piece Legal OK but I just wanted to test your mettle.' His words grew quieter, before he concluded: 'Very good. You did very well. I'm sure you'll make the grade. You'll be sitting here with these two old lags on your own before they can say "Why can't journalists write anymore?" Well done.'

There was something unconvincing about Flack's speech. Its initial liveliness seemed to taper off into a cul-de-sac from which even a tried and trusted joke at the revise editors' expense provided no relief. His cheeks were again wan, his eyes flat and dull. Dixon and O'Donoghue exchanged another worried glance; Berlin chose to ask if there was anything else she could do to help.

'Why, of course!' exclaimed Flack, leaping up and waving his arms in the air. Once he had sat down again, a bare three seconds later, he continued. 'Newspapers are never dull. That's the thing about them. Something is always happening, even if it's a fiction, or a wicked invasion of someone's privacy, or a scurrilous piece of phone hacking, or the product of an evil editor whose motives we can only imagine and who might even be having an affair with another editor. Ours is not to reason why but there is always something for the likes of us to do. Isn't that right, Mr Dixon?'

Urged to say something, Dixon came up with a toneless 'Quite so, Harry, quite so' before continuing to write an e-mail. A moment or two later it pinged into the inbox of every single employee of *The Record*, and, indeed, that of its night lawyer. Flack read it, and chortled freely, as if he didn't have a care in the world.

'Here, have a read of this,' he said to Berlin. 'Very good, Richard,' he added.

Hi,
Yes, this is a kneejerk reaction to any potential lawlessness on our
pages, but we'll opt for the unhyphenated modifier of the Collins
Dictionary *rather than the hyphenated preference of the* Oxford.
     P.S. Obviously no caps needed.

Levity again, thought O'Donoghue, as he too read the e-mail. He
wondered how long it would last. Something was awry. He'd never
known Flack to be inconstant in any aspect of his life. Flack was as
safe as houses, or maybe it would be better to say that he was a safe
pair of hands, or even, thought O'Donoghue – who could never resist
the urge to find as many tautologous idioms as possible, once he'd
alighted upon one – it was best to say that he was as steady as a rock,
but whatever the cliché one thing was true: Flack was a man you could
rely upon to keep a firm hand on the tiller, he was a man who would
keep his eye on the ball, he could be counted on, he'd be the last man
standing come rain or shine or a late night phone call from an angry
lawyer, or editor, or judge, and this was vital in the fraught business
of pre-publication risk assessment given the consequences of hare-
brained advice, or even monkey business, for there is many a slip twixt
cup and lip and tonight the fact was that O'Donoghue's colleague of
so many years seemed very likely to make just such a slip, what with
his jumping up and saying he was a night lawyer, his speech about the
Cerne Abbas giant, his lingering looks at the young trainee and his
bizarre comings and goings, not to mention his morose silences and
ludicrous pretence that he'd set the poor young woman a test. Had he
lost the plot? And what must the girl think of all this? *OK, she's not a*
girl, but I'm old enough to be her father, thought O'Donoghue, *and to*
me she might as well be a girl. He felt protective towards Berlin, and as
much as he was worried about Flack he was vexed with him, too. This
was not the way to treat a young woman who'd come in to learn the
ropes. The metaphor made him think of boxing, and the novels of F.X.
Toole, which he'd commended to many people including Flack, though
he had no idea whether the night lawyer had taken up his suggestion
and read anything by the former cornerman turned scribe; this literary
journey in turn prompted O'Donoghue to wonder if a clip round the
ear might be the best way of knocking some sense into Flack. But then
he heard Dixon speaking, to the room as much as Flack.

'Hyphens are a perennial problem,' he declared. 'I have no idea why but they seem to cause such difficulty.'

O'Donoghue heard himself agreeing. 'Very true,' he said.

'The Style Guide is clear,' continued Dixon. 'We should be ...'

'Sparing with them,' interrupted O'Donoghue

'Exactly,' said Dixon. 'Sparing is the word. The right word. We should be sparing with hyphens. We should run together words which look right together, and where there is sense in doing so, like *intercontinental, motorcycle* and *takeover*. I'm sending another note on this now.'

As good as his word, the inboxes of O'Donoghue and Flack, and everyone else at *The Record*, pinged again:

Hi,
...*a hyphen is rarely needed for words with the -esque suffix.*
Trusting that, like Gregor Samsa, my counsel has legs.

'Another gem,' said Flack. O'Donoghue looked across at Berlin. To his relief, she was smiling. What she made of the evening so far was impossible to tell, but mercifully, for now, she seemed happy. So did Flack, but disconcertingly so. Perhaps Dixon and the girl saw it, too: a look of derangement in Flack's eyes.

A moment later, again as if an extraordinary idea had just struck him, Flack all but shouted: 'Kafkaesque, Richard! Kafkaesque! No hyphen! But hot-water bottle – there's a hyphen there, and that's the truth. But as for hotpants, a pair would look very good on the lovely lady sitting next to me, better yet next to her, she having removed them, but either way were they to appear, on or off this gorgeous female – if this were to be the most miraculous of evenings at *The Record* – they wouldn't have a hyphen, would they? They'd look good, and we'd all admire them, but if we were to commit our thoughts about hotpants to writing we wouldn't use a hyphen. Don't worry, there's no need to answer. I've picked up a lot over the years, working with you and Denis. I should know what to do with hotpants by now. But that was a lovely little note about the *esque* suffix. You're on form tonight, Richard.'

The room was thick with embarrassment. No one knew what to say. But O'Donoghue muttered: 'Which is more than can be said for you.' He said it loudly enough for everyone in the small office to hear. He was certain that Dixon and Berlin had heard him, and he hoped that the girl might thank him for it, silently, at least. Flack, though, was humming a tune and had evidently heard nothing.

*

'This is the letters page,' announced Flack, a few minutes later. 'It's a bit like the obits. There's never anything on it to worry about. You can just call them up and tell them it's Legal OK.'

The letters page had been delivered by a messenger, a young man of about twenty whose job it was, from 4pm each day, to ferry things from place to place in *The Record*. For the most part, his cargo comprised internal memoranda, newsletters, invites from PRs and letters from readers, but sometimes his help would be enlisted in getting copy to the night lawyers and revise editors. Pippa Kennedy, the paper's deputy letters editor, had done just this at approximately five past six. 'Here, would you mind?' she'd said, as the man, whose name no one knew, still less thought to ask, passed with his trolley. 'If you could pop this page down to Harry I'd be ever so grateful.' On the proof, she'd written her extension number. The young man had taken the proof and said 'No problem'. In the ordinary course of things, Flack would read the page promptly and tell her that it was acceptable – or not, for sometimes even the letters page threw up legal issues, as in the infamous case of Telnikoff v Matusevitch, which was the consequence of a letter written by Mr Matusevitch and published in *The Daily Telegraph*. Flack knew of this case well; it had gone on for ten years. Even if it had finally resulted in a pyrrhic victory for Mr Telnikoff – whose award of damages was ruled unenforceable in the state of Maryland, to which Matusevitch, a Russian like his courtroom adversary, had moved – it remained a textbook reminder of the dangers posed by the letters page.

Berlin knew the Telnikoff case too. Everyone in libel law did, save for the chancers. It and other precedents were ample evidence of the need to take care over letters. It was all very well for The Maryland Court of Appeals to declare that upholding Telnikoff's award of £240,000 would be 'repugnant to the public policy of Maryland' – and also to note that 'American and Maryland history reflects a public policy in favor of a much broader and more protective freedom of the press than ever provided for under English law' – but it was another to jettison time-honoured principles of domestic jurisprudence. How could Flack possibly suggest signing off the letters page without even reading it?

'Is this another test?' asked Berlin. To Dixon and O'Donoghue, her voice suggested that she had not enjoyed Flack's vision of her wearing hotpants, or taking them off, one iota. She sounded tense and clipped; acid, even. Both of the revise editors had every sympathy with her. She'd turned up in good faith for her first training shift, clearly knew the law and was a decent person, but the man she was supposed to be learning from was all at sea. Both Dixon and O'Donoghue had inwardly made identical resolutions: to find a way of having a quiet word with Flack, and with Berlin, too.

Flack's answer to Berlin's question made them feel that their quiet word could not come soon enough.

'No, it's not a test. It's a statement of fact. There's never anything to worry about in the letters page and this particular example is the most risk-free page you'll see all night. Now, in order that you get to know people here, I suggest you show a bit of that initiative of yours and go off and find Pippa Kennedy. She's the letters editor. Or deputy letters editor. I can't remember. But it's her number here, and her name, so she's in charge of this page tonight. Go and see her and tell her the page is Legal OK.'

At this, Dixon and O'Donoghue stopped what they were doing. They were mesmerised by how Berlin would respond to Flack's aggressively conveyed order. But instead of the scowl they half-expected, instead of any objection, instead of even a huff, she looked almost sorry for Flack. Gathering up the letters page, she departed in search of Pippa Kennedy.

O'Donoghue seized the moment.

'Harry,' he said, 'what on earth has got into you?'

Flack did not look up from his PC.

Dixon echoed his colleague. 'Harry, come on, snap out of it. Denis is asking a reasonable question. You don't seem yourself at all. What's up? Has something happened?'

'Tell us, Harry,' implored O'Donoghue. 'It's your last shift. You've got a lovely lady in for the night. You're saying things that are upsetting her. You're not right. What is it?'

Slowly, Flack turned to look at the two men. There was Dixon, with all his hair; hair that Flack imagined he'd have until he drew his last breath. Next to him, his face as eager for reassurance as his colleague's, was O'Donoghue, his large frame leaning forward in a pose of solicitude and worry. Flack felt as if he'd been knocked off course. What was he playing at? How could he act so objectionably?

There would be casualties. Hell, there were already casualties. The two old lags. The girl. He'd spoken offensively to her, in a way that he had never countenanced in all his years in the law or anywhere else, for that matter. He'd spoken like his old boss, Dr Tax – full of sexism which could easily be described as outright misogyny. He couldn't blame Berlin if she'd gone off to file a report with HR about him.

No, this had to stop. If Flack was going to engineer a contempt of court so heinous that Eddie Conrad would go to prison, he needed to smarten up his act.

'I'm sorry, gentlemen,' he said. 'You're right to upbraid me. You're right to be concerned. The fact that this is my last shift isn't the problem. It's just that I've seen a ghost. But it's nothing to be concerned about. It was essentially a benign, if sexist, ghost, called Dr Tax. I never expected to see him again, least of all here. But that's it. In speaking of this unwelcome intruder from the past I've performed an exorcism. Let us return to our respective tasks.'

Dixon and O'Donoghue did not feel reassured.

*

Upstairs, on the first floor, Berlin had found Pippa Kennedy. An unexcitable character with a flamboyant dress sense, Kennedy listened intently as Berlin, leaning over her desk, explained that one of the letters posed a legal risk. Her reasoning, thought Kennedy, was impressive.

'Have you just joined the legal department?' asked Kennedy, when Berlin had finished explaining why a letter about a well-known peer could not be published. 'It's just that I haven't seen you before.'

'No,' said Berlin. 'I'm here doing a shift with Harry Flack. The plan is to join the rota, but I'm a qualified barrister already.'

'So Harry got you to come and see me instead of picking up the phone himself? He's getting lazy in his old age.'

'He's busy on some other stories. Besides, he wants me to get to know people.'

'Well, it's a pleasure to meet you. But are you *sure* we can't run this letter? Is it really so bad to call His Lordship a paedophile?'

The second question was delivered in such a deadpan tone that, for a moment, Berlin took it seriously. Just as she was about to reply, Kennedy broke into a smile.

'Don't worry,' she said. 'I'll get rid of it. I only put it in as a joke for

Harry's last shift. I know he'd never have let it through. It'd cost us a fortune in libel damages.'

*

Henry Garms had been *The Record's* diarist for as long as anyone could remember. An Old Etonian, he seemed to know half of London – the half worth knowing, at any rate. His charm was as expansive as his liking for fine wine and it, together with the wine, was one of the reasons he received so many tips, but as well as being well connected, ever so slightly suave, sometimes intoxicated and certainly polished he could write, too. His diary was always elegant, often erudite and unfailingly witty, and it was rarely the cause of a legal issue, as much because Garms only ever gently ruffled feathers: his barbs, when he made them, managed to be kind rather than insulting, or complimentary even as they debunked their recipients. Granted, his diary had prompted one or two letters before action over the years; it had even been the subject of a writ on one occasion, when something Garms alleged about a politician having snorted cocaine during Prime Minister's Question Time turned out to be wholly untrue, a base lie and without foundation, not to mention very hurtful and damaging (thus spoke the politician's lawyers). Usually, though, Garms's copy was marked 'Legal OK' by Flack and the other night lawyers – who received it anytime between 6.00 and 6.30pm from a Monday to Friday – without any great expenditure of legal skill.

On Flack's last shift, however, the ordinarily equable diarist strayed into dangerous territory. Flack at once spotted the problems with the lead item on a page of A4 delivered by Garms himself:

> *One of m'learned friends is in touch. She tells me of despair among the judiciary. Judges at the High Court and the Old Bailey are apparently quaffing too much claret of a lunchtime. Their prodigious intake has been disclosed in an audit, and the good justices are now urged to forego their midday tipple. Said Mr Justice Stafford: 'The good old days of being pissed for the afternoon session are over. The law has changed out of all recognition. It is a scandal.' It is, m'lord, it is indeed.*

Flack turned to Garms, who, as was his wont, stood waiting for the verdict on his work.

'Henry,' began the night lawyer, 'where has this comment of Stafford's come from?'

'I had a feeling you might ask me that,' said Garms. 'It's from my source. She's a QC. She heard His Lordship say it. It's cast-iron, Harry. There is not a shadow of doubt about its accuracy. It is, as the modern generation like to say, 110 per cent true.'

Flack murmured something inaudible and again read the piece. As he was doing so, Berlin returned from her trip to see Pippa Kennedy.

'Ah, you're back,' said Flack. 'Everything OK with the letters page?'

Berlin confirmed that it was.

'Excellent,' said Flack. 'Here, have a read of this. It's the diary, as written by Henry here. Tell me what you think.'

Berlin glanced at Garms before sitting down next to Flack. She studied the piece of paper and its various stories. After a couple of minutes she suggested there might be a problem with the lead item. 'It may be true that Mr Justice Stafford said this, but have we got admissible evidence to prove it? If not, we have a problem. There's no way that a judge is going to like being on record as apparently being worse for wear for afternoon court hearings.'

Garms sighed ostentatiously. 'Lawyers! Why do you always have to find problems with my stories?' he asked. He feigned upset, before adding: 'I mean, I go and get a nice, juicy, kosher quote from a brilliant source, turn it into a little bit of knockabout fun, and you query it! Harry, can't something be done about this young lady?'

Flack was quick to reply.

'There is nothing to be done,' he said. It seemed as if he was about to say more, but then he stopped.

'Excuse me?' said Garms.

Flack's silence continued. He looked stern and resolute. Garms – a man who liked to get on with everyone, even if his profession entailed taking them down a peg or two – felt as if he were being criticized for an unintentional but serious mistake.

'Harry,' he offered, as Flack's stony face grew harder, 'I was only joking. I didn't mean to offend your colleague here. I'm sorry.'

'There's nothing to be sorry about,' said Flack. 'The diary is Legal OK.'

Garms looked stunned. 'Really?' he said. 'Even the piece about Judge Stafford?'

'All of it is fine,' said Flack. 'I happen to know of Stafford's habits. There's no way he'll sue. Half of Fleet Street would give us witness statements to stand the story up. It's Legal OK.'

'Thank you, Harry,' said Garms, taking the piece of A4 held out to him by Flack. He departed the office with a look at Berlin that asked if the old man was all right; deftly, she indicated that he wasn't, and that she'd find Garms shortly.

Minutes later, Berlin stood up. 'Excuse me for a moment or two,' she said. None of the three men in the office said a word. In their different ways, each was too discomposed to muster the smallest pleasantry. For Dixon and O'Donoghue, the natural order of things had been turned upside down; Flack, the architect of the subversion, was no less disquieted. Each fidgeted with pens and paper, or files, or busied himself with staring at his computer screen and pointlessly manipulating the cursor. Dixon started to write a note about the distinction between firms and companies, which he planned to end 'Yours firmly', but was unable to concentrate on it. O'Donoghue tried in vain to correct the racing page, which was always one of the first to arrive from sport. Flack absently rifled through a folder containing injunctions.

As soon as she left the revise editors' office Berlin saw Garms. He had not gone far. She noted, with surprise, that he was a well-kept man – trim and healthy-looking despite what she imagined were an awful lot of liquid lunches. And as she approached Garms, who was talking to Clare, the South African sub-editor, Berlin realised he was younger than she had first thought: perhaps in his late thirties, at most. She overheard a snippet of their conversation, something about 'Harry seems to have gone bonkers', before her arrival led Garms to adopt an amiable grin and offer an introduction to Clare, 'One of the paper's real troopers, without her, we'd hardly ever get an issue out,' said Garms. To this, Clare merely nodded.

'I'm sorry to interrupt,' began Berlin, 'but I wonder if we could have a word about the Stafford piece in the diary?'

'Of course,' said Garms. 'Fire away.'

Berlin seemed to hesitate. At once, Garms understood.

'Oh, don't worry about Clare,' he said breezily. 'Clare knows Harry as well as anyone in the building.' Then he checked himself. 'Assuming, that is, that you've sought me out to discuss Harry's advice?'

'Yes, that's right,' said Berlin. Again she dithered: was it right to have this conversation in front of Clare? But then she made up her mind.

There was no time to lose. *The Record* had to be put to bed. Pages had to be got off stone. And at this rate, it was going to be a busy night. She had to be decisive.

'My advice is that you lose the Stafford piece. It's a hostage to fortune. Unless you can tell me that your QC will take the stand on the paper's behalf, I can't see that it's a fair risk for publication.'

Garms stepped back a little. He seemed to puff up his chest, only to exhale audibly.

'Thank God,' he said. 'I thought Harry had gone mad. Maybe he has. But I'll happily take your advice. *Very* happily.'

Clare grimaced at the flirtatious import of Garms's last words. To Berlin, she said: 'How are you finding it here? Full of dinosaurs?'

Berlin laughed. 'They seem harmless enough,' she said.

'Don't be so sure,' said Clare. 'This place redefines "old-school". You'd think the twentieth century hadn't happened. But I'm glad it's going well, though I hear Harry isn't responding too well to the jokes that are coming his way.'

Was that what Garms's diary was – a joke? As Berlin's mind analysed the possibility she recalled the words of Pippa Kennedy, the deputy letters editor: *I only put it in as a joke for Harry's last shift. I knew he'd never let it through. It'd cost us a fortune in libel damages.* So was it a game? A game that Henry was in on? A game that other journalists would be in on for Flack's last shift? And if so, was Flack's agitation all part of the fun?

As soon as she gave credence to the idea Berlin rejected it. Kennedy may have been joking but Garms wasn't. He was relieved to be told that his skit on judges had been spiked. He had known it went over the line. Judges, drinking claret over lunch and then presiding in court? Preposterous. He'd written it not in jest but as part of the daily badinage that went into creating a newspaper, the jostling between journalists and lawyers to produce copy that someone, somewhere, wanted to read. He was playing a role, and the role demanded that Flack, or whichever night lawyer was on duty, said 'No'.

Instead of which, and in deadly seriousness, Flack had said 'Yes'.

It struck Berlin that if it was a game, it was being played by Flack alone.

*

'Ah, there you are. The old lags have been very worried. I was starting to fret too, you know. We thought you'd been spirited away.'

As Berlin sat down she offered her apologies. Dixon and O'Donoghue looked genuinely concerned; for a second, the same look was evident on Flack's features. It soon disappeared, to be replaced by a teasing twist at the corners of his mouth and a wicked twinkle in his eyes.

'Now then, this is a good one for you. It's the City diary. Its author loves nothing more than to be provocative. He likes to make *The Record's* lawyers earn their keep. Would you mind earning yours and telling me what you think of it?'

Flack gave Berlin a proof of the City diary. Like the letters and obit pages, and Garms's diary, it was always one of the first items to be ready for press. Flack did not misrepresent its author's style. Wallace Munroe Moravia was as eccentric as his name. He had a knack for finding nuggets of gossip that enlivened what, in lesser writers, was sometimes a dull part of the newspaper, tending merely to tales of who'd settled the bill in the City's best restaurants or predictions of boardroom reshuffles. Moravia went further, for like Garms he was such a master of both charm and networking that stories seemed to flow to him as inexorably as the incoming tide. But unlike Garms, he was deliberately caustic, self-consciously as sharp and stinging as he could be. As a consequence, his copy often needed the night lawyer's finessing; tonight's was no exception.

Berlin read the City diary with mounting alarm. Each of its five nibs contained legal problems. Three were defamatory, a fourth was a clear contempt of court, the last mocked Portakabin for its well-known insistence on its intellectual property rights. Berlin didn't know where to begin. She was, however, thankful that Moravia – whose mordant wit she had heard of long before she arrived at *The Record* – wasn't hovering above her, waiting for her verdict. Eventually, she turned to Flack, who was looking at her expectantly.

'I think each story has a problem,' she said. 'They could land the paper in varying degrees of hot water. I'd want to have a chat with the diarist and see if there's evidence to stand up the first three nibs.' As she said this, she gestured at the stories – the first, a snide snippet about the CEO of an oil company who had failed to fly to the scene of a major slick because he was booked on a week's golfing holiday; the second, about a well-known advertising executive who, wrote Moravia, 'insists on fighting the ravages of time with that most ineffective of implements – hair dye. If only he was as diligent in representing his clients as he is in plastering it on and looking like a vain old fool'; while the last piece to strike Berlin as libellous was an *ad hominem* paragraph on a soon-to-be-retired supermarket CEO whose wife, it was alleged, had three lovers – one a musician, the other a professional footballer, the last a poet. *Before you ask, it's all true,* said a scrawl of Moravia's handwriting, next to this tale of marital discord which, noted Berlin, was blamed entirely on the husband: 'To lose one's wife to one lover, Mr Worthing, may be regarded as misfortune; to lose her to three looks like impotence.' If these stories struck Berlin as bad enough, the one about Portakabin surely went well over the line:

The Hyde Park Hideousness – or, as its organisers like to call it, The Very Big Party in the Park – is upon us. This weekend superstars from bands like The Rolling Stones, The Stone Roses and Queens of the Stone Age will stone-facedly boogie the night away in an event which is sponsored, for the first time, by major City institutions. Quite what the likes of Goldman Sachs and Coutts will get out of lending their names to a rock festival eludes your diarist but he can report that the lawyers for Portakabin are as busy as ever. This week they have sent missive after missive indicating that on no account must anyone describe the stand-alone relocatable buildings which will be used at the festival as Portakabins for the simple reason that they are not Portakabins but stand-alone relocatable buildings created by a competitor. This sort of thing is important. Thank the Lord for Portakabin's lawyers. They provide a wonderful service. Your diarist will be mindful of their injunctive zeal when he steps into a Portakabin on Hyde Park in a matter of days. He will not, for a second, think: 'Good grief, they really are a bunch of twerps in the Portakabin legal department. I mean, haven't they got anything better to do?' No, he will enjoy every moment of his time in the relocatable Portakabin even if he cannot but help observe that it does smell awfully bad.

Lastly, Berlin drew Flack's attention to the fifth story in Moravia's City diary. She had been relieved to see that Flack studied the text of each story intently. His eyes were just as focused as he read the fifth and final piece, a Moravian skit on a case soon to come before the Old Bailey. The managing director of an international hair product manufacturer was accused of defrauding shareholders and inflicting grievous bodily harm on a whistleblower who'd tried to alert the authorities to his boss's malfeasance. 'Davenport-Hides has form for this sort of thing,' wrote Moravia. 'Who can forget the time he punched an employee in the face for saying 'Good morning' in a lift, when he felt it was not a good morning, or the infamous case of the missing millions when a Cayman trust he'd set up slipped from its mooring and ended up in the Bermuda Triangle? Both times a criminal conviction followed. And surely any right-thinking jury will convict again when this waste of taxpayers' money is finally over.'

Flack tutted. 'Well, well, well,' he offered, to no one in particular. 'It seems that our friend Wallace has pushed the boat out tonight.'

'You agree then?' asked Berlin.

'Oh yes,' said Flack. 'Yes indeed. These stories amount to a mini legal minefield. It doesn't take a genius to work out why but well done anyway. Good job you're paying attention.'

Berlin ignored this comment. She felt unable to do the same with Flack's next statement.

'Four of the pieces need a bit of work. By all means go and find Wallace and sort them out. You know what you're doing and I'm sure you'll do well. But tell him the thing about Davenport-Hides is Legal OK.'

'What? You can't be serious!' said Berlin, raising her voice so loudly that Dixon and O'Donoghue turned to look at her. 'It's a blatant contempt of court! We can't go round publishing details of his previous convictions and speculating on what the jury will do. It's just not on!'

'Oh yes, it is,' said Flack, brightly. 'Don't you worry about a thing. A directive came round about this case from the court. The normal rules don't apply. It's absolutely fine. Legal OK.'

Berlin pushed her chair back violently and stood up. She glared at Flack, who returned her gaze with mock innocence.

'Trust me, I'm a night lawyer!' he all but bellowed, as Berlin strode from the room with Moravia's diary in her hand.

*

'Harry, I'm troubled by this story on page five. Do you think we can run this picture with it?'

The speaker was a woman in her mid-thirties called Lisa Halls. A fine journalist, she had risen through the ranks at *The Record* as effortlessly as a house on fire, or, if O'Donoghue were to have been tasked with supplying a synonymous idiom, like a knife through butter. She knew her law almost as well as she knew how to write; only rarely did she ever need a second opinion. On Flack's last shift, she sought advice on a picture of a celebrity who had been arrested on a charge of being drunk and disorderly. It was illustrated by a photograph of him taking an evidently soothing and much-needed gulp from a bottle of Heineken. He was clearly the worse for wear.

'I've been debating this with the picture desk,' said Halls. 'They've dug it out and say that it can't possibly cause a problem, because it's true – our favourite drunken celeb really was drunk at the Munich Beer Festival, at which this pic was taken. But if he's just been arrested for being drunk and disorderly, surely it's not a good idea to have this as the accompanying image, even if it is true?'

Flack stared at the proof, with its potentially dubious photograph, for at least a minute. He then opened his mouth to speak, only to say nothing and return to intently scrutinising the page. The silence went on for so long that Halls was moved to make a hesitant prompt.

'Harry,' she said, 'er, do you have an opinion? I'm sorry to press you – it's just that the page needs to go as soon as possible.'

Flack startled her with the bombast of his reply.

'Of course I do! I'm a night lawyer, aren't I? The picture is fine. I know what you're thinking – that it might be prejudicial, that somehow a jury, in the dim and distant future, will conclude that our man must have been drunk and disorderly, not just because of the facts of which he is accused but because of his prior form, that which we have chosen to illustrate so unsubtly here. But the truth is otherwise. There is no danger of contempt of court. An advisory note from the Attorney-General came through about this very matter earlier today. It has been decreed from on high that this picture is absolutely fine.'

Halls looked dumbfounded. She looked first to Dixon, then to O'Donoghue, for confirmation. As Flack waved her away and re-engaged with his computer, both men surreptitiously shook their heads. O'Donoghue added a hand motion to suggest that their colleague had gone mad.

Picking up the proof, Halls quietly thanked Flack and left the office.

*

Flack was laughing when his mobile phone rang. Deciding against reading any of the stories that were now arriving thick and fast from various quarters of *The Record*, he had been reacquainting himself with Dixon's notes on style. He had just discovered, in an e-mail folder in which he stored 'Dixon's gems', the following:

> Another example of fluvial illiteracy has managed to meander past us and pollute the pure pool of our published labours.
> *The Style Guide notes:*
> Teesside no hyphen, double 's' in middle; but note Deeside in both Scotland and Wales.

The voice on the end of the line brought him up short.

'Hello, Harry, it's Pat here. How are you?'

Momentarily lost for words, Flack recovered well enough to realise that the voice belonged to his boss, Patricia Phillips. But why was she calling, at 6.30pm or thereabouts, just as his work as a night lawyer was about to enter the most critical phase of the evening?

'I'm very well, Pat, thanks.'

It was all that Flack could think to say. Phillips was surprised: even when he was under pressure, Flack was unruffled and courteous. He never failed to ask how things were, or to enquire, a gentleman in every situation, to what he owed the pleasure. Immediately, Phillips regretted calling him. She'd done so principally to check that all was under control, but also because she felt for Flack, having to come in for the entire day on his last shift. But now, as the night lawyer she most respected was tongue-tied – so much so that she could sense his discomfort – she felt guilty. Flack was obviously having a hell of a night; worse, she'd rung just as the op-ed pages would be arriving, not to mention the news stories and tricky regulars like the City diary.

'Good, Harry, jolly good,' she heard herself saying. 'I just rang to check that everything was OK. I feel so awful for landing you with such a beast of a day. Are you sure you're all right?'

'I'm absolutely fine, Pat, absolutely fine,' said Flack. 'Don't you worry about me. Don't worry about a thing. It's all under control.'

*

The office was quiet. Each of its occupants – Dixon, O'Donoghue, Harry

Flack and Maya Berlin – was superficially rapt in their respective tasks. In fact, three of them were merely relieved that some fifteen minutes had passed without incident. The fourth – the possessor of years and years of legal experience, perhaps London's best exponent of practical, at-the-coalface media law, the man looked up to by so many other Fleet Street lawyers and known even to journalists – this man was quiet because, once again, he was reading his folder of Dixon's gems. There he discovered a note from the past on the dread subject of relocatable loos:

> Sources with their ear to the ground, so to speak, inform me that the lavatory facilities at the Glastonbury Festival are not supplied by Portaloo.
> So please refer to them by the generic portable toilets or other appropriate phrases.
> Yours, rockin'n'rollin'

This time, Flack did not laugh out loud. Instead, he focused on the sign-off chosen by Dixon. It was an allusion not just to Glastonbury, but also to Dixon's hobby in his spare time: he was a DJ, playing often in clubs and wedding venues which were, ideally, within a radius of three hours' drive from Central London (though he was happy to travel further for the right event). Not only was he a DJ, he was also a drummer and percussionist. Whether DJing or playing the drums, congas, bongos or tambourine, Dixon's preferred musical genres were soul, blues, jazz and Latino. 'He sings pretty well, too,' O'Donoghue had once told him.

Why hadn't he, Flack, ever heard Dixon playing, or singing, or seen him at work as a DJ? It struck him as somehow negligent that his view of Dixon, a colleague and friend for so long, was one-dimensional, that he knew Dixon to be an eloquent and witty pedant but that he knew nothing of his musical side. How, for that matter, did the two things co-exist? Witty though he was Dixon's pedantry was finite, exacting, indisputable; Flack, a jazz-lover, saw music as something lawless, improvised and ambiguous. If he had made an effort to get to know Dixon outside work, perhaps Flack would understand how two things which were ostensibly antithetical could prosper in one man – but he hadn't made that effort. He'd drifted along, amiably enough, conversing happily with Dixon – and O'Donoghue and a number of other journalists over the years – at work, sometimes in The Rose, sometimes in other Wapping pubs, but virtually never accepting their invitations for supper, or to go to a football match, or to attend some other event which would move the friendship along.

Why had he been like this? Flack looked over at Dixon, who was absorbed in his work, professional to the last; then he looked at O'Donoghue, the gentle giant who loved boxing and, if the rumours were true, could boast of a distinguished record as an amateur in his twenties. True or not, O'Donoghue was no less preoccupied, every bit as professional as his colleague, staunchly marking sentences in front of him with a red pen that he insisted was 'every pedant's best friend'.

Flack knew neither man well. He regretted the distance he'd kept, and he regretted the upset he'd caused them on this, his last shift, a night when they'd probably organised a farewell card and a collection. In a flash he understood just how unnerving his behaviour had been – not just to the two old lags but for the girl, too. What had he been thinking of, coarsely talking of hotpants, even going on to imagine them taken off (by whom he couldn't say) and lying next to her and, yet worse, letting everyone know that this was in his mind? How gross and insulting, how base an example of the sexism he'd hated all his life, how all the more regrettable given that he was old enough to be her father. And yet, even as he felt mortified, his mind meandered into an altogether different arena, the room in his Fulham flat into which he'd stealthily crept only to find Eddie Conrad on top of his fiancée, naked, her knickers discarded at the end of the bed, a black, sheer pair that he'd never seen before, mocking him as inadequate, as a failed lover, as a man who even when confronted by his partner's betrayal couldn't help but think of a famous libel case involving the heaving buttocks of a large and ugly South African for he, Flack, was the prospective husband who knew too much about the hidden byways of defamation law and nothing of the secrets of his woman, of her willingness to wear and remove racy underwear, of the desperation she felt to be with another man.

Conrad. There he was again. Conrad, the author not of novels of renown but of Flack's misfortune. If it hadn't been for him, how different life would have been. He'd have been happy. He'd have had pride. He'd have been capable. He'd have avoided humiliation. He'd have let his guard down and made friends and perhaps even had another relationship, one that meant something anyway (perhaps with Martha – what on earth had become of her?). He'd have lived.

In front of him, in the pile of proofs that was growing by the minute as journalists rushed in, deposited them and rushed out, were the op-ed pages. These, too, were always among the earliest pages to be given to the night lawyer and revise editors. Flack looked at them in despair. Should he continue with his plan? Or should he abandon it as nothing more than a doomed slice of Saturnalia, a throw of the dice that had no meaning because the game had long since ended? Worse, Flack's uprising was in danger not of hurting its object, Eddie Conrad, but of alienating those closest to him – the two revise editors with whom he'd worked for so long, not to mention a number of journalists whom he could, in his own peculiar way, count as friends and the young woman who'd come in to learn the ropes. Perhaps more than anyone else she didn't deserve to be caught up in Flack's attempt to engineer what the Roman poet Catullus called 'the best of days', when a sacrifice in honour of Saturn, the god of many things including dissolution, liberation and renewal, at the Temple of Saturn in the Roman Forum culminated in a riotous public banquet that turned society upside down, so much so that masters apparently provided table service for their slaves. Would Flack's subversion achieve the best of days? He reviewed his efforts so far. He had signed off Garms's diary and the City diary despite both containing blatant examples of contempt of court. The girl had beaten him to it with the obit and the letter about the peer. He thought he'd done enough to convince Lisa Halls to run the photograph of the celebrity who was drunk – another nice little slice of contempt. Flack smiled: a fabric was emerging, tomorrow's paper would be so full of disregard for the contempt laws that the Attorney-General would have no option but to prosecute. After all, there was the Leveson Inquiry rumbling away; if ever there was a time when the media should behave well, it was now, and yet already Flack had engineered a series of willful acts of contempt, flagrantly ignoring the Contempt of Court Act 1981. The night was still relatively young; there would be other opportunities soon, added to which he had no doubt that he could facilitate a few indefensible libels, perhaps also a copyright infringement and – praise be to Portakabin – a trade mark violation, too. It was too good an opportunity for revenge, and why, when all was said and done, should he not proceed with it? The discomfort felt by his colleagues would be temporary; they would recover and get on with their lives; most importantly, no one could accuse any of them of having anything to do with *The Record's* unique appearance the day after Flack's last shift as the newspaper that spawned the highest number of legal complaints in history and saw, for the first time in decades, the imprisonment of an editor.

Flack felt the muscles in his forearms twitch – nerves, perhaps – as he resumed his scrutiny of the proofs on his desk. The op-ed page contained a piece on the government's economic policy for inner cities, another on the rise of the far right, and a third on a relatively recent phenomenon, the super-injunction, the inhibition on freedom of speech that was so secret that no one, save a select group of lawyers, even knew about it. Those who did know about a given super-injunction were prohibited from mentioning its existence, a judicial development of which *The Record's* writer did not approve. Virginia Whitton, a respected political commentator, went for the jugular:

> *It is time to stand up to one of the most rank developments in English legal history. The super-injunction sneaked in by the back door and must now be cast out, set alight and destroyed. Not even its ashes should remain.*
>
> *We're not supposed to know about super-injunctions but, of course, we do. People talk. In today's age, people don't just talk – they tweet. They go online and use all manner of social media. A super-injunction – or just your common-or-garden injunction – is no sooner granted than it is gossiped about.*
>
> *What, then, is the point? On a practical level, it is absurd to think that anyone can go to court and obtain an order that restricts the publication of certain information to the extent that the mere fact that the order has been granted cannot be talked or tweeted about, let alone formally reported. On a jurisprudential level, the super-injunction is a gross injustice. It is a time-honoured principle that justice must not only be done but be seen to be done. The existence of super-injunctions flies in the face of this and with our essential rights to free speech. How is it right that merely mentioning the existence of a court order amounts to a contempt of court?*

Whitton went on in a similar vein, adding her personal experience of one or two individuals who had sought and obtained super-injunctions – without naming them. And then she dropped a bombshell.

I can tell you, now, about Axel Austin. I have only met the American

celebrity chef once or twice but the self-styled Drawl from the
Deep South is as full of charisma in real life as he is on screen. A
straight-talking family man, as honest as the day is long, and such
an Anglophile! No wonder we're buying his books in bucketloads,
desperate to learn how to make Mississippi Comeback Sauce
and Hoppin' John Jambalaya. We've fallen for Austin, but there's
something we didn't know about him. Two years ago, he took time
out from cooking up a storm to acquire a nice and shiny super-
injunction.

Why did Austin need a super-injunction? For a reason as old
as the Alabama hills – he didn't want anyone to know about an
extra-marital affair he'd had with the woman who ghosted his
bestselling books.

Ultimately, though, Austin proved that he was a good 'ol boy,
after all. He withdrew his super-injunction, saying he'd made an
error of judgement. As he put it, as the leaks grew and social media
lit up with details of what no one was supposed to know: 'I come
from the United States of America. We have the First Amendment.
I got it wrong.'

At this point in the text Whitton had appended a Post-it note. On it, in
her meticulous handwriting, was a question.

To tonight's lawyer: everyone knows who Austin was shagging.
Can we name her? She has a super-injunction too but it'd be great
if we could put it out there.

And the text ran on:

Austin saw the error of his ways. But what of the ghost? The
woman behind Austin's endless books, magazine and newspaper
columns? She's a ghost no more. Her name is Bonnie Farrow, she's
also married, and she lives in London. And Bonnie, it's time you
did the right thing, too.

Flack chuckled. *Of course,* he thought, *of course we can reveal the ghost's*
identity! The consequences are irresistible! How wonderful! He wrote
on the page: 'Great news – it's Legal OK to name Farrow. We received
word from the court a couple of hours ago. She too has given up her

injunction. It's open season!'

Then he stood up, cleared his throat, and announced to the room:

'Excuse me while I go and discuss an important and delicate matter with Virginia at op-ed.'

*

'Excuse me,' said Berlin, once Flack had gone. 'What's "op-ed"?'

Dixon was the first to answer.

'Harry should have told you,' he said. 'It stands for "opposite editorial". And it does what it says on the tin.'

'As in, the op-ed page is this page, the one that sits opposite the leaders, which are otherwise known as the editorial,' added O'Donoghue. He held his op-ed proof up, next to the page of leaders. It seemed to Berlin to contain innumerable red marks.

'Are there always so many mistakes?' she asked.

'Oh yes,' said O'Donoghue. 'This specimen is actually quite good, in comparison with what we usually get.'

'I'm afraid my friend is right,' said Dixon. 'Sometimes we wonder if anyone here ever studied English.'

'It's just as well that we're here, toiling away on the frontier,' said O'Donoghue.

'The frontier?' said Berlin.

'Yes, the frontier. The final frontier. After us there's nothing but the printers and the presses. And then the readers.'

'We are the last bastion of linguistic orthodoxy,' declared Dixon.

'And harmony,' offered O'Donoghue.

'Is it fun?'

Berlin's question seemed to surprise the two men. Both took a few moments to collect their thoughts. Dixon spoke first.

'It is not so much that it is fun, but that it is necessary.'

'Vital,' said O'Donoghue.

'Necessary and vital. It is something that we have to do.'

'For our wellbeing. That's wellbeing without a hyphen.'

'And our wellbeing mirrors that of the readers.'

'But do you read every single page?' asked Berlin. 'You'd be here all night if you did, wouldn't you?'

'We don't read every page, no,' said Dixon, wearily. 'We can't.'

'You're right, it would be too much,' said O'Donoghue. 'We have to let some things go. Or be.'

Berlin was curious. Were there certain pages that the revise editors always let go, or be?

'Sport does not get the attention it deserves,' said Dixon.

'It is a shame, but nor do the pages which lie deepest in the business section,' said O'Donoghue.

'We have to let them go. We look at the headlines and captions but that's all.'

'There's not enough time, you see,' said O'Donoghue. 'Unless, as you say, we decided to stay here all night. And that would be no kind of life.'

'We certainly wouldn't be paid for our extra labours,' said Dixon. 'Besides, it is not as if we will be here for much longer. There is no point in going the extra mile.'

'None at all,' said O'Donoghue.

'What do you mean?'

'The powers that be will do away with us soon,' explained Dixon. 'We cost too much. Soon newspapers will not have revise editors.'

'Or sub-editors.'

'Or journalists.'

'But how on earth will they get written?' asked Berlin, laughing at what struck her as an idiotic conceit. The revise editors had to be pulling her leg.

'Press releases.'

'What?'

'Press releases,' echoed O'Donoghue.

'The news desk will just churn out press releases, topped and tailed to suit.'

'With a few things from the wires.'

'And Twitter. It's the next big thing when it comes to news.'

'So there won't be a need for us,' concluded O'Donoghue. 'You heard it here first.'

'I can't believe for a minute that's true,' said Berlin. 'A newspaper like *The Record* will always need you, not to mention proper writers. It can't just rely on press releases from PRs.'

'We wish we shared your confidence,' said Dixon.

'We certainly do,' said O'Donoghue. 'But the media as we know it is dying.'

'It will be very different in less than five years,' said Dixon. 'The internet is killing us all off. Not a single newspaper is profitable anymore, they're all losing money and no one has worked out how to survive. In the short term, the powers that be go round cost cutting where they can. That means the like of old lags like us. Our days are numbered.'

'If you're right, that's very sad,' said Berlin. To her, there was something noble about a paper employing revise editors; it was a badge of its commitment not just to good writing but factual accuracy. She wondered whether to say more but O'Donoghue called time on the discussion.

'What will be, will be,' he said. 'The night is slipping away from us. Back to work.'

The three occupants of the small and cramped office turned back to the reams of newsprint on their desks, and got on with what they were doing. In Berlin's case, this meant re-reading a list of instances of strange or (and she didn't like to admit it) plainly incorrect advice given by Harry Flack, supposedly Fleet Street's most reliable night lawyer but a man who seemed, tonight, anything but.

*

'Excellent, I see that you are all hard at it!'

To Dixon and O'Donoghue's dismay, Flack sounded once again as if he'd been surreptitiously gulping from whisky from a hip flask. He bounced into the office so energetically that he may as well as have been a sixteen-year-old running onto a football pitch. To O'Donoghue's astonishment, as he turned round he saw that Flack was about to ruffle Dixon's hair. For a second, the night lawyer's hand hovered above Dixon's curls, only for Flack to think better of what, by the standards of the trio, would have been tantamount to an assault. Moving rapidly away from Dixon – who deliberately, it seemed to O'Donoghue, refused to divert his attention from his computer screen in front of him – Flack all but skipped the few steps to Maya Berlin. Seeing him standing over her, O'Donoghue gasped. Was he about to touch her? The fingers of Flack's hands snapped back and forth, first behind Berlin's head and then, again for a split second, before her face when she turned to greet him; O'Donoghue feared the worst, some quasi-sexual touch and an offensive comment; mercifully, Flack shoved his hands dramatically into his pockets, before declaring: 'It's about time we all concentrated. There's been too much nonsense tonight. How can we expect this poor young lady to learn a thing? The only thing I would say is this: you can never trust a judge. Especially a French one. I've just been talking to Frances. She has confirmed my suspicions.'

Flack revealed that on what he called a 'tour of duty – I've been round the houses tonight' he had bumped into 'our estimable friend Frances – she's the legal editor, for those who are new here. That's you, young lady. Frances is an excellent person and a brilliant journalist. She told me of a French judge who used to sketch portraits of people in court. They were very good. He even painted people too, from advocates to defendants, clerks and clients. For years his collection was barely known but now it hangs somewhere in Oxford. There's even a book about him, Cavellat he was called. The book's by a professor called Watt. Frances was telling me that Watt is keen, thinks the Frenchman's scribbles and paintings are wonderful. I don't agree. To me, they're indicative of everything that is wrong about the judiciary. They're always up to something on the side, whether it's drinking too much claret or drawing pretty pictures of those appearing before them. Typical. Frances didn't agree, thought Cavellat was charming, said that she was sure he served the law well, that his art was merely incidental – a harmless pleasure. I put her right with the tale of the other barking mad French judge, the one from Angoulême who was suspended for 'performing unmistakable movements' under his gown when he was supposed to be listening to a female lawyer. Disgraceful, and absolutely typical not just of our Gallic friends but judges everywhere.'

No one said a word. Flack stood in the middle of the office, as if he had just delivered a sermon.

'Does anyone remember the war?' he asked.

Silence.

'It is our duty to educate our young friend. Chatting away about France, as we were then, reminded me of the war. Of both wars. And the fact that whenever we publish commemorative pieces looking back on the war, especially the First World War, we need to be careful.'

The silence persisted. But Berlin looked at Flack inquisitively. She felt sorry for him; exasperated, but sorry. The least she could do was to appear interested in what he was saying.

'I see that you are interested in the reason why we have to be careful,' continued Flack, to Berlin alone. 'Well, let me tell you. It is so that we don't get a copyright claim. You see, most of the famous First World War poets were knocked off their perches during or straight after the war, so their poetry is out of copyright. Do you know how long copyright lasts?'

'Seventy years from the death of the author,' said Berlin.

'Excellent! They have taught you well up there at 9BR. Do you also know which poet's estate might have a go at us?'

Berlin shook her head.

'Sassoon's. He died in 1967 so his work is still in copyright. Wrote a poem called 'Alone' and was known as Mad Jack. Bet you didn't know that either.'

Abruptly, Flack sat down with a moan. It was as if he was disappointed in a small and impious congregation.

Adjusting his cuffs, Flack then attempted to resurrect a semblance of poise, perhaps even authority: 'Ms Berlin, would you kindly assist me by libel-reading the pile of pages that have arrived, as if by a sinister and malign force, in my absence. I will meanwhile go through what people here delight in calling the 'Murder of the Century' story, as if there is something glorious about murder which, save in connection with one man whom I heartily wish were dead, I very much doubt.'

'Of course,' said Berlin. Her tone surprised Dixon and O'Donoghue. It sounded as if she had made a decision of some kind, that she knew something they didn't; more to the point, it paid no heed whatsoever to Flack's tirade about errant French judges. Her voice had a strange blend of resolve, superiority and – what was it? – compassion? Or its opposite? The revise editors shot each other a look. Without saying a word, they were in agreement: *The girl is going to get on with her job for the rest of the night, and then she's going to make one hell of a complaint.* Moreover, each privately thought: *Who could blame her? Harry Flack, tonight, has been a nightmare.*

*

The hours passed. To the relief of Dixon and O'Donoghue, and, it must be presumed, Berlin, nothing happened. Nothing unusual, anyway. Journalists came and went, bringing copy, asking questions, going away again. Berlin dealt with the majority of their queries. Ordinarily, the revise editors would have blanched at the prospect of a trainee night lawyer taking the helm, but Berlin was clearly capable and besides, for some unaccountable reason Flack had gone mad. For a while, that is; from roughly 7.30pm he seemed to have recovered his senses, or rather, found a new focus for his quicksilver mind. He sat quietly, lost in thought, occasionally writing, sometimes reaching for a textbook on contempt of court, muttering once or twice 'that should do the trick', then writing again. To the extent that he gave any advice it sounded measured and sensible; there was only one occasion for concern, when he calmly wondered whether accusing someone of fraud was defamatory in today's world, when everyone, from bankers and brokers to tradesmen and footballers, seemed to be on the make, grasping away at money as if there were nothing else of importance in life. 'Seriously,' said Flack, to a relatively young male journalist, 'if the test of defamation is that the allegation will lower the subject in the estimation of right-thinking members of society generally, and we live in a society in which there are now very few, if any, right-thinking members, can it be defamatory to say someone is a fraudster?' But if his words perplexed the young man, they lacked clout; they were rhetorical. Better yet, so far as those sharing the office were concerned, they were not followed by an imperious, but hollow, 'Legal OK'.

Berlin had been busy all night; now, as the clock struck 8.30pm, she was surprised to see Dixon and O'Donoghue shut down their computers and prepare to leave. As they gathered their things, she saw that there were no more proofs on either man's desk. Their shifts were over. Sport, and the deeper recesses of the business section, may not get the attention they deserved but it was time for the revise editors to go home. As Berlin sought a pithy phrase by which to thank them, they surprised her again.

'We're off,' announced Dixon.

'Off home,' said O'Donoghue.

'But we have something to do before we ...'

'Leave,' concluded O'Donoghue.

'Yes, we have to eat,' said Dixon. 'We're starving. And given that you must be pretty peckish too, we wondered if you'd like to ...'

'Join us.'

Berlin laughed. She liked the revise editors. They were diligent, and funny, and kind. She said she'd love to join them, but feared she still had plenty of proofs to read. At this point, Flack, putting aside his pen and what looked like a letter on The Record's headed notepaper, intervened.

'Don't worry, my dear, you go ahead. I'll hold the fort here. We're nearly done, anyway. In fact, let me have those last couple of stories. I'll deal with them.'

Berlin asked if he was sure. Flack said he was, and that all things being equal, he would join the trio in the canteen.

'I'm pretty peckish myself, you know,' he said.

*

Within minutes of their departure Flack was sitting at Dixon's desk. He started up the chief revise editor's computer, tapped in his password – trusted by Dixon to none other than O'Donogue and Flack, in case of emergency – and swiftly found the queue of 'Done' stories, divided into various sub-sections. The first edition of the paper had just gone; the timing, now, was perfect. Flack could rewrite the second edition – *The Record's* biggest-selling, key edition – to his whim. He found the leaders. He pulled up on screen the first leader, about foreign policy in the Middle East. Highlighting the entirety of its text, he pressed 'delete'. Then, looking at a handwritten note that he'd created over the past two or three hours, he typed in the following:

> The Record *has long stood for impartiality. It has been our watchword. Like Switzerland with its hordes of Nazi gold, and Costa Rica with its dens of online gambling iniquity, we stand for neutrality, so long as the price is right. Give us this day our daily diet of sleaze, phone hacking and illegality, and we,* The Record, *will stand like a barber's pole in the high street, red and white and fairly arbitrary and not really meaning all that much.*
>
> *The same goes for the rest of today's papers, but it is a competitive world and we have to do what we can to get ahead. Moreover, as the Leveson Inquiry rumbles pointlessly on, we have been confronted with one of the most shocking murder trials in British legal history. The case of Peter Terry and his barbaric serial murders has rightly caused all of us to wail and gnash our teeth, and it has caused me, Eddie Conrad, installed today as your new editor, to make a stand.*
>
> *The jury has yet to return with its verdict in this case but I can tell you now that Terry is guilty. He has a list of previous convictions for violence that is as long as my manhood and that, let me tell you, is pretty damn long. It is as clear as day that he has murdered these poor unfortunate women over a lengthy period of time. His defence is a shambles and as for his dress sense, it is*

rivalled for hideousness only by the suits sported by that idiot of an Attorney-General.

As for the A-G, he will not like me writing this Leader. But I believe we, the citizens of Britain, have had enough. Our laws of contempt of court and libel are arcane and archaic. Why can't we be like certain overseas jurisdictions, and say what we like without fear of reprisals? Do we live in a democracy or a Stalinist third world banana republic?

I say to the Attorney-General: come after me if you dare. I am not afraid.

I say to The Record's *readers: buy this paper on Monday. We will have an exclusive on the Terry trial. Several exclusives, in fact, from a unique source: the jury room. They will reveal the machinations of our so-called justice system in a vile case in which the accused is as guilty as sin.*

And I say to my man on the jury: like hacking phones, you justify the means. Thank you.

As soon as he had entered the last full stop, Flack pressed 'save'. That was it. That was all that had to be done. This would be *The Record's* first leader.

Quickly, Flack scanned the 'Done' list for other stories. There was Garms's diary; there was the City diary. There was the news item about the drunken celebrity and the story about the Titian painting. And although, when he went to see her, Virginia Whitton had baulked at naming Axel Austin's former lover, Flack had convinced her. 'Look, I want to have a pop at super-injunctions', she'd said, 'But I've had second thoughts. Austin seems to be a good man. He made an understandable mistake because he was thinking of his wife and kids. That's the problem, isn't it, Harry – this fine line between what the public ought to know and what's private. I don't know. Are you really sure we can do this?' Flack had all but ordered her to name the woman. There were other stories, too, that he'd quietly corroded as the night wore on.

The Record's second edition would be a tissue of contempt, libel and other legal infractions. Eddie Conrad might plead innocence, but there was no way he would survive this.

Flack thought of opening one or two of the stories: his mouse wavered first over Moravia's provocation of Portakabin, then a story about a footballer who'd been having an affair that he'd ensured would delight the libel lawyer instructed to sue over it. But a scruple made him stop, lean back, and stare at the screen. The girl would be having supper with Dixon and O'Donoghue.

He ought to go and see her. Problems would flow from what he had done; she, not to mention the revise editors, would be livid with him. At least, on his last shift, he could try and be charming in person. He could offer to pay and crack some jokes. Perhaps, one day, they'd understand.

Omitting to shut down Dixon's computer, Flack set off for the canteen.

*

At that precise moment Dixon and O'Donoghue were reeling from a revelation by Berlin. Halfway through their meals, both men had put down their cutlery. The silence, as they stared at Berlin, was overwhelming.

'So you see, I had to do something,' she said, as if interrupting a blackout.

Dixon was the first to speak.

'I understand,' he said simply.

'So do I,' said O'Donoghue.

'I couldn't sit by and watch him ruin the paper, not to mention his life's work. I had to do something.'

Her audience adjusted themselves. They sighed. They fiddled with hair, cuffs and jackets. They scratched their temples and chins. And then, they laughed.

'You did the right thing,' said O'Donoghue.

'I agree,' said Dixon. 'You did absolutely the right thing.'

'Do you mind me asking, what will you do next?' asked O'Donoghue.

Berlin shrugged her shoulders. 'Tell him, I suppose. And then it depends on him.'

'Perhaps, perhaps not,' said Dixon. 'You're far from powerless, you know.'

'I know,' said Berlin. 'I know. But what happens has to be right.' She paused. 'By the way, I hope they don't make you two redundant. The place wouldn't be the same without you.'

'It won't be the same without Harry Flack,' said Dixon. 'But don't worry about us. All good things come to an end.'

He seemed about to say more, but stopped when nudged by O'Donoghue. 'Talk of the devil,' said the latter, gesturing towards the door of the canteen.

*

Flack entered the canteen with a spring in his step. Unaware that Dixon, O'Donoghue and Berlin were watching him, he reached for a tray and proceeded to admire the evening's fare. It was unusual for him to be in the canteen at this point in a shift; there were still pages to read, including those he'd taken from Berlin and sport, which were always the last stories to reach his desk. Normally, by now Flack would be alone in the revise editors' office, ploughing through the last few proofs. Ordinarily, he'd finish his shift anytime between nine and 9.30pm; only then could he think to walk for almost ten minutes through *The Record's* maze of corridors until he found himself at the canteen. Tonight, he had broken with the habit of a lifetime in deciding to abandon his office at 8.40pm. Conscious that this was unprecedented, Flack made another bold choice: instead of the light salad that was his preferred evening meal, he opted for roast beef with all the trimmings. The attendant at the till was treated to an explanation of why, tonight, things were different.

'That'll be £7.50, Harry,' said Avril, a middle-aged woman who had worked in *The Record's* canteen for the past twelve years. She and Flack were on first-name terms.

'How are you tonight, love?' enquired Avril, as Flack searched for his wallet.

'Never better, Avril,' replied Flack. 'Never better. Tonight's my last shift. I am looking forward to a new life of freedom and fun.'

'That's nice, Harry,' said Avril. 'But I'll miss you! Will you pop in from time to time? The food here is very good, you know.'

'I cannot testify to that assertion, Avril.'

Avril's easy manner was replaced by a frown. Flack had spoken with such seriousness, as if – she thought – he was in court.

'No, Avril,' continued Flack, handing her a ten pound note, 'it is impossible for me to confirm that the food here is very good. All I have ever eaten – as you must know, having served me for so long – is salad. Anyone can rustle up a salad and so *The Record's* chefs would look to me in vain in search of a testimonial. But tonight, to celebrate, I am having roast beef. Once I have eaten it, I will let you know what it was like.'

Again, it seemed to Avril that Flack was speaking to a jury, presenting evidence in anticipation of a verdict. Phlegmatic by nature, Avril concluded that lawyers were a curious breed – even nice ones like Harry. 'Whatever, Harry, whatever,' she said, giving Flack his change. 'Enjoy your meal.'

Flack said that he intended to ('for that is the point of having this meal, now, tonight – is it not?'), picked up his tray and set off. Seconds later his gaze alighted upon his colleagues. Each of them had witnessed his exchange with Avril, albeit from a distance. To their dismay, although they couldn't hear what had been said it was evident that Flack's inner disarray was as pronounced as ever. They dreaded what would pass when he joined them, but even as he approached Flack's countenance changed, morphing from a determined, even offended scowl to a canvas on which sorrow, sadness and regret were etched in deep charcoal creases. As he sat down, Dixon was the first to note that his eyes were welling up with tears. He wanted to put an arm round his friend and tell him that it didn't matter, everything would be fine, but before he could move Flack was in full flow.

'I'm so sorry. I'm so, so sorry. I don't know what happened to me. No, that's a lie. I do know what happened to me. But I shouldn't have done what I've done. I wish everything was as it was. But it's too late now. I've sabotaged the paper. I've ruined tomorrow's edition. Please believe me when I say I didn't mean to harm anyone. Anyone other than that bastard editor. But what I've done is an insult to you and your hard work. It's an insult to everyone here. I've picked up our friendship and stamped it into the ground. I'm so sorry.'

Flack paused. Tears were running down his cheeks. Amid his upset. he stuttered the truth – that all night long he had engineered any number of legal problems by way of revenge on Eddie Conrad, that he had been unable to bear the arrival of the man in his life, after all these years and what he'd done, that he wanted the Attorney-General to prosecute *The Record* for several unpardonable contempts of court and imprison its new editor.

Again, there was a pause. O'Donoghue broke it, saying as gently as possible: 'Harry, it's OK.'

Flack couldn't agree. 'It's not, Denis, it's not OK. I've behaved as if the law means nothing. And what I've done will affect us all. On top of everything the last thing I did was open up Richard's computer and rewrite the main leader. I wanted to make a mockery of Conrad but all I've done is destroy myself, and you, and the girl, and the paper.'

At this, Dixon and Berlin jumped up.

'Bloody hell, Harry!' exclaimed Dixon. To Berlin, he said, 'Quick, come with me'; to O'Donoghue, he said 'Look after Harry.'

Flack pushed the tray of food away and slumped onto the table, his head in his hands. He was vaguely aware of Dixon and Berlin running from the canteen as O'Donoghue's heavy arm hugged his shoulders.

*

'What's the rush, you bloody idiots! Running around like that could cause an accident!'

Conrad spoke from the floor of a corridor. He had been on the wrong side of a door that Dixon had thrown open as he and Berlin sped back to the revise editors' office. The impact had knocked him flying.

Dixon did not stand on ceremony. 'Sorry, got to dash,' he said. He ran off down the corridor as Conrad picked himself and his briefcase up. Berlin, whom Dixon had breathlessly exhorted to accompany him 'just in case we need a bit of legal gravitas', was left with *The Record's* new editor.

'Christ almighty!' shouted Conrad. 'The fool knocks me flying and then runs off! Who the hell is he, anyway?'

Berlin eyed Conrad calmly. 'His name is Richard,' she said. 'He's the paper's chief revise editor.'

'He's a fucking idiot, shoving doors open like that.'

Now upright, Conrad brushed down his raincoat. He had been on his way out of the building, to find a cab to ferry him home. He groaned again, for good measure, and then absorbed the image of the woman standing before him. Her presence pleased him.

'Who are you?' he asked.

Berlin explained that she was a trainee night lawyer.

'A trainee night lawyer? Good grief. You're far too pretty for a job like that.'

Berlin's face was inscrutable. Conrad was not deterred.

'Why don't you come and work for me? You don't want to be a bloody night lawyer. I sacked that excuse of a man who was tonight's night lawyer earlier. Always so serious, always so full of conviction that what he was doing meant something, when it's all a game – you know that as well as I do, don't you?'

'I don't know what you're talking about,' said Berlin.

'Sure you do. If you don't, you soon will. It's all a game. That's what keeps us going.'

'I really don't know what you're talking about.'

Conrad looked Berlin up and down. 'Once upon a time, a very long time ago, I didn't think it was a game,' he said. 'I believed in things like books, and writing, and truth; bearing witness, the need to report, all that jazz. But the real world taught me what a load of bollocks all that stuff is.'

He made the last statement in such a way that Berlin was invited to respond. She did not take the bait. Her refusal to speak seemed to provoke Conrad.

'Do you know who I am?' he demanded

'Yes.'

'I'm the fucking editor of this paper, that's who I am.

'I know.'

'As the editor of this fucking paper, I can say and do what I like. Do you understand?'

'I understand that's what you think, yes.'

'It's not what I think. It's fact.' Conrad paused. 'You're quite insolent, aren't you? You think you're better than me. Why? Because you're pretty, and because you're a lawyer?'

'I don't think I'm better than you. I'm sorry if that's the impression I gave.'

'So you should be.' This time Conrad heaved a large sigh. 'Anyway, it doesn't matter. You remind me of someone. Someone from the past.'

Berlin said nothing. She merely stared into Conrad's eyes until *The Record's* editor looked away.

'Bloody hell,' muttered Conrad. Then he rallied, albeit on a different tangent. 'Don't tell me the old git has worked his magic on you! That you believe in him? Jesus Christ! You've spent an evening working with Harry Bloody Flack and you believe in something like virtue.'

'What has my work with Mr Flack got to do with what I think? And why do you dislike him so much?'

'It's not so much that I dislike him. It's that he did nothing, and means nothing, and in his almighty nothingness he thinks he's achieved nobility. "The Nobility of Nothingness" – that should be on his gravestone.'

The strength of Conrad's feelings was a surprise. Berlin looked upset. Conrad continued, like an animal going in for the kill, sensing weakness:

'It's his last shift here. I sacked him today.'

This time, it was Berlin's turn to rally.

'He was leaving anyway,' she said. 'And so am I. Goodnight.'

Conrad watched her walk away. There was definitely something familiar about her. He wondered if they'd met previously, perhaps at a function of some kind, one of those talks that media lawyers are fond of hosting at their swish and trendy offices.

*

'I've done it,' said Dixon, when Berlin entered his office.

'Thank God for that,' said Berlin.

'It was close. Far too close for comfort.'

'I know. But Richard: thank you.'

'It was my pleasure,' said Dixon. 'Thank you, too. Between us we've managed to avert a total disaster.'

'Was it easy?'

'He hadn't closed my computer down so I didn't need to reboot it. I got into the queue as quickly as I could, then rang the production editor and told her to hold the presses because there was a problem with the leaders. Then I just deleted what he'd written and replaced it with the correct copy.'

'I'm sorry I didn't tell you what was going on earlier,' said Berlin.

'Don't be,' said Dixon. 'You had more than enough on your plate. No one has ever gone into the queue like that and done what Harry did. We couldn't have anticipated it.'

'What did he put there instead, just out of interest?' asked Berlin.

'A chaotic rant about Eddie Conrad,' replied Dixon. 'Something about bugging the jury room in the Terry trial. It was bonkers.'

'Thank God you got there in time.'

'Yes, thank God, or whoever manages our destinies. Shall we go now? We'd better go and find Harry.'

Part 4

CHAPTER 22

Obit

Archie Lewis was walking to work when he heard the news. His mobile phone sounded; he saw that it was Richard Dixon. At once, Lewis feared the worst. Flack had been hanging on for months, battling terminal cancer with the kind of pugilistic determination that O'Donoghue so admired. But there was no reason, other than to pass on news about Flack, for Dixon to call him at this hour – especially given that he'd long since been made redundant. Lewis's fears were confirmed within a couple of seconds.

'Hello Richard,' he said.

'Harry passed away last night,' said Dixon. 'I've just heard. I thought you should know.'

Lewis was well aware of the subtext to Dixon's call. He'd had a long time to get used to this day, and knew what he would do when it happened.

Once in the office, a survivor of so many redundancies and changes that he wasn't the only person to suggest that he would never leave 'because the dead need their Charon', Lewis remembered a question Flack had asked him, many, many years ago.

'Do you ever have fun with the obits, Archie?'

Lewis had asked him what he meant.

'Well, obits are very formulaic. But do they ever contain in-jokes, or depart from the norm?'

Now, twelve years or so since Flack's last shift, Lewis knew the answer. *Only occasionally, Harry, and only when deserved, for example when a colleague dies, or a friend of the family. In such circumstances we might have a little fun, do something a little different.*

He also knew the truth. Only Lewis knew what had happened on Flack's last shift; only he had been told, sworn to secrecy by Dixon and O'Donoghue. He'd been dumbfounded when they told him, over lunch one day in The Rose; amazed when he'd discovered that Flack had tried to destroy the paper he'd worked for all his life, only for the young female lawyer to correct each of his deliberate mistakes save for one about that blasted portable loo company and for Dixon to delete the disastrous first leader and reinstate the original just before the presses rolled. But most of all, he'd been astonished by what had passed between Conrad and Flack, by the fact that Flack's fiancée, Helen, had been so cruelly treated by Conrad; that Flack had been cuckolded; that Helen had moved abroad and remarried; that she'd told her daughter everything when she graduated from university and that it was this, more than anything so prosaic as the desire to be a libel lawyer, that led Maya Berlin to *The Record*.

Lewis sighed. 'The threads we weave,' he said under his breath, staring into nothingness. Then he sat down at his computer, turned it on and retrieved the obituary he'd written for Harry Flack. He couldn't make it the lead obit but he could give it a fair bit of space, perhaps 600 or even 700 words. He had a decent photo of Flack, and pleasingly, unless the day took a turn for the worse, no one of significance had died. Flack's obit would therefore be contemporaneous rather than held over for a week or two, perhaps longer, as was sadly the case for obits of lesser figures because, like it or not, there is a pecking order when it comes to obits and Charon's ferry works most efficiently for the rich and famous. It would, in any event, be nice to get the page away nice and early. Lewis pressed 'send' and committed Harry Flack's obituary to *The Record* for the following day:

> *With his tall and wiry frame, clad always in an immaculate black suit, Harry Flack cut an elegant, if for long unheralded, figure in legal London. From relatively austere beginnings he went on to become one of the most respected Fleet Street lawyers of his generation.*
>
> *Beginning his career at the respected mid-tier Holborn firm of Bowles & Parkes, Flack soon grew tired of conventional legal practice. The routine of clocking up time, billable hours and climbing the ladder to partnership was not for him. Instead, he opted to become a night lawyer for several national newspapers, a role that gave him the freedom to indulge his passions for jazz and cricket and the satisfaction that he had matched a philosophical commitment to free speech with earning a crust.*
>
> *Harry Flack was born and raised as an only child in Islington. Little in his upbringing suggested a predilection for the law: his*

father was a taxi driver, while his mother, from whom he inherited a love of books, was an English teacher. But Flack – a promising cricketer at school, though he did not pursue the game as a player in adult life – obtained an excellent law degree from Oxford. Having secured articles of clerkship with Bowles & Parkes with ease, his move away from the firm caused some consternation; it is even rumoured to have played a role in the breakup of his engagement at the time. But it was among the Fleet Street newspapers of old that Flack thrived. There, at a variety of titles as a freelance night lawyer, he was respected for the incisive accuracy of his advice, his phlegmatic bearing and his stewardship of legal issues in emergencies, when a given paper's staff lawyers were unavailable.

It was at The Record *that Flack made his reputation. Here, he worked for a quarter of a century without once presiding over a legal howler. The excellence of his judgement became legendary, but so too his sense of professionalism. Journalists trusted him; fellow lawyers admired him, even as they envied his perspicacity and unruffled nature. Everyone liked Flack, even if, when pressed, they might acknowledge that they didn't know him very well.*

Flack's time at The Record *spanned huge changes in the media. In legal terms, it began when the great show trials of the libel bar were still a feature of the front pages, included the era of forum-shopping by overseas, especially Russian, oligarchs and took in the rise and fall of privacy actions and the unpalatable, unlamented heyday of the super-injunction. Journalistically, Flack's career coincided with what some commentators characterise as the death of good writing but which all agree was the era of the unstoppable rise of the internet, a time when newspapers had to reinvent themselves at dizzying speed just to break even.*

Flack's career also saw the phone hacking scandal and the imprisonment, for contempt of court, of Eddie Conrad, an editor who would stop at nothing in pursuit of a story. Conrad's extraordinary decision to bug the jury room in the notorious Peter Terry murder trial took journalistic excess to a level unforeseen even by the most trenchant critics of the press. Remarkably, it would never have come to light had Flack not turned whistleblower, alerting the Attorney-General to his suspicions in a letter which he penned during his last shift at The Record.

Today, the media is a different place. Twelve years after Flack's last shift for The Record *journalism has mutated out of all recognition. Newspapers are not the same as they were in Flack's time: many no longer even exist. But the nadir was reached by Conrad; thereafter, Fleet Street became, once again, a place whose ethics were at least on a par with those of other professions.*

Flack never married. He kept his personal affairs to himself, sometimes quipping, if pressed, that he had accepted his fate of 'a long and strange kind of viduity'. However, he went on to find a degree of familial happiness when his legal career ended, moving to Cornwall and becoming an expert in the paintings of the Newlyn School artist, Albert Chevallier Tayler. At the time of his death, and despite being ravaged by cancer, he had managed to complete a book about the artist which he had provisionally entitled 'The Old, Old Story: The Uncertainty of Truth in the Work of Albert Chevallier Tayler'. While the book's fate remains to be seen, Harry Flack's status as one of Fleet Street's finest lawyers is not in doubt.

He is survived by his daughter, Maya Berlin, herself a night lawyer.

Acknowledgements

This novel would never have been written if I had not been fortunate enough to spend many years working on Fleet Street. I owe a debt to everyone in the newspaper trade for their generosity, knowledge and experience, but there are a few people I must thank by name:

Richard Dixon and Denis O'Donoghue, and, before them, Tim Austin – revise editors who made the night shift a pleasure as much as an education. Thanks to Richard and Denis for lending their names to versions of themselves – who are nevertheless not themselves – in *Flack's Last Shift*.

Gill Phillips, Pat Burge, Alastair Brett and Tom Crone – lawyers who not only have great judgement, but are great people too. Thanks to Gill and Pat for a name each, to create someone who isn't either of them but who might bear a passing resemblance to someone like them.

Frances Gibb – who appears as herself. Likewise, Clare Hogan. Thanks also to Mary Ferrant, Donna Boultwood and Sarah Rook, and to Alan Kay, Sandra White and Richard Whitehead.

I'm grateful to Nigel Tait and Alasdair Pepper of Carter-Ruck both for their tutelage at the outset of my career, and for their brief appearances in this novel. Thanks, too, to Razi Mireskandari of Simons Muirhead & Burton for his support.

Thanks to all of London's night lawyers, but especially Simon Heilbron, Stuart Patrick and Mary Byrne.

Thanks to Keith Carabine, for his careful reading of the manuscript, advice and friendship, and thanks to my mother and father, for the same. And to David Milner – thanks for an important brainstorm, many years ago.

Thanks to my publisher, Blue Mark Books, and editor, Toby Fountaine, for their patience.

And finally, thanks to Caroline Davidson, for her own patience (which was tested), care and wise advice.

Permissions

The author is grateful for permission to reproduce the following extract: